True Fiction (Volume Two)

ALSO BY AVTAR SIMRIT

TRUE TIME TRILOGY:
A Dream of True Time
The End of Truth

TRUE FICTION:
True Fiction (Volume One)
True Fiction (Volume Two)

POETRY:
Shackled to Creation
Break Every Chain

THE COMPLETE LYRICS
OF AVTAR SIMRIT:
Nilotic Years
The MC Pan Era

True Fiction (Volume Two)

Avtar Simrit

Apocalyptic Rhymes

For
Jordyn Veronique;
May the darkness
always create
the brightest art.

Contents

The Tell-Tale Tail

Gaping Black

The Pariah and His Dark Passenger

Fluxing Uranus

Begotten

"History is bullshit; it is as indeterminate as the future."

-Peter J Carroll

"Need I add that, as the book itself demonstrates beyond all doubt, all persons and incidents are purely the figment of a disordered imagination?"

- Aleister Crowley

Dead Ears

Dead Ears (Short Story)

I knew this was the day I would finally do it. I could feel it in my bones. I could feel it in my loins. And it burned, but it was a good burning, one that might be described as fascinating. Whatever the case might have been, it was a mix of excitement and curiosity. The semester had just ended and winter break had begun. I was looking forward to going to stay at my friend's house that weekend. It was cold and the hustle and bustle of the holiday season only made me more anxious to get away from my normal routine.

I was going to sleep over at my friend Carl's house for two days. We didn't get to see each other that much, so he always invited me over whenever we had a break from school. We were going to hang out with a couple of other people once I got there. Me and Carl headed over to Rob's house to hang out with him.

When we got to Rob's house, he opened the door to let us in. I eyed his ears, they did not look cold and dead. They looked excited and innovative. He had two diamond earrings poking out of each lobe. I wanted them. I wanted to feel the needle piercing through my skin. I wanted it to hurt.

"So, Rob," I said. "Your girlfriend did that for you, right?" I indicated his ears.

"Yeah." Rob touched one of his lobes.

"Do you think you could get her to do that for me?" I said.

"Sure, I'll call her up and see."

Rob called her and it was fine, she said she'd do it. Carl, Rob, and I went to the HIP mall to get some earrings and antiseptic. When we got to the mall parking garage, there were so many cars because it was the holidays. It looked as if we were gonna be waiting at least a half hour to get a parking space. Lucky for us Carl's car came equipped with an intermolecular sylocone-chrome vaporizer. This handy little device comes out like an arm from under the car whenever the driver is in dire need of a parking space and none can be found. We found a space on the third floor that was occupied, however Carl set coordinates for where the intruding car matter would be relocated to. He hit the button and the car dissembled into tiny fragments of hidden spawned black matter. All evil cars are made of this vile substance.

After achieving the commandeered parking space, we headed to Spencer's gifts to see if I could find some earrings. The ones I liked where crescent moon shaped and looked like supernatural fingernail clippings. However, they really were supernatural and gave the wearer eerie powers. These powers would only come if the wearer's blood mixed with the metal of the earring. But what the power does is unknown until the wearer bleeds.

I bought the earrings and headed to Claire's to buy the antiseptic. Rob and I looked at the earrings on the rack in Claire's just for fun to see if anything looked cool. Rob saw some amazing looking Rhino Tusk earrings and saw his chance to take what he wanted. He slid them in his pocked and thought no one noticed. When he took his hand out of his pocket, it was stained completely blue. His eyes went wide and he shoved his hand back into his pocket where his stolen goods slept.

We walked up to the counter and I asked for the antiseptic. The cashier pulled out this gigantic pink bottle of some foreign liquid that I wasn't really sure I wanted to put on my ears. Rob pulled me to the side and whispered in my ear.

"You know, that's just sulfur water. It's made to control your mind. It's a trap. She's an enemy spy."

We turned back to the cashier.

"How much?" I said.

"Nine dollars," said the cashier.

"WHAT?" I screamed. "OUTRAGEOUS!"

I grabbed the bottle out of her hand and chucked it directly at her fucking face. In super slo-mo I saw the bottle collide with her bottom lip. Her head flew back, her eyes clenched shut, as blood broke out of her lip. She fell to the floor.

"You will never get me, arch fiend. My mind is too strong for your puny animal tactics. My mind will be liberated through piercing. You will forever whimper, damp and forgotten on the sunless ground of belonging." I said.

I turned away satisfied. My work was done there. Rob followed me out. After that moment, a freeze frame and a jump cut entered into my day to day existence. Nothing mattered after that until my eyes shot open and I was in the back seat of Rob's car with a girl on either side of me ready to penetrate my tender flesh.

"Make it hurt as much as possible," I said.

Kelly, Rob's girlfriend didn't seemed phased. But she did say, "I never heard that before."

"Make it excruciating so that the flashes of sunset can become one with my cerebellum and into the fiery moments of understanding can awaken my consciousness." I pleaded.

"Whatever the fuck that means," Kelly said as she wiped the sewing needle with alcohol. She put the needle up to my earlobe and pushed it through. The doorway was open. The doorway of pain to the other side of purpose and truth and density was mine now. I gasped as I felt pangs of knowledge radiating out of my being. I could see the electric blue waves of energy wafting off of my arms like steam from a radiator. I knew now the meaning of life. I knew who I was.

I turned and the other girl just used the other earring to punch a hole in my other ear. I moaned from the pleasure. Climax is achieved when all the world is a stage in my own mind, inside my own movie house where I can make my own lives on a silver screen. But they still hadn't gotten the supernatural toenail earrings through yet.

Kelly was trying to shove the curved metal through my ear as I felt warm blood drip down off of it. This is it, I thought, this is the moment when the power reveals itself. I knew. A flash of light suddenly blinded me, my teeth bled, and I finally knew who I was if only for just that moment. For now, just for now, and for only this long, I am Batman.

The Scribbling Vagabond

The Scribbling Vagabond
(Fact or Fiction?)

My name is David Sherry, but they call me Nilotic. This may be because I am one and a half parts masculine, one part feminine, and two parts pseudo-Egypt. However, if you want to get super factual about it, I was hatched just like everyone else; if you trace back far enough. On the day of Creation I was excreted from the vaginal prison at Hinsdale Hospital. It was October 24, 1989. I remember it vividly.

After my expulsion, Mother, Father, my sister, and I all lived in a little blue house in Lisle, IL until the age of six. My sister is two years older than me, so she would have been eight. Afterwhich we departed the burbs to go settle down closer to the heart of the city. The place agreed upon was a skinny brick house on LeMoyne street in Wicker Park. Now, you are missing a vital piece of information necessary for understanding this story. But have no fear for I will enlighten you.

After my mother gave birth to my sister and I, she decided that in order to fill the steadily growing hole in her soul, she must embark on a spiritual quest. This search led her to becoming a born again Christian, dedicating her life to doing the work of the Lord. My father went along for the sake of keeping the family together (or so he says in hindsight). That being said, the reason that we decided to move into the city in the first place was because my mother said she had been called to go into 'urban ministry.' They had already joined a church in the area. The congregation was called Freedom Church.

The first year we lived there, I had one of those moments in life where you know that that one single event altered the fabric of your entire existence. One of those cataclysmic events where you know it's either the work of God or some devils. If absent, I may not have become the writer I am today; which is very well likely because it was while living in that house that I first put pen to paper.

The Gift of Writing runs in the Sherry blood. My father's father is a published author himself. He started out as a journalist and also published fiction and nonfiction books. And my father is a lawyer, so I guess you could say it technically passed to him. Lord knows how many briefs he's written in his life.

I changed schools five times before I turned twelve. By then I was in sixth grade at some private school called Catherine Cook. This was when my parents' marriage started to dissolve. My mother had moved on from Lutheran, to Baptist, to Messianic Jewish; finding herself part of a little congregation called Temple Shalom. After a while I refused to go and just stayed home with my dad while my mom and sister went. My dad was also seeing another woman on the side (whom he later married).

So there was a divorce. Irrevocably splitting our family like a fault line in a desert. Each half ended up states away from the other. My mother and sister in Missouri, and my dad, his mistress, and I in Illinois. All these problems and turbulence sparked some sort of angst in me which I then transferred to my pen, spilling forth stories and poems I did not know were in me.

To make a long story short, we moved. Again. To Park Ridge at the beginning of eighth grade. I was the new kid again. That seemed to be the story of my life. But at the end of that year I shot my first short film. So I guess the year wasn't a total waste.

There was a relatively traumatic summer before high school though. I had spinal fusion surgery to correct my scoliosis. There were thirteen vertebrae fused. That's no small potatoes. Throw some physical pain into the mix with that emotional pain. Before I had the surgery, I was a little hunched, and for the first few months after the surgery, I had to wear a plastic brace. Both of these things contributed to the fact that all my classmates called me 'turtle.' All of this was fuel for the creative fire.

I coasted through high school, making a few films here and there and writing quite a bit. All the while living with a step-mother who I knew wanted to get rid of me. It was like a combination of every evil stepmother from every Fairy Tale by the brothers Grimm. She finally got her chance on Halloween my senior year of high school. What happened was that there was sort of this misunderstanding and my father caught infor-mation that he misinterpreted to mean that I was plotting to kill my stepmother--which consequently I wasn't.

By this point in my life, my mother and sister had moved back to Illinois and were living in a one bedroom efficiency apartment in Crete, IL. That being said, my father dumped me off with my mother. I remained there until my father made me two appointments to get me psychoanalyzed by two different doctors. He tried to use my writing as proof that I was violent. That tactic failed miserably. Both doctors said I was not a threat to anyone and it was not a crisis situation. Nonetheless, my father refused to take me back unless I agreed to take medication. I flatly refused. Hence, I had to go live with my mother and sister.

After that I went through a period of almost three years where I didn't speak at all to my father. My mother supported my wish to attend a two year film school after graduating from high school. Needless to say, my father didn't. He had his heart set on me going to a four year university. To me, that seemed like the most dreaded prospect.

My mom and I decided to just say "Fuck it" and enroll me at Flashpoint Academy in the film department. The only kickback from that was a lawsuit between my mother and father that dragged out for years to come; all over who had to pay for my tuition.

I graduated from Tribeca Flashpoint in 2010 with an Associate's Degree in Film, spending a brief two months over the summer of 2009 working as an intern at TriCoast Studios in California. They promised that there would be jobs for us when we graduated; but if you did not wish to go into corporate media, advertising, or reality television, then you are shit out of luck.

But I moved out anyway, getting a job at a movie theater in Chicago, and moving in with another filmmaker I met during my travels. We had a good run, shooting some music videos and documentaries, but his time in America was abruptly cut short. What I failed to mention is that he was an illegal Mexican immigrant. He finally got deported for too many arrests and DUIs.

Around this time I caught wind that my father was going through another divorce and finally coming to his senses after all these years. He wanted to see me to discuss some things. So I met with him. The impression I got was that he wanted to make up for some of the ways he had treated me and how he had made things worse in our family. So his proposition was to put me up in any city that I wanted to live in, for two years, all expenses paid, while I tried to get my freelance filmmaking business/record label up and running.

I humbly agreed, afterwhich I found myself in Providence, Rhode Island of all places. I drove straight there from Chicago in the dead of winter through blizzards and nor'easters. Believe it or not, I fell in love with the city and decided to stay.

To make a really long story really short, in that first year I lived there: I managed my own record label, recorded lots of music, worked with other artists, performed several shows, shot videos, and wrote a gratuitous amount. But good things must sometimes change or come to an end. A strange spiritual struggle descended on me at the end of that year. The outcome of this was an ordeal which left me frozen and hospitalized for two and a half weeks. The consequence of this was that my dad completely cut me off (he couldn't pay me anyway since most of his money was being stolen by his ex-wife). He took my car back and left me with no way to pay for my apartment and my bills. Looking back on this, it was one of the best things that ever happened to me.

Eventually I found my way down to the Occupy movement

in Providence during early 2012. I absorbed their struggles and their stories until I decided to take a bus back to Chicago in late May.

After a failed romance over that summer, I ended up moving back in with my mother in Crete, IL. My sister had already married and moved out. Even though I deliver pizza now and am taking a Journalism class at the local community college, I have no plans on slowing down. I will write, I will write, and I will write some more. And maybe perform some shows on the side until I am regularly read, listened to, and watched. Which is not far on the horizon.

I would venture to say that that's me in a nutshell, but to be more accurate, I'd be in more like one of those Russian dolls. Layer upon layer upon layer upon layer... until you get to the moment of conception, and that's where it ends.

- or very well starts over again -

Powers of the Metasexual

A *Dying Fetus* Origin Novella

1

"Sorry I'm late. I got held up explaining to my daughter again about how it's not our place to question God's will," Toni explained to the pastor as she walked down the steps into the basement of his house. Toni could sense from the pastor, whose name was Evan, his excitement from the anticipation of their encounter.

This was the first time Toni had been to Evan's house. They had been speaking for weeks extensively about the possibility of converging their energies for the purpose of deeper spiritual work, but this was finally the day their plans would actually come to fruition. The hour was 9 PM, and after the unfortunate argument with her fifteen-year-old daughter Shelley, Toni had left her in the care of her grandparents for the night.

The stairs leading to Evan's basement were covered with cheap gray carpeting, but at the bottom they gave way to a linoleum flooring—good for easy clean up. Toni trailed behind Evan as they entered his dimly lit basement, already set up for their ceremony. The room was bare except for a few lit candles scattered around the periphery. Evan felt the bulge of his crotch grow with the thought of how the night would unfold.

Evan turned to face Toni as he walked to the center of the

room. He smiled at her as if she where the most glorious jewel he had been lucky to stumble on amid dull stones and rubble. "That's all right, my beautiful prophet. I hope you are prepared to be parted even as Moses parted the Red Sea," said Evan with lust and revelation in his eyes. Toni's body shook with chills of rapture. She wore a long white hooded robe and nothing else. The robe was low-cut and exposed her pale cleavage. Evan was still wearing his clothes from the day: a white button-up dress shirt tucked into his slim-fit jeans. He also wore aviator glasses to correct his vision. God had not yet been able to heal his poor eyesight. Evan began to rub his crotch in a clockwise circular motion.

"I am ready for whatever our Lord commands." Toni was already on her knees with her head between Evan's legs, her fingers on his fly.

"Jesus spoke to me in a vision," Evan continued. "And he says for me to lie with you. He wishes for me to be his human vessel, his avatar, so he can physically enter you." As he said this, Toni unzipped Evan's fly and stroked his already hard penis a few times before sliding it deep into her throat. He moaned and put his hand on the top of her head very gently. "Jesus has chosen you, my child. God wants a grandson. You are to be the immaculate mother of the new messiah."

Toni was so overcome with an indescribable rapture at hearing this that she instantly secreted fluid from her vagina with such force she had a trinity of orgasms at once. As she licked the underside of Evan's cock, Toni pulled a small dagger out from a pocket in her robe. As her tongue flicked the tip of Evan's erect member, a dribble of pre-cum made its way into her mouth and it tasted sweet on her tongue, like communion wine.

Finally Toni spoke after a long silence where they both bathed in the electrified air they had charged mystically with their shared intention of God manifestation. "Lo, the Immaculate Conception! A conception is only immaculate if it is clean. The seed of Jesus is made of pure immaculate light, to penetrate my womb for the purpose of your glory on Earth. Jesus, we call you in to use Evan's body as your vessel. We are open to you completely and totally. We are your avatars. We are your light. Oh, Jesus; the Way, the Truth, and the Life. Through only you I come to the Father. Take me now!" The Holy Spirit gripped her body with orgasmic ecstasy, and she began speaking in tongues as she used the dagger to carve a cross between her breasts.

The blood was like the river of life. The Living Water. Toni discarded her robe as the beauty and red bliss spilled down her open body, she was as one ready to be encircled by the wings of Gabriel. After Toni disrobed, she wiped her warm blood on her hand and began to stroke Evan to full erection again. Her naked body was that of a middle-aged mother, which was what she was. She was not a virgin by any stretch of the imagination, but this didn't matter to Evan or Toni. The only thing that mattered was their devotion to God and their Lord and Savior Jesus Christ. Her breasts were large and sagged as a woman's do after breast-feeding two of her own children. Toni also had a round belly left over from her baby weight of her two children. Evan didn't care about this either. Her blind faith and devotion where what turned him on, not her body.

As she continued to stroke Evan with her blood, she slid her other hand down between her legs, through her hairy bush, and onto her moist labia. She breathed heavily as the pleasure in the room continued to build. "Take off your clothes," she whispered.

Toni watched and fingered herself as Evan slowly stripped his jeans off and unbuttoned his shirt then discarded them in the pile with her robe. His body was that of a forty-year-old man, not fat, but it had definitely seen a lot of life. By this time the whole front of Toni's body was red with blood. But she wasn't in pain. She was in so much pleasure that it was all she could do to try not to convulse with all the multiple orgasms she was experiencing. Toni cupped her hands under the flow of life and filled them to the brim. She started to draw a symbol on the floor with her blood like finger paint. The finished work was a streaky Celtic Cross.

As if they were communicating telepathically, Evan slowly laid down on his back on top of the blood cross as Toni began to get off her knees and stand over him. Evan continued to stroke himself with her blood as Toni straddled him, standing. Her blood continued to drip onto his stomach and penis. The Holy Spirit was strong in the room, they both could feel her presence. And Evan could feel the spirit of Jesus possess his body. He surrendered completely, body, mind, and soul.

The time was perfect. They were ready to make love to God. "Come to me, Jesus!" Toni closed her eyes and felt the waves of spiritual ecstasy ripple through her body like mystical MDMA. Her eyelids fluttered and her eyes rolled back into her head, exposing the whites of her eyes for a fleeting moment. Just as Toni dropped to her knees next to Evan, a river of semen came gushing out of Evan's erect member. The flow was endless. Toni tried to stop the stream with her mouth, swallowing as much holy cum as she could without choking. The supernatural ejaculation was too much for her esophagus and spilled out the corners of her mouth and began running down her chin and neck to meet with the river of blood still flowing between her tits. "Jesus!" Toni screamed in pleasure.

Suddenly the creamy flow ceased to squirt. The time had come for Jesus to part her Red Sea. When Evan spoke, his voice had taken on a quality that was not his own; it was other-worldly, almost celestial. "I have made woman," Jesus spoke through Evan, "and see that she is sexy." His rock hard cock throbbed as he watched Toni, crouched naked beside him, blood and semen mixing together at her heart and running down into her sex. "I give the gift of life and I can also take that life away. I alone hold the power of life and death. I have chosen you to be the bearer of this new life. You will hold the New Earth within your womb." Toni laid down on her back in anticipation for Jesus's immaculate seed.

"I am ready, O Lord. I am but your humble servant. I am honored and humbled to be chosen to carry your seed for the New World." Toni closed her eyes as she said this and Jesus with Evan's body got on top of her, spreading her legs so he might gain entrance to her chamber of life.

"I am the Son," he said. "And no one comes to the Father except through Me." Then he penetrated her hard and deep.

Toni was one of those women who thought having children would give purpose to her life. She would forever try to fill the hole that was inside her soul. Toni was not an unintelligent woman by any means. However, her smarts were all of the type we call book and she was not very worldly-wise, much to her own detriment. She graduated from Virginia Tech with a degree in Chemical Engineering. And after she married Samuel, whom she met at Virginia Tech, she went on to get her Master's Degree in business with a focus in finance from the University of Chicago. But all of this achievement and subsequent high-level jobs did not bring her the fulfillment she so desperately wanted.

Samuel wasn't a stranger to this feeling either. However, he thought that being a good husband and provider was the most important thing for a man to be, so he went after that instead of his true passions, whatever they might have been. Samuel also graduated Virginia Tech with a chemical engineering degree, but then went on to law school. Law was something he had a natural knack for and he was a talented persuasive speaker. That seemed like the field most likely to yield results and wealth for him. And he was right...for a time.

Their life was beautiful by any standards. They had a big house in the suburbs of Chicago which had an ample back yard perfect for barbecues and get-togethers. They both had good jobs and status in the community. Toni as a business manager at a chemical factory and Samuel as a intellectual property attorney at a small law firm in the city. They were both making money and living comfortably. They both thought they were happy...for a while.

After a short time Toni began to have this itch, something tugging at her, a feeling of emptiness and dread that something vital was missing from her life. Her first revelation—or false epiphany—was that she wanted to have children. Maybe that would fill the gaping hole in her life. Samuel thought this was the normal progression: lucrative job, nice house, then children and family. So he didn't see any warning signs yet at this point.

In November of 1987, Toni gave birth to a toe-headed girl, whom they named Shelley. Toni liked biblical names. Even though she wasn't a raging Christian yet, she was fond of things that reminded her of her faith-based upbringing. A lot of people drift through life never knowing or having a purpose to their lives, and I can imagine how painful of an existence that would be. Other people know that they want to have a purpose so they search endlessly to find one to fill their meaningless life. They will start out simple at first, and if those 'normal' things don't bring them the fulfillment they crave, then that's when they start the descent into the rabbit hole. They must search harder and crazier to fill that vacancy that lingers without res-pite. And if that doesn't work, they'll latch on to whatever and every purpose that they can to satiate the lack within their soul.

Toni thought that maybe having children would fill that emptiness, so why not give it a shot? For a time Toni was happy.

Less than two years later she felt that itch, that sinking feeling in her stomach again, the dread and despair. Toni decided to get pregnant again. Maybe having two children, a girl and a boy, would bring her purpose and a sense of belonging. So two years after Shelley was born, in October of 1989, she gave birth to a son and named him David. In her eyes they were both beautiful, equal gifts from God. She had a loving husband who provided for all of her needs, two children whom would love her, and all the comfort and security she could ever want. What more did she need? And for a time Toni was happy.

By the time Toni had given birth to her son David, she decided that she didn't want to work anymore. She figured it was more important for her to raise a family and search for her purpose in life. Her job had failed to give her that. Even despite all of this, she voiced to Samuel her feelings about there being something still missing from her life. "What could you possibly be missing?" He responded. "You have two beautiful children, a nice house in the suburbs. You had a great job where you made almost as much money as I do. And you have a husband who loves you and provides for you and your offspring. What more do you want?" Toni just shrugged. She didn't know. She just knew that there was a gaping hole within herself that needed to be filled with something—anything. This worried Samuel.

As her children grew, Toni continued to become more and more depressed. Even though she didn't always outwardly show it, Samuel could feel her restlessness and he started to develop a sense of foreboding as well. He kept his mouth shut about it, but was aware of the changing atmosphere and her growing disinterest in him. The sex slowly dried up and Samuel was lucky if he even got one night in a whole month to be intimate with his wife. Toni was definitely out of sorts, he concluded, but was there anything he could do to combat it?

Around the time David and Shelley reached Preschool and Kindergarten age, Toni started coming to the conclusion that religion was the missing piece in her life. A spiritual life was what she was lacking, and more specifically, Christianity. That was the easiest ideology to gravitate back to since she was raised in a home with Christian philosophy. Toni's parents still went to church every Sunday, for God's sake. She found a Lutheran church not too far from their home and began attending services and taking Shelley and David along with her. At first Samuel was uneasy about his wife hanging around with a bunch of magical-minded Christian loonies. After all, he wasn't raised in a Christian household like she was. So he let her do her thing and remained separate for a while.

However, there came one Sunday where Toni invited Samuel to join them for a Bible study that one of her friends from the congregation—Michael—was going to be conducting at his house. It's just a normal get together, she explained to Samuel, some good people, good food, good vibes. Reluctantly, Samuel agreed to go.

Outings with the whole family were becoming rarer and rarer, so Samuel took this opportunity to enjoy time together with his wife and children the way healthy families do. And he enjoyed the fellowship with the other families as well. Samuel was actually surprised by how normal they seemed. They weren't the Christian loonies that he had made them out to be in his mind. While the children went off to play in the backyard of this upper-middle class suburban home, the adults spoke briefly about how the teachings of Jesus could be interpreted and practiced in today's world. It was basic golden rule stuff, treating others as you would want to be treated; common sense of being a human being. There was no hocus-pocus being slain in the spirit speaking in tongues crap—not yet anyway. After the short Bible study, the get together just turned into a regular suburban family party. They drank beer, talked politics and sports, and ate hamburgers and hot dogs. Michael even had a Playboy magazine in his study—his father-in-law had gifted him with a subscription as a joke. Samuel actually found himself enjoying the party and these people. *Hey*, he thought to himself, *maybe I can do this Christian thing and get closer to my wife again*. If this is what they were like—just normal folk—then he could be part of that world too, especially if it meant keeping his family happy and together. When it was over, Samuel drove back home with his family with a sense of optimism, for the first time in a long time.

And for a while, Toni was happy.

After a short time Toni became discontent with the Lutheran church they had been attending. This seemed to be the pattern that was developing in Toni's behavior. She would try something out for a while and then get bored with it, having to move on to something more extreme. To her the Lutheran church wasn't 'spiritual' enough, wasn't 'charismatic' enough. For her there wasn't enough emphasis on the healing power of Jesus and the spiritual gifts of the Holy Spirit. So Toni found a new church. Calvary Church. This was a much larger congregation and slightly more charismatic than the Lutheran denomination. The congregation even put on spiritual plays such as *Heaven's Gates and Hell's Flames*. Toni liked this new church for a while and dragged her family along with her. By this time David and Shelley were old enough to get baptized and consciously accept Jesus into their hearts at the pulpit. They did this obediently, never questioning their mother. Samuel went along, trying to ride out the storm, hoping that this was all just a phase that Toni would soon come out of. How wrong he was. And for a time Toni was happy, and that was all that mattered.

Samuel went along for the sake of his family, but in the back of his mind he knew that the marriage was doomed, he just didn't know when exactly it was destined to crash and burn. He played the part of the Christian husband for as long as he could stomach it, and he played it well. He even had a story of his conversion which happened on a plane, and I think for a while he even believed it himself. Samuel even delivered a speech once at Calvary church; his subject was the evils of patenting life, and especially pieces of human life. More specifically sequencing and patenting parts of the human genome. At the time Samuel was doing work at his law firm for a biotechnology company called Genentech. His thesis was that once a company owned the fundamental blueprints for life, it would open a whole Satanic can of worms. This technology led to evil corporations like Monsanto that created genetically modified crops, and they owned the patent for those life forms. If an independent farmer happened to have his crop contaminated by Monsanto GMO corn, then technically his whole crop became property of the Monsanto Corporation. That's how Monsanto put lots of independent farmers out of business. Where else could this technology lead in the future? What if a company owned a genetically modified piece of the human genetic code? Then by the same logic, if our bodies where corrupted to become modified by this patented gene, then we would become the property of that Corporation. Samuel was a highly intelligent man and he had foresight that went beyond Christian mumbo-jumbo. This is probably why ultimately he couldn't stay part of a cult like Christianity.

Day after day having to pretend to be someone he was not left Samuel more and more depressed and he could feel the distance between himself and his wife was growing. Toni never listened to him and didn't notice or didn't care that he had to force himself to be someone he wasn't for her sake. This eventually became a bone of contention between them. However, Samuel didn't let it show right away because he thought there might be a glimmer of hope that his family could still be saved and they wouldn't have to split up. If only Toni would come out of her religious trance. Ultimately he did not believe the same things his wife did and that fact was bound to come to light sooner or later.

At the same time Toni was slipping farther and farther down the rabbit hole. She became more obsessed with Jesus everyday to the point where it would have been more accurate to say she was married to Jesus more than she was to her own husband. Their family were members of Calvary for quite some time, and at this point David was in Kindergarten and Shelley was starting second grade. They both attended Christian school, of course. Shelley was a good little Christian girl, innocent and pure. David was also, for the most part. The pastor even had said that he felt like David particularly had the fire of the Spirit raging within him and that he was bound to grow to be a strong leader. However, there were a couple episodes where he exhibited strange sexual behavior. Toni wrote this off as little children just being curious about their bodies and he would grow out of it. One particular time, at church, while the adults were having their Bible group, the children played in the play-room. David had gone under the plastic slide and exposed himself to one of the little girls playing with him. The chaperone became aware of this and mentioned it to Toni, telling her that she should have a talk with her son. She never mentioned that incident to him. But there was another incident where she did question him at their house. The little daughter of one of their friends from church came over to play with David and Shelley, and when David was alone with her they both pulled down their pants and took turns touching each others private parts. When the little girl left, Toni took David aside and asked him, "Did you show your private parts to that girl?" David shook his head. "Okay," said Toni. "I don't want you doing that, it's very inappropriate." She patted his head and told him to go upstairs and play with his sister.

Toni continued to increase her time studying the Bible and praying. She talked to God as well as listened to His replies to her conversations with Him. Her dialogues with the Most High revealed to her that the pastor and the leaders of Calvary church were not delivering God's message the way that they should be. God was not speaking to them because they were not listening. What they had were several pre-written sermons and lessons that they recycled and updated briefly in order to seem like they coincided with current events. There was nothing new in their sermons, nothing that was relevant to the congregation and to today's world. This was Toni's point of view and she had to do something about it. So Toni started to give to the pastor the messages that she was receiving from God. She had been chosen to be the conduit and what God spoke to her was for the entire congregation and it was her responsibility to make sure they were delivered to the body of Christ, God's people. Not surprisingly, this did not go over well with the leaders of the church. Who was this frumpy mother, with no Master's in Divinity, to tell them what God wanted them to say to their congregation, the ones who paid their bills and allowed them to go golfing every day of the week? So they —as respectfully as they could to maintain their image as good Christians—asked Toni to leave the church and never come back. They said that she was disrupting the peace and they were worried about her stability. The leaders suggested that she may benefit from seeing a therapist. Toni was shocked at this response and was not pleased with the outcome of what she knew God wanted her to do. Why would He do this to her? Hadn't she done all that He had asked? Hadn't she spent hours and hours a day talking to Him and writing down everything that He wished to be shared with His people? At first she could not reconcile this whole affair in her mind. It just didn't make sense. If God gave her a task to do, why hadn't he allowed her to do it? Finally she came to the conclusion that she was right and the leaders of Calvary church were wrong. She decided that her visions were needed elsewhere, that was why God had sent her away from Calvary. But she didn't know where it was she was supposed to go. She left that up to God and waited.

For a time, she was depressed.

999

A year passed in very much the same pattern. Of course the children were too young to really understand what was going on with their mother spiritually and psychologically. They were just pulled along, as kids are, having absolutely no control over their own lives. Samuel spent most of his time working and was exhausted when he returned home at the end of the day, so he had limited energy to engage with his wife. She was more interested in Jesus than she was in him anyway. Toni's journey through the Christian religion remained largely a mystery to Samuel, and he just let her do her thing, trying to be supportive in the ways that he could.

When Toni voiced her desire to go into urban ministry, to share the gospel with the inner-city people, Samuel went along with her swings from here to there, still being the supportive husband. Toni had met Pastor Robert who operated a small storefront church on the north side of Chicago. He named it Freedom Church. Pastor Robert had a pleasant wife and two young daughters around six, David's age. Samuel and Toni were quite a bit more wealthy than Robert and his wife, so Toni got it in her head that it was her mission—and Samuel's—to help the church financially so that the congregation could grow and they could have a legitimate outreach program. Samuel quietly grumbled to himself about all this, but he secretly harbored a suspicion that the whole arrangement—and Freedom Church itself—would come to a bitter end.

So Toni uprooted her family and moved them to Wicker Park, a neighborhood right off of the Damen stop on the Blue Line. Things were a lot different in the city than in the quiet suburbs. Toni was very naive about those sorts of things and always assumed the best of people when she should really have expected the worst. One thing they had to get used to was having gang activity in the alley right next to their new house. They even would hear gunshots from time to time. Samuel hoped that all this shit they had to deal with was worth it for Toni to have her Urban Ministry.

The parents and their children, at this point, were largely in different worlds. Samuel had his law job, which took up the majority of his time, and when he got home at night all he wanted to do was relax or play his flight simulators on his computer. His participation with Freedom Church was already at a minimum and he wasn't sure how much longer he could keep up feigning interest. Toni remained absorbed in her Bible study, even more vigorously this time because she had the souls of inner city families on the line. She was engaged in a Spiritual War and she was a soldier to the end. The existence of these separate adult worlds forced David and Shelley to become close and to forge their own worlds out of the wonders of their young imaginations.

David and Shelley formed a collection of over one hundred dolls of all kinds. They had Barbies, GI Joes, baby dolls, those little troll dolls; they were big and small, boys, girls, white, and some black babies. They created families and elaborate stories for these characters to play out. The main doll was named Mrs. Greenleague. She had a family and all the other dolls were extended offshoots of that main family. They even had a fantasy scenario that they would play out on long car trips. There was one little black baby doll that they called Queenie, and the car was her moving palace and she had servants and assassins who conspired to kill her and take over her throne. They knew, maybe not consciously, but they could feel that Jesus was always their mother's top priority. David and Shelley continued to escape into their own world which they had created, and their bond remained strong during that time of their lives.

In another sphere, the seed of aberrant sexual behavior continued to grow within David. On the whole his mother continued to be oblivious to this part of his growth, his childhood innocence becoming corrupted. At first it was only mild experimentation masturbating. He would stroke himself in front of the mirror for hours and hours and maybe slide a finger or two up his anus as he did so. This was before he was old enough to ejaculate, of course. Yet he did experience something that was not unlike an orgasm. After stroking himself for a long while, his body would jerk and he would feel a spasm of ecstasy travel up his spine and then dissipate. In spite of the orgasm, his erection still would remain so he would continue to stroke until he had two or three more orgasms as he admired himself in the mirror. David even developed a technique where he would lay on his back on his bed then flip his legs over his head, almost like plough pose in yoga. He was able to lower his buttocks just enough that the tip of his penis reached his lips, and he would lick the tip of his cock until he came. On top of all this, one of his favorite things was to take this toy ventriloquist dummy, that he had cut a hole in between the legs, and fuck it doggy-style with his little hard seven-year-old boner.

David mostly enjoyed playing with himself, but occasionally he would experiment with other children as well. One Sunday, after church, Pastor Robert and his family came back over to Toni's house for a meeting about their Urban Outreach. The pastor's daughters, Millie and Mandy, went upstairs to play with David in his bedroom. Shelley was off in her room playing with paper dolls and wanted to be alone. So Mandy, who was six, laid on David's bed, pulled her pants down, and began to rub her vagina with her middle finger. David watched her and felt a slight movement in his pants. Millie, who was the older one—she was eight—leaned up against the bed in front of David and smiled at him mischievously. "Have you ever seen what adults do in their bed at night?" Millie asked David. She giggled as he shook his head. She pulled her leggings down slowly, showing off her small bald vulva to David. Millie bit her lip, smiled, and gave a shy look as David enjoyed the view. "They rub their privates together," Millie laughed. "Isn't that silly?"

David slid his hand into his pants and felt his little boner start to grow. Then Mandy spoke as she continued to touch herself on the bed. "Daddy likes to tickle us down there sometimes. We like it."

Millie spread her legs apart a bit, her lips parted slightly. "Lick me," she said to David. "Lick me down there." David dropped to his knees in front of her, leaned forward, and lapped at her cunt as if licking a lollipop. It wasn't a long lick since he had never done that before and wasn't aware of what adults did with each other. It was just a taste and the tip of his tongue, just for a second, found its way between Millie's lips. It tasted salty on his tongue. "What do I taste like?" she asked.

"Like skin," was all David said before he pulled his own pants down. He was hard by this point. "You want to taste me?" Millie was more than ready and willing to give the tip of David's dick a lick like a popsicle. David couldn't believe how good that felt. It was even better than when he licked it himself. "What do I taste like?"

"Like pineapples," Millie said as she stood up and took his hand. "Come here, I want to show you what Mommy and Daddy do." She led him into his closet, pants still around their ankles. David's closet wasn't a walk-in closet, but it was big enough for two kids to hide in easily. They slid the door closed behind them. Millie kissed David on the lips and pulled his body close to her. His dick poked between her legs and rubbed against her pussy lips, slightly spreading them. Millie began to grind her hips back and forth on his cock and christened the length of it with her not-yet womanhood. She was slightly moist from the excitement. Then Millie began to vocalize a strange musical tune that sounded like a ditty from the Gameboy game Mario. "Doo doo doo doo doo DOO." She continued to vocalize this strange tune as they grinded on each other. There was no penetration involved that day, but both David and Millie enjoyed their play day together.

They never told their parents or anyone else about their closeness in David's room that day, and their parents never found out. It was their delicious little secret. That was the only time that something like that ever happened between them, but whenever they would see each other at church, they would smile fondly as they thought of their beautiful secret.

Shelley never had a sexual awakening the way her brother did. And David never tried to experiment anything sexual with her, it just never occurred to him to do something like that. They were close in other ways and sharing a world of elaborate imagination was enough for him during that time.

IV

Freedom Church eventually crumbled largely because of the pastor's shortcomings. Toni tried to salvage the sanctuary and the ministry as much as she could using Samuel's money. Pastor Robert, it turned out, was a sexual deviant and was sleeping with more than half of the women who came to his church. Toni was so naive as to the true nature of people that she was blind to Robert's activities until it came blatantly out in the open and the church began to crumble around them. Even though Toni wasn't sleeping with pastor Robert, many people thought that she was since she worked so closely with him. When all this came to light, Toni was shocked at Robert's indiscretions and left the congregation. And without her money—Samuel's money—to hold them afloat, the whole ministry sank under its own perverse weight.

Toni started to become disillusioned and questioned herself and God for bringing her to the city. Part of her wished that they had stayed in the peaceful suburbs. But she knew that the spiritual war did not stop just because she was having her doubts. She could see the spirits of light and the spirits of darkness battling eternally on the streets of Chicago and she knew that she was needed in that battle.

The next project God wanted her to do, she decided, was to lead a Bible study group at her house every Sunday. This lasted for a short while, but eventually Toni started becoming too radical for the average Christians who lived in the city. She also lacked the charisma to keep a loyal following. So her little congregation would come and go. Toni would tell her followers that they weren't strong enough in the Spirit. That they needed to become radical with their prayer life. She told them that she could see the battle waging between angels and demons. Toni would regularly speak in tongues and then translate the message sent from God. And she would be slain in the Spirit, overcome with the power of Christ. Most of the women who came to Bible study just wanted a little club, a group of other older women they could get together and gossip with. That wasn't what Toni was trying to accomplish in the slightest. Eventually she had no congregation at all, and she was forced to look for another avenue to get her spiritual rocks off.

Toni prayed and meditated days and nights trying to find guidance from God to where He wished her to go next on her spiritual journey. She had always been intrigued and fascinated by the Jewish roots of Christianity. However, her unwavering faith that Jesus is the Risen Christ, the Son of God, prevented her from converting to full-fledged Judaism. Instead, she became exposed to a movement called Messianic Judaism, or its other moniker *Jews for Jesus*. Toni was instantly in love. She had always enjoyed watching *Fiddler on the Roof* and embraced the Tradition with new-found enthusiasm. The congregation that she found was called Temple Shalom Yisrael, or Temple Shalom for short.

By this time David was twelve and Shelley was fourteen.

For Shelley the Messianic Jewish traditions took hold firmly, she even found a Hebrew teacher and started learning to read and speak the language. David, on the other hand, was starting to assert his own personality at this point. He went along for a while since his mother insisted, but he was tired of all this religiosity and Jesus dogma, especially since he had already been sexually awakened. Samuel didn't even bother going at all. He had become disillusioned with the congregation of Christianity when Freedom Church fell apart and hadn't been able to bring himself to pretend and go along much more after that incident. The divide between Toni and Samuel was complete and there was no going back. Toni had found a renewed happiness with Temple Shalom, and Jesus always took precedence over her husband and family.

Toni and Shelley enjoyed celebrating Passover and Yam Kippur, as well as all the other traditional Jewish holidays. Shelley even had herself a Bat Mitzvah, which is a Jewish rite of passage into adulthood, which usually is done around the age of thirteen or fourteen. Toni vocally wished that her son would also embrace Messianic Judaism like his sister had and get a Bar Mitzvah himself. But David would have none of it. He was done, completely and utterly finished. The fracture was complete; Father and son versus Mother and daughter.

David started to assert his autonomy from Toni by reading books that she disapproved of, authors like Clive Barker and books on Magic and Esotericism. Toni would frequently tell him that these books brought demons into the house and he was being possessed by the Devil. David also started watching *South Park* and other movies and shows deemed inappropriate by his mother. He stopped going to Shabbat service on

Saturdays with Shelley and Toni. Instead he stayed home and would watch action movies with his father. Naturally Toni disapproved of this behavior but she knew that her son was now too old for her to force him to come to church with her. In truth, she was relieved not to have to deal with her rebellious son, at least on Saturdays and other times they went to Temple.

Samuel knew that his marriage was now beyond all hope of repair. They had what is called an irreconcilable difference. It had been a long time since they even had slept in the same room, much less had sex. Toni had kept the master bedroom while Samuel slept in the bunk bed on the top floor of their house. Toni had also let herself go, becoming frumpy and unattractive to the point where Samuel didn't even want to be intimate with his wife. She gained a lot of weight, leaving her with a little potbelly. She didn't wear make-up anymore and she started wearing ugly bibbed overalls all the time. Her justification for this was that focus on physical appearance and the body is materialistic and against a life of pure spirituality.

As the schism intensified, so did the clash between Toni and David. She thought that the books, music, and movies that he was into were all Satanic and would lead him down the path of Darkness. She would regularly tell him that if he didn't worship Jesus then he worshipped Satan. To Toni there was no middle ground, you were either a saved Believer, or you were possessed by demons and worshipped the Devil. All this kind of talk did was make David more and more rebellious. A rage started to build inside him. He wasn't close with his sister anymore and for him that was heartbreaking; that their mother was driving a wedge between siblings that were once so happy and close, building imaginative worlds and stories with dolls and toys. David felt the destruction of his family and the anger continued to increase. He started drawing pictures depicting horrific violence and graphic sex. He also began to write, channeling all of his rage into healthy creative outlets; poetry, short stories, music. Toni was far from encouraging, she became more and more convinced that her son was possessed by legions of demons. He might even be the Antichrist himself.

Toni decided then to end it once and for all. While Samuel was away at trial for his law job, she seized the opportunity to serve him with divorce papers. This was the final nail in the coffin. Samuel knew this was coming, but to serve him with the papers while he was away and under so much stress from the case he was working on, was just cruel. He lost all respect for her. Not that he had much respect for her anyway, she had lost that years earlier when she started going down this path and pulled away from her husband to follow Jesus above all other things in her life. Samuel was left so desolate from the failure of his marriage, to the point where he felt there was nothing left to lose. Still spinning from the audacity of his wife serving him with divorce papers at trial, he had no qualms going after an attractive co-worker who was twelve years his junior. It had been years since he had gotten any affection from his wife, so he thought, *why not go for it*. To his shock and surprise this secretary, whose name was Wendy, responded in kind to Samuel's advances and his romantic initiation soon led to an intimate relationship.

Their family cracked wide open like a dead clam with no pearl inside to make any of it worth anything. After the divorce, David and Samuel stayed living in Illinois. They were joined by Wendy soon after, who became David's stepmother. Toni took

Shelley to live with her out of state, in the Missouri Ozarks. They changed from city people to rural folk. Shelley and Toni still maintained a bit of their Messianic Jewish traditions, but they found a church down in the Ozarks that they liked and became more and more fundamentalist, adhering to a strict literal interpretation of the Bible. It would seem that they finally found where they belonged. And for a time, they were happy...

V

Toni bought the 40 acre property adjacent to the 40 acres that Samuel's parents owned and lived on. Since they each owned so much land, they were neighbors, but they weren't right next to each other where Shelley could see her grandparents' house. She had to walk up the gravel road and then up the hill into the forest. It took about fifteen minutes. There were a few reasons why Toni decided to move to this boondocks location. First of all she wanted to get as far away from Samuel as possible and to keep his daughter away from him. In her mind he was a filthy adulterer. She also wanted to get away from David, who in her mind was possessed by demons and would grow up to be a rapist serial killer, or God knew what. Toni's other assumption was that it might be easier to find a church community more in line with her own beliefs in a rural area than it had been in the city of Chicago.

The first thing they had to do was renovate the house, because basically it was a garage that had been half-assedly turned into a living space. The two bedrooms that had been set up in the 'house' were basically cubicles and their walls didn't even reach the ceiling. With the money that she had gotten from the divorce, Toni started the building project right away. Toni and Shelley had also brought their pets with them when they moved—a Pomeranian named Frisky and a orange striped cat named Milo. Shelley would put them into their cages when the construction guys came through to work on the house.

Shelley was fifteen when she and her mother moved into the Missouri house. A couple days after they moved in, Shelley decided to start up a journal of her experiences in this new place called the Ozarks. She never kept track of the date or the day, just the number of whatever entry she was on. Shelley would hide her journal under the mattress of her bed so that her eyes were the only ones who would see it.

FIRST ENTRY:

We just moved in to this house a couple days ago and haven't gotten to know many people around here yet. My mom isn't a very social person. I'm not either, it's against the Bible to have friends that don't share the same Christian beliefs as you. Everyone on Earth should be a Christian because Christianity is the only right religion and I wish that everyone was a Christian because that would make the world a happier place. My mom says that anyone who doesn't worship Jesus worships Satan. She thinks this about my brother. He doesn't believe the same things we do and I don't want him to go to Hell. That makes me sad because I don't understand why people would not want to worship Jesus in all his glory instead of burn in Hell for all of eternity. I know that I would. My mom says to be good and obey Jesus's teachings and not to talk back to her because she knows more about everything than I do in my 15 years of being on God's great Earth. My mother is the smartest person I know and I look up to her. They're supposed to start construction on the house tomorrow. Mom has been writing Bible verses all over the concrete floor in the kitchen, but that will be covered up by the wood that they are going to lay. All the verses will protect us from evil spirits. I'm excited to explore this new place.

This was Shelley's mindset throughout most of the time. She viewed her mother as a very wise figure, someone she could always look up to and trust. The illusion that she had built up around her mother had not yet proven to her to be a delusion. But that was coming, it was unavoidable and that would shake the foundations of all that Shelley believed in. Her entire life growing up, she had learned never to question her mother's authority because it came from God. Teenagers were supposed to question their parents, as children come of age it is healthy to do this. But Shelley had started to become very capable of bottling her questions and feelings inside. She suppressed a lot of what came up within her and fell in line with her mother, because if she didn't—she had seen how well that worked out for her brother.

After construction started on the house, it took about three months to create it how Toni had envisioned. A whole second floor was added to the house which contained one bedroom, an office, and a bathroom. They fixed up the two rooms on the ground floor by extending the walls to reach the ceiling. One of the rooms became an office and the other became Toni's room.

Between the two rooms on the ground floor was the living room where Toni put in a large blue L-shaped couch and a TV. The whole kitchen was also redone to add linoleum flooring and an island in the middle.

Toni and Shelley took the time while their house was being renovated to get acquainted with the town and to find a church that they could fit in to. Shelley had never lived in the country before and she was enraptured by their neighbors who had a goat farm. She loved to go over there and visit the old couple, Diane and Billy, who owned that farm. They would teach her how to milk the goats and butcher chickens. Shelley was starting to turn into a country girl.

Toni decided that they should be dressing more modestly as well. So they started wearing pastel colored dresses—mostly blues and lavenders—along with a cloth to cover their head. Toni had gotten this idea in her mind that God wished for women to cover their hair with cloth as a sign of respect for their religion, similar to what nuns would wear. To be honest, Shelley didn't really like the way her mother dictated how they should dress, but she went along with it so as to not make waves. Shelley learned early on that it was better to just get along then to make problems and arguments. Especially with her mother.

Toni also found a church called *The House of Christ* which they started attending. The pastor was Evan, and the building was small and modest compared to some of the suburban churches that Toni had been to in Illinois. The pastor and congregation took a fundamentalist view of the Bible, insisting on a literal interpretation of scripture. Pastor Evan was not married, and from the first time Toni met him, she felt a strong connection between them. If it was spiritual or sexual—or both—she hadn't quite determined yet.

They met a lot of other families there from the church community that they became friends with. Shelley especially took a liking to the Howell family who owned and operated a dairy farm not too far from where Toni and Shelley lived. The Howells had three girls around Shelley's age and a couple years older, and they had three boys ages eighteen, thirteen, and nine. They asked Shelley if she would be interested in helping them around the farm and they would pay her for her work. Shelley was more than happy to be a part of the farm lifestyle. She got very good at butchering chickens and turkeys and eviscerating their guts. Shelley really enjoyed being around a large family and having kids her own age to socialize with.

Toni and Shelley had their two indoor pets Frisky and Milo. But Shelley started to want more outdoor animals around their property, so she asked her mother if they could create a little animal farm. Toni obliged, and they got a couple ducks, chickens, a flock of guinea fowl, a couple outdoor cats, and a border collie that would be an outdoor pet as well.

Shelley and Toni were very happy in their new environment, much more than they were in Chicago. Their house was finished, they had a church and they were part of a community, Shelley had friends and work, they were surrounded by animals and God's creation all day, and they also had family just up the road. They were very fulfilled. What more could they want? Toni wanted a partner, and Pastor Evan was the one she wanted to have, spiritually, sexually, emotionally. She was going to have to be more aggressive if she was to make her feelings known and get what she wanted. Pastor Evan would be with her, it was just a matter of time and prayer.

VI

Several Sundays later Toni had built up the courage to ask Pastor Evan to meet. They had had many conversations in the interim. They were becoming more and more intimate, as much as talking can make you with another person. Toni could feel the sexual tension growing and growing. She knew that the connection and tension would be so great that Pastor Evan's defenses would be down and he would be powerless to her advances. Little did she know, Evan was the one who was really planning this the whole time.

Evan stood by the door of the church, saying goodbye to his congregation as they filed out of the chapel. Toni pulled Shelley to the back of the line so she could have a chance to talk to him without other members of the flock gawking around.

"That was a great sermon today, Brother Evan." Toni smiled as she and Shelley approached him, straggling at the end of the line. He smiled back. "That verse about principalities and evil wickedness in high places. That's something that has been on my mind lately. God has been impressing on my heart questions about secret cabals and conspiracies that go on even right under our noses," Toni extrapolated.

Evan raised his eyebrows. "You know about that?"

"Yes, I know about the Shadow Council," Toni continued. "And the secret Circles of Satanism that have infiltrated every branch of our government..." She trailed off for a second, trying to think of how to initiate this meeting. "I was thinking we could get together to discuss this in more detail. How we can get the church involved, and our prayer warriors to escalate so they can weaponize spiritually... Maybe tonight, if you're free." Shelley just stood next to her mother silently looking back and forth from Evan to Toni. A smile teased to pull at the corners of Evan's mouth. He briefly glanced in Shelley's direction and then back to Toni.

Pastor Evan cleared his throat. "Yes, well," he started and then gained his composure. "I think that is a wonderful idea, Toni. I'll be free tonight if you want to meet to discuss and pray." He looked at his watch. "8 o'clock good for you?"

At first Toni was a bit stunned that this was actually about to happen. After a second of her mouth half hanging agape, she composed herself. "Y-yes. That sounds great. I should meet you at your house?"

Pastor Evan nodded then shook Toni's hand and held the door open so Shelley and Toni could go find their car in the parking lot while he locked up the church for the night.

"Mom, why do I have to have a babysitter? I'm fifteen years old. If you want to go see the pastor, that's your business. I'm all right to stay here by myself. Besides, Grandma and Grandpa are right up the road if anything happens. All I was saying is that I have a bad feeling about your meeting with Pastor Evan and it might not be a good idea for you to go," Shelley pleaded with her mother just before she was about to leave for Evan's house.

Toni threw her hands up in the air. She had been trying for hours to find a babysitter to watch Shelley while she was gone, but was having no luck on such short notice. "I just can't win with you!" Toni was trying hard not to yell, but her religious indignation was getting the best of her. "I told you once and I don't want to have to tell you again. Don't question me. God knows what is best for you and he speaks to me. It's getting late and I have to go. Fine, you can stay here by yourself. If anything happens or you need anything, call your grandmother and they'll take care of you." Toni shook her head as she walked out of the door to rendezvous with Pastor Evan.

As Shelley stared at the closed door and the spot where her mother was standing just a second ago, she couldn't shake the intuition that strange events were coming and her mother's meeting with Pastor Evan would be the catalyst for all of them. Shelley clenched her fists together and trembled, her internal rage not quite evident. She had gotten very good at hiding her true feelings from herself and the people around her. One silent tear rolled down her cheek and her inner turmoil was suppressed once more.

Toni got in her car, determined to have this encounter with Pastor Evan. She drove off toward his house, a subtle tingling feeling began to build between her legs. And we find ourselves back where our story began.

VII

Toni awoke on the floor of Evan's basement. She was naked and his arm was around her shoulders, she had used his chest as a pillow. Dry coagulated blood clung to her breasts and stomach. "Oh, no," Toni said with a start. "What time is it?"

Evan groaned and slowly opened his eyes. "It's early," he muttered. "What's up?"

Toni slowly detached from Evan's embrace and made it to her feet. "My daughter. I wasn't planning to be out all night and leave her alone." She glanced around the sparse room for somewhere she could get cleaned up. Evan pointed to the far corner of the room. There was a door there that Toni hadn't noticed before.

"There. There's a bathroom," Evan said through a yawn. "You can go wash the blood off and be on your way in five minutes."

Toni nodded, grabbed her clothes and rushed to the bathroom to clean herself up. After she was done, she kissed Evan goodbye and rushed back home.

When Toni got back to her house, Shelley was already awake and eating cereal at the island in the kitchen. Shelley stared at her mother as she walked in the door. "You were gone a long time," Shelley said after chewing her mouthful of cereal.

Toni sighed, walked over to the island and put her purse down on a chair. "I know," Toni conceded. "I'm sorry. I didn't mean to be out all night. But... time just got away from me, I guess." She stared off into space as if deep in thought. Shelley furrowed her brow and studied her mom's face while she chomped away at another bite of cereal.

After a minute of silence Shelley spoke again. "Dad called." For a second the statement didn't register on Toni's blank face, then she seemed to snap out of her daze.

"What?" Toni wasn't sure she had heard Shelley correctly. "Sam called? For what?"

Shelley shrugged. "Said something about David coming to visit us. Dad said to have you call him back as soon as you got home."

"Hmm," was the only response that Toni gave to this. She went to her bedroom to call her ex-husband back.

"David's going to be flying out here tomorrow," Toni said when she returned to the kitchen. Shelley still spooned cereal into her mouth as she eyed her mother. Milk dripped into her bowl out of the corners of her mouth. "Apparently your father wanted David to have a full time job over the summer or his stipulation was that he had to spend the summer down here with us. Obviously he decided this without checking in with me about it." Toni shook her head.

"Who would give a thirteen year old a full time job?" Shelley asked after a moment of silence.

Toni looked over at Shelley as if she was just pulled out of a daze, taking a second to register what her daughter's comment had been. "Huh... That's an interesting point. It seems like an unrealistic expectation to me." She shrugged her shoulders. "Probably just an excuse to dump him on us for the summer so he doesn't have to worry about what he's doing."

"Might be good to see him," Shelley said between bites of soggy cereal, getting to the end of the bowl then slurping the milk down. After a gulp she continued. "It's been a while. I dunno, I kind of miss him. Don't you?"

Toni chewed on her lip, determining how to respond to this. "Yeah... I guess. You know he can be difficult to deal with sometimes though. Lord knows what dark things he's been into since we left."

"Don't be so hard on him, Mom." Shelley got up and took her bowl to the sink. She ran some water on it and then left it there for later. "He went through a hard time. We all did." Shelley turned around and leaned on the counter, looking at her mother.

Toni sighed, raised her arms and then let them drop in a gesture of resignation. "That's true. I'm just worried that Satan has got a hold of him. But then again, maybe Jesus is giving us this time with David in order to minister to him and pull him back to the light of God's love."

Shelley walked over and gave her mom a hug. "I think that's best," she said. "He's still my brother and I love him. Besides, he asked Jesus into his heart when he was a little kid. His salvation is there still, whether he knows it or not, right?"

They detached from each other's embrace and Toni looked into her daughter's face, eyes shifting back and forth. "You're right, Shelley. Once you're saved, you're saved for all eternity.

He can't lose his place in Heaven. God forgives all sins." Toni smiled and kissed Shelley on the top of her head. "I better get the office upstairs set up for David to sleep when he gets here tomorrow." She gave Shelley one last squeeze on the arm and then went upstairs to get the office set up as a guest room.

SECOND ENTRY:

My brother is coming to visit us! He'll be flying into Missouri tomorrow. I'm actually really excited to see him. I don't reveal to Mom all of my feelings because I don't want to make her feel bad. But splitting up me and my brother in the divorce has really affected me more than I let on. I really miss him. We used to have a really close relationship when we were younger. Playing with dolls and making up elaborate imaginative stories to entertain ourselves... It makes me sad thinking about how far apart we are now. We're in two totally different states, for gosh sake! I don't get to see Dad anymore. Our family is completely destroyed and I don't think I'll ever be the same. If I had told Mom that I wanted to stay living with Dad and my brother, I don't think she would have been able to live with that. So I don't want to start trouble. It's easier to live with Mom and our beliefs line up. They don't when it comes to my dad and David. I don't really know what they believe anymore. It's nice to have my grandparents so close, right down the road. But they don't agree with the way my mother raises me, especially my grandpa. He actually doesn't even talk to me as much anymore because he thinks I should be studying other subjects and not be so focused on the Bible. But that's who I am. I want to be a traditional conservative woman, one day be a wife and mother, and follow Jesus's teachings. Mom is smart and teaches me a lot of good things, but she's not perfect.

The next morning Toni and Shelley woke up bright and early. David was arriving on the 9 AM flight into Springfield, Missouri. It was about an hour and a half to two hour drive back to West Plains from there. They finished their breakfast of oatmeal and strawberries then hit the road at 7 am to be at the airport before 9. Toni still drove her white minivan that she had in Chicago before the divorce. The area under the back windshield was completely covered with Jesus themed bumper stickers. No one could ever doubt that this mom van was driven by a devout believer.

Shelley enjoyed long drives. She could sink into daydreams, gazing out the window at the passing countryside. They would pass the time by listening to Messianic Jewish folk music on the car CD player. Shelley would smile and sing along, enjoying the opportunity to practice her Hebrew. Sometimes when she was so engrossed in singing uplifting music and watching the beautiful scenery roll by, she could forget for a moment that her family was no longer intact, and that it never would be again.

They arrived at the airport fifteen minutes before David's flight was supposed to land. As far as they knew everything was on time. Toni and Shelley had to wait in the meeting area below the escalator where the passengers had to come through on their way out. They weren't allowed to go to the gate—which they used to be able to do—since security at airports got a lot stricter since 9/11. Before that incident, David would fly as an unaccompanied minor and always be greeted by his family right at the gate, wherever he was flying into. That luxury was gone along with most other human rights. There was even a time long ago and far away when people could fly without getting their crotches groped by TSA.

As Shelley and Toni waited, watching the escalators for any passengers who had recently gotten off of a flight, they sat in silence. Toni seemed to be somewhere else, lost in her own thoughts, worries, or fantasies. Shelley couldn't tell which one it was.

"Thinking about Pastor Evan?" Shelley asked her mother after a while of trying to decipher what was on her mind.

Toni was shaken out of her trance by the question, a little shocked by her daughter's intuitiveness. Her mouth hung agape for a second then she regained her composure. "Well... Yes, actually," she confessed.

"Ha! I knew it!" Shelley smiled, pleased at her deductive skills. "You like him, don't you? Like, more than a friend?"

"I don't know... The thought of having a man in my life is appealing." Toni laughed a bit awkwardly. She was being purposefully cryptic. "But that's ridiculous. It's way too early for me to be thinking about the possibility of getting remarried." Toni waved her hand as if brushing the idea from her mind. However, her face flushed red just the faintest amount for Shelley to detect it.

"Mom," Shelley smiled compassionately, as if saying *It's okay to have feelings.* "I know you better than you think I do. And I'm not a little kid anymore. I can pick up on adult things. I mean, you even stayed over at his house all night."

"Nothing happened," Toni responded hastily. "We just

discussed passages from the Bible that Evan is thinking about doing a sermon on. And different ways to grow the congregation and expand what's offered at the church. And before we knew it it got so late I fell asleep on the couch... That's it." She didn't want Shelley to know any of the true details about their relationship. To be honest, she felt like she was sinning with Evan. But she didn't want to stop. Toni felt excited and uncertain about where their interactions would take them. Down what dark rabbit hole and what forbidden pleasures she would have to keep a secret. From everyone. She felt guilty, but she loved it so much she didn't want to stop. It made her wet just thinking about the things she wanted to do with Evan. He had some sort of power over her that she couldn't explain. There was a part of her mind that told her that what she had started with him was wrong, but the pull from the other urge was stronger.

Passengers with carry-on bags slung over their shoulders began to come down the escalator. Toni was relieved that this put an end to the conversation that she didn't want to continue with her daughter.

They scanned the faces of all the people making their way down the escalator until David's familiar features came into view. "Look! There he is!" Shelley yelled. David jerked his head around, recognizing his sister's voice. He smiled when his eyes found where they were in the group of all the other family members who were also waiting for their kin. David was still short, about 5'5". He hadn't grown at all since the last time he'd seen his mom and sister. However his hair was a little longer, it hung below his ears trying to make its way to his shoulders but not quite getting there. He wore wire-rimmed glasses and an enormously baggy South Pole shirt that could have passed as a short dress. David's jean shorts were oversized as well, almost reaching his ankles. They looked like capri pants—if they had been skinnier. He had also lost a little weight since the divorce. Stress can do that to a person. Or stress could contribute to putting on weight, depending on what a person reaches for for comfort. David had started smoking weed to deal with his stress, but he wasn't going to be able to smoke any this summer being around Toni and Shelley.

After David got to the bottom of the escalator, he rushed over for a heart-felt family reunion like a good son and brother does. He briefly hugged his mother and then wrapped his arms around his sister as if he hadn't seen her in years. Endorphins swam in their brains as David kissed Shelley on the neck and then on the cheek. The scene was like two long-lost lovers reunited. "I missed you," he said and squeezed her one last time before letting go.

Toni kissed her son on the top of the head like she would to a small child. "I missed you too, D!" She squeezed his shoulder as they left the waiting area and started walking toward baggage claim. "You ready for the long drive home? Even though you were on an airplane for a long time?" Toni asked.

"Oh, yeah," David replied. "I love Missouri. I'm ready for the hills, and the trees, and the country. I was so tired of the same boring Chicago scenery. I can finally relax out here."

VIII

On the drive back to his mother and sister's house, David reflected on how much more peaceful it was out in the country. He felt like a weight had been lifted off of his chest. Even though nowadays his beliefs differed from that of his sister and mother, David still enjoyed spending time with them. There were even splashes of instances where he could forget for a second the reality of his family being in disarray, and be transported back to an earlier time when things were simpler and he was allowed to just be a kid. Unfortunately that time had been ripped away from him far too early. David sighed, staring out the window from the back seat of Toni's van. *I'm just glad to be away from my stepmom*, David thought to himself.

The deep well of sadness that had been growing within him was now giving way to a seething rage that he had to manage for fear of losing more of the life he had, which was rubble as it was. Sometimes when David closed his eyes, he would see this sadness as a pool of blood growing larger and larger as if the ground itself were bleeding. Then he himself would emerge naked from the center of the blood—that's when the rage began. The rage within him, in the vision, would become black tentacles of destruction that would whip out of his back, destroying anything that came near.

"We got some new boardgames that we all could play together," Toni's voice jolted David out of his trance.

"Oh, yeah?" David replied flatly.

Toni looked at her son's reflection in the rear-view mirror and continued. "Uh-huh. That could be fun. And I know you'll enjoy playing with the animals we have on our property. Is there anything in particular you have in mind that would be fun to do while you're here?"

David sat in silence for a moment, recalling what he had in mind to do while he had the peace and clarity of the rural landscape. He was forced to grow up fast and learn quickly, so his intelligence and activities far exceeded his thirteen years. "Yeah," David said after a while. "That sounds like fun. I've got this idea for a fantasy adventure novel. The time I spend out here with you guys might give me the push I need to start writing it."

"That's ambitious!" Toni said with a wide smile. "But I'm sure it'll be great. You're very creative."

"Ma," Shelley interrupted. "Do you think David could help me with the little vegetable garden we started?"

"Maybe, why don't you ask him?" Toni said, her eyes shifting between her two offspring.

Shelley turned around in the front seat to face her brother. "You want to help me with the vegetable garden?"

"Sure, maybe. That could be fun."

Shelley smiled and turned back around to the front, then leaned down to turn the volume up on the Christian music playing through the car stereo.

They arrived home in less than an hour and a half, traffic was light. All David had as far as baggage was a rolling suitcase that he hauled into the house when they got there. There was a lot of land, David noted, and a lot of forest surrounding the property. Those things made him feel comfortable, like he could finally relax and slow down. Tall buildings and concrete always caused him to feel unwanted anxiety.

"I set up a little bedroom for you upstairs in the office there. We pulled out the inflatable mattress and put sheets on it for you to use as your bed." Toni indicated the stairs on the far side of the house, past the kitchen, that led to the upper part of the house. "Why don't you go get settled in and put your things away and I'll get dinner started."

David nodded and made his way over to the stairs, rolling his little bag behind him as he went. Shelley kicked off her shoes at the front door and then flopped herself down on the couch, her dress trailing behind her and then dripping down the side of the couch as she splayed out. Toni was already in the kitchen poking around in the refrigerator for something easy to cook.

David dragged his bag up the stairs and peeked into the first room on the left at the top of the stairs. The bedspread was light pink and the wallpaper was flowery—Shelley's room. Her cat Milo was curled up asleep at the foot of the bed. Across from Shelley's room was a bathroom. At the end of the hall was Toni's office that she had set up as David's room for the visit. Before he entered the room, he turned back and noticed a small circular window at the top of the stairs. Golden sunlight washed in, illuminating the hallway like a waterfall made of gold coins. *At night this whole floor could be bathed in moon- light*, David thought and then went into the office.

The carpet was the standard, boring cream-colored. The inflatable mattress was neatly placed in the middle of the room and made up with lavender sheets. There was a shallow closet with a sliding door. And in the far corner was his mother's desk and old Microsoft desktop computer—probably from the late nineties. David had been using an Apple computer since he was eleven, but he'd make due with what he had to work with. And the desk was right next to a large window that looked out over the front yard. This was a perfect place for him to work on writing his book.

David put his bag down on the floor next to his bed. He unzipped the side as he sat onto the carpet cross-legged. He had mostly packed clothes and a couple notebooks to keep notes in for his writing projects. Underneath his neatly folded t-shirts, David had smuggled in two books that he knew his mother wouldn't approve of. He slid them out from their hiding spot to look at them lovingly and flip through their pages like a devoted student. The first book was *The Book of the Law* by Aleister Crowley, and the second book was *The Tree of Life* by Israel Regardie. They both were books on the occult and magic. David knew his mom would freak if she knew he had brought them with him, so he slipped them silently back under his t-shirts into their hiding spot.

David was in deep thought and was jolted out of his contemplation by a wet tongue licking his elbow. He looked over and beside him was a fluffy ball of fur with a little head sticking out of it with buggy black eyes. It was Frisky, their pet Pomeranian. She yapped at David a couple times and looked at him with those soggy puppy dog eyes, wanting him to pet her. David scratched the dog's head and behind her ears. Frisky was getting old, she was as old as he was—thirteen years in human years. David wasn't sure how old that was in dog years.

"Hey, Frisky!" David said to the dog in a playful voice. She twirled around in a circle several times. "You want some food? Let's go down and see what Mom's making for dinner!"

THIRD ENTRY:

My bother flew to Missouri today to join us in our humble country home. It's nice to have him around again. I didn't realize how much I had missed him till I saw him come down that escalator at the airport today. Even though the divorce wasn't that long ago, it seems like forever ago that I had seen David. He's different somehow. I mean, we all are... different. I don't know how a family can split apart and still remain the same and not be damaged somehow in the process. I feel like there is a lot of pretending going on when it comes to me and Mom. We like to pretend everything is okay, but really there is a raging storm below the surface that isn't allowed to be let loose. I don't know... The difference I see in David is more subtle somehow. It's in his demeanor and his energy, I guess. I don't really know how to describe it. He seems more calm somehow, like he's gained some much needed strength that I haven't been able to find yet. We used to be so close and tell each other everything. Now he seems more reserved. But I want him to open up to me again like he used to. Share with me how he's coped with everything. Maybe telling me that secret that lies in wait silently below the surface.

It didn't take the three of them long to fall into somewhat of a normal routine. David was pleasant and interacted with his mother and sister, playing games, playing with the animals, and helping Shelley in the garden once in a while. But he still seemed to be playing his cards close to his chest. He didn't really reveal how he was actually feeling about the whole situation, and neither Toni nor Shelley pried anything out of him. To be honest, the only one who even thought about that was Shelley. The divorce had affected her and David in a profoundly different way than it had Toni, and Shelley intuitively felt that. Toni was too absorbed in her study of the Bible and what she wanted to pursue as far as a relationship with Pastor Evan.

A couple weeks passed like this. David would spend long stretches of time on his mom's computer typing out this fantastical story that had come bubbling up in him like a well in a flash flood. And as he composed his prose, David would occasionally glance out the window that overlooked the front yard, and watch Shelley digging in the dirt of her little not-so-secret garden. In a way he felt like Shelley had become his muse, unlocking hidden gems and treasures of beautifully written passages that David wasn't aware were within him. And the pages came flowing out from the tips of his fingers.

On Sunday David even accompanied his mother and sister to church. Toni introduced him to Pastor Evan after the service was over. David was quiet but polite. He shook Evan's hand and said, "Nice to meet you."

"It is a pleasure to meet you, son!" He shook David's hand with a smile that was a little too wide, a little too white. David looked down at their extended handshake, noticing that Evan squeezed just slightly too firm and too vigorous. "Your mother has told me all about you!" The smile did not leave his face.

"Has she?" was David's only reply. He sensed something was off about Pastor Evan. The part within himself that was slightly askew could easily connect to a piece in another that was also off kilter.

Pastor Evan finally let go of David's hand and looked back up at Toni. "We'll have to all get together soon and have dinner," Evan continued. Toni smiled warmly at him. Was that a slight blush that David noticed on her cheeks? As if his mother and Evan were already secret lovers. "My place? I'm cooking!" As Evan waited for a response in the affirmative, that fake smile never once faltered or left his face.

"That sounds great!" Toni responded after a second of awkward smiling, as if they were UFC fighters competing for the title of the Colgate Championship. "Actually, we've been raising a flock of guinea fowl—have you ever eaten one? They're a little more gamey than chickens, but we like them." Toni glanced at Shelley who concurred with a nod. "Maybe we can, you know, butcher one up and bring it by to cook."

"That sounds perfect," said Evan as he gave Toni a hug. "I'll call you."

IX

"Mom," David started between munches of his breakfast of Froot Loops. Toni was puttering around the kitchen doing dishes and cleaning up. Shelley hadn't yet come down from her bedroom that morning. "Frisky has been sitting in the kitty litter box again." *Munch munch.* "I wouldn't bring it up, it's just that I've seen her doing that the past few days. I think I even saw her eating Milo's poop one time... Is this, like, normal?" David looked up at his mother with concerned saucer eyes while he continued to chomp his soggy cereal.

Toni sighed and turned around to face her son from the other side of the island. "Yeah... It seems to be getting to be a more and more common thing. You know, she's getting old. And I don't think she can see very well either. The vet said that she was developing, um, cataracts. That was it." Toni paused, mourning the fact that her beloved pet was coming to the end of her life—or so it seemed. "I wish I knew what I could do to help her." She sighed again and shook her head.

"You know," David began with a mouthful of cereal, slurping milk from his large silver spoon. "You could always put her down." Toni studied David's face but came up empty. He continued, "You know, *bang*, quick. Out go the lights."

"Huh..." Toni looked like she was actually contemplating this solution as if David was making a serious proposition. He was joking, obviously. However, it seemed Toni was not quite astute enough to pick that up.

The next morning, bright and early at 5 AM, just as the sun was peaking over the horizon, Toni took Frisky down to the meadow on the side of the house. The one with the blackberry bushes. It was beautiful in the summer time, and Shelley always enjoyed picking blackberries for hours, her fingers stained purple by the time she would come back to the house with baskets full. Toni held her shotgun against her shoulder like a American Revolution soldier about to go into battle for freedom. She walked ahead while the Pomeranian waddled behind her panting and exited, unaware of its fate.

Toni stopped almost to the tree line, near the blackberry bushes. She turned around. "Sit!" She commanded. Frisky sat, she yawned and continued panting. The dog looked around the field, as if she was anticipating to play a doggy game. Toni's eyes were shiny, and tears threatened to pour from the corners of her eyes. It was still dark, but the sun was beginning to peek up over the trees. Toni swung the shotgun off her shoulder and aimed at the dog's head. Just as she pulled the trigger, Frisky moved, distracted by a rabbit or some such creature.

Because of this sudden movement, the shotgun's aim didn't quite hit the center of its mark. Instead, the shot only blew off half of the dog's head. Dog blood and brain matter spattered against the dewy grass. Frisky began to whimper as much as she could with half of a face. Blood was squirting out of the side of her shattered skull as she tried to crawl away from her murderer. Now tears began to liberally pour down Toni's cheeks as she fumbled to put another shell into the shotgun. She didn't want this poor creature to suffer more than it had to. Finally she got the shell into the gun and pumped it, aimed, and fired. This time the rest of the dog's head blew off, staining the grass in front and around it like a Jackson Pollock painting. The rest of Frisky's body lay still, like a ball of hair ripped off a Troll doll.

Toni sighed. "God, please forgive me for taking this dog's life," she whispered to the rising sun. She said a short silent prayer over the fallen pet, and then walked back toward the house, sobbing softly, leaving the carcass to become food for the coyotes.

FOURTH ENTRY:

This morning I was woken up by the sound of two shots from what sounded like a shotgun. It wasn't even that far away, I think it might have been in the field with the blackberry bushes. I know Mom has used that shotgun before to kill pests like possums and armadillos. Maybe that's what it was, I'm pretty sure. I'll have to ask her about it later. I think I was having a wonderful dream too. Can't really remember now what it was about... Don't you hate that? When you're having a really nice dream, maybe even about a boy you have a crush on, and you get woken up and interrupted just at the good part? That's so annoying.

David barged into Shelley's room, interrupting her writing in her journal. Upon seeing her brother, she quickly closed her journal and slid it under her pillow, hoping he wouldn't have seen it. Of course, he did notice. Yet, David filed that information away in his mind for future use. There were more pressing matters at hand.

"Don't you ever knock?" Shelley asked, perturbed.

"Sorry," David replied quickly. There was a distraught look on his face. Shelley wondered what on earth could possibly have happened. He began speaking very rapidly, almost manically. "Mom killed Frisky and I'm pretty sure it's my fault. Me and Mom were talking about the dog yesterday and how she seems to be sitting in the cat's little box more and more everyday, not seeming to know where she is and occasionally eating the cat's poop. I kind of suggested as a joke that she could put Frisky down, you know—bang—one shot to the head and it's all over. But I was joking. I didn't think that she would actually do it." David stopped his rapid-fire monologue and sat there panting, his thirteen-year-old eyes pleading with his sister to absolve him of his transgression.

"Whoa, slow down. She did what? Is that what those gunshots were this morning?" Shelley put her hand on David's leg to try to comfort him and calm him down. "You know, David, on a farm sometimes we gotta do things like that. Life can be brutal on a farm. I mean, I cut off chickens heads and pull their guts out." She laughed and David gave a weak smile, looking slightly relieved. "It wasn't your fault, little dude!" Shelley gave David the look and then pounced on him, tickling him under his armpits viciously. David began to laugh uncontrollably.

"Stop! Stop! Mercy!" David wheezed the words out between bouts of laughter. This was kind of nice actually, it reminded

David of the simpler times when they were younger and would play like this without a care in the world.

"No chance!" Shelley laughed mischievously and continued to tickle-attack David even harder. "Are you gonna feel better? Are you gonna stop blaming yourself?"

"Yes! Yes!" David gasped, but his sister wouldn't relent. She was having too much fun. After Shelley had thoroughly abused David's armpits, she moved down to his most ticklish spot, the joint sockets where his legs met his pelvis, right on either side of his penis. David shrieked and couldn't stop laughing to the point he was gasping to get a breath, but he liked it in a masochistic sort of way. Shelley also used this opportunity to feel up her brother. She would sneak squeezes of his penis as she tickled him, Shelley could easily feel it under David's sweatpants. She loved feeling his cock swell with blood under her hand, it made her tingly between the legs. She could never vocalize this forbidden perversion, so she had to pretend like she wasn't actually doing what she was doing. Her dirty little incestuous secret.

"This is it?" Shelley asked in a disappointed tone.

"This is it." David replied.

They studied what was left of Frisky's carcass. Most of it had been picked clean by turkey buzzards and coyotes before the time the two of them got out to the field to look for it. There was no head, just pink smears on the grass, brain matter and blood that had been picked at by the predators. There was some fuzz-ball fur still stuck to the bones that blew softly in the breeze like dried grass.

"Huh..." Shelley grunted as she stared at the mass of bone

and mutilated organs that had once been their family pet. David shot her a glance as if she was a peculiar creature studying a homicide crime scene.

"What?" David raised his eyebrows.

"No, I," Shelley shook her head but didn't take her eyes away from the mutilated corpse. "I was just expecting..." She trailed off for a second, searching for the right word. "More."

"More?"

Now she finally looked over at her brother who was staring at her like she was a crazy person. Shelley chuckled. "Yeah, now this just looks like the chicken carcass I eviscerated earlier and that we're gonna eat later."

"Eww, gross, sis." David stuck out his tongue and pretended like he was vomiting. Shelley laughed again and playfully punched her brother on the arm.

David looked uncertain for a moment, thinking about his mother. "What is it, David?"

He looked up at Shelley with genuine concern in his eyes. "Does Mom ever, you know, act weird? Or seem weird?"

"Weird? What do you mean?"

David scratched his chin—where he wished some facial hair would start growing—deep in thought. "I dunno how to say... Just, like, off or not right somehow. Strange... Like, you know, if she thought that I became too much for her to handle or I was too much of a burden on her, that she would put me down too." He indicated the corpse.

David's face was so serious, but his notion was so ridiculous that Shelley burst out laughing. "That's crazy! Mom would never kill you. She loves us, she's our mother. Yeah, you can be a pain in the neck sometimes, but that doesn't mean she wants you dead. Where do you get these crazy ideas? You've been watching too many movies."

"Oh, yeah... Ha, ha... I guess I just feel weird because I was the one who suggested this."

"You're thinking too much. Come on, little bro." She said suddenly. "Let's get out of here." David nodded in the affirmative. Shelley grabbed a handful of blackberries off the bush and they left the corpse of their once beloved pet to rot and decompose into the earth.

That night David couldn't sleep. He felt as if there was a ghostly presence of the dead dog haunting him. Frisky couldn't rest in her nonexistent grave because she harbored anger toward David, the one who gave the idea of killing her. He tossed and turned on his inflatable mattress, his heart racing and sweat beading his brow. "I'm sorry. I'm sorry," David whispered, his eyes squeezed tightly shut. The moonlight poured into his room through the window, bathing him in a bluish glow. David could swear he could hear an ethereal barking coming from the woods. Even though his sister had tried to ease his mind, he still felt guilty about the death. They had even discussed it briefly with their mother who assured them both that what she did was the most humane thing to do. Needless to say, he was less than convinced. David was reminded of the time he had watched the movie *Panic Room* and was so scared that he couldn't sleep the whole night. Actually, he was so freaked-out that he crawled into his Dad's bed and stayed there the rest of the night.

David slowly crawled out of bed, half expecting Frisky's ghost to fly out of his closet and try to maul him to death with translucent fangs. He was only wearing his bedtime clothes, pajama pants and a t-shirt. There was a chill in the air and David felt like he should run to the bathroom and splash cold water on his face to see if he could get a grip and calm down.

Cautiously he stepped out of his room and turned down the moonlit hallway. Suddenly David froze, petrified, and stared at the small circular window at the top of the stairs at the end of the hall. When he saw it, he pissed himself. Warm urine ran down David's leg and pooled on the carpet. Then he started to shake as if he had tremors from an allergic reaction to psych meds. There, hovering outside the window like a semi-transparent Peter Pan, was Frisky's ghost, silent and staring him down. David clapped his hands over his mouth to keep from screaming so loud that it would wake the dead. His teeth began to chatter.

The ghost of the dead dog suddenly swooped down through the wall straight for David. The sound of barking was a cacophony in his head, but the snout of the ghost dog was not moving at all. The ectoplasmic apparition went straight through David's body. He spun around just in time to see it exit through the far wall and disappear. "Holy shit!" David whispered under his breath and ran back into his room.

With speed that would make a competitive racer proud, David pulled off his pee-soaked pajama pants and whipped on some clean boxers. "Fuck. Fuck. Fuck." He said under his breath, terrified that he was actually going to die. David zoomed out of his room and into his sister's as if he literally had the Devil on his heels. He dove under the covers next to Shelley, shivering and almost crying from fear.

Shelley slowly woke up as she felt someone invading her

bed. Rolling over slowly, groggily, she saw her brother in a fetal position, shaking and looking like he was about to be inevitably murdered. "Sorry, sis," he whispered. "I thought I saw Frisky outside the window. I'm scared. Can I sleep with you?"

Shelley yawned, still pretty much asleep. "I guess. I'm sure it was just a nightmare. I told you not to worry about the dog."

"Thanks," David began to calm down and came out of his fetal position, stretching out under the covers. "I know it's silly. I think I was just freaked-out about what we saw..."

"Now go to sleep." Shelley turned over, giving her back to her brother. She was wearing a thin pink nightgown with just panties underneath. David scooched up against Shelley's body and put his arm around her waist, hugging her like a teddy bear. Even though she was a bit taller than him, he did his best to be the big spoon. David's face was squished up against her back as he scooted his crotch against Shelley's soft round butt. She didn't make any move to pull away. *This feels nice*, David thought as he began to relax into sleep. And just as he fell deeply into sleep, his erection became fully hard against his sister's slender body.

X

FIFTH ENTRY:

David slept with me in my bed last night. When he cuddled with me I didn't push him away. I actually liked it. Does that make me gross? Am I going to go to hell for this? God, please forgive me for my perversity... This is something I could never tell anyone else. Only you, Diary. God knows too, but will he judge me for this? I could feel David's hard penis against my body. I could feel myself having impure thoughts, and maybe a little lubrication between my legs. Jeez, what am I saying? Please give me strength against this temptation and perversion.

David was sitting on the couch in the living room reading a book, *Pilgrim's Progress*. It was a title from his mother's book-shelf. He couldn't risk being caught reading the occult books that he had smuggled with him in his suitcase, so David chose his favorite Christian book Toni owned. Shelley was laying on her stomach on the carpet, her face in a sketch pad doodling farm animals with colored pencils. It was early afternoon.

Toni emerged from her bedroom to come talk to her

progeny about plans for the night. "Hey, Shelley," Toni began as she came into the living room. Shelley looked up from her drawing. "You still want to go see that presentation of *Little Women* at the theater tonight, right?"

"Yeah, that'll be fun," Shelley replied.

"What? You didn't tell me about this?" David interjected.

Toni addressed his question before Shelley could. "I figured it was a girl thing. You wouldn't be interested. Did you ever read the book?"

"No. It's cool. I was just surprised you had plans to go out tonight and didn't tell me till the last minute."

"I'm sorry, sweetie," Toni said. "It just slipped my mind... We gotta be there by five. And Pastor Evan is coming over to babysit while we're gone."

"What?" David exclaimed, shocked. "I don't need a baby-sitter. I'm not a baby!"

"I know you're not, honey." Toni softened to show genuine concern for her son's opinion. "But you're also not an adult either. Besides, this will be a good opportunity for you two to get to know each other. You know, before we all have dinner together."

David rubbed his forehead and then waved his hand at his mother in a dismissive fashion. "Whatever," he said. "I guess that's fine." David stood up and tossed the copy of *Pilgrim's Progress* he was reading onto the couch. "I'm gonna go upstairs and work on some writing." He exited stage left and left Toni and Shelley alone in the living room.

Toni looked down at Shelley who was sketching again. "Is he okay?" Toni asked, eyebrows raised.

Shelley looked up, half registering the question. "Huh? Oh,

yeah, he's fine." Shelley affirmed and went right back to her colored pencils.

And David *was* okay. Okay as he could be. Okay as any of them were.

"Evan's here and we're about to leave." Toni was in the doorway to the office which was now the guest room. David was typing away furiously on the word processor. He swiveled around in the desk chair he was sitting in.

"Yeah, okay," he said, his attention still on his work. "Let me just finish this paragraph I'm writing and I'll be right down." David swiveled back to the computer and continued to type with ardor, as if he was composing a masterpiece that, if not exorcised, would be a tragic loss to the human race.

Four minutes later David descended the stairs to see his mother and sister off and to greet his babysitter. Evan was standing near the door speaking quietly with Toni. He had just recently kicked his shoes off and he was wearing a white dress shirt buttoned all the way up to the top and tucked into his dark navy blue jeans. David had a feeling that this was going to be a strange night. The missing piece within him was somehow connected to the missing piece within Evan. Shelley was sitting in a chair at the island, ready to leave. She was wearing a modest blouse and a long skirt.

David walked closer to where they were all congregated. He gave a weak wave and a smile. Shelley jumped up from her chair, shoes already on and ready to go. Toni and Evan ended their conversation as David entered the room.

"Hey, sport!" Evan greeted David with a fake cheery smile. He put his hand on David's shoulder and gave it a squeeze.

David didn't pull away even though he felt uncomfortable with the physical contact.

"You two will be good together?" Toni looked back and forth between her son and the pastor.

"Of course," Evan replied. "We'll have lots of fun. I like playing board games, or whatever kids like to do these days." He gave Toni a hug and a light kiss on the cheek, like a respectful Christian man who wanted to give the impression of wishing to court instead of the worldly 'dating' that secular young people engaged in.

Toni smiled warmly at the affection. Evan was the only man who had expressed any interest in her romantically since before her marriage to Samuel had fallen apart at the seams. "Well, help yourself to any of the food in the refrigerator or pantry for dinner. There are some frozen pizzas or macaroni. Whatever David wants is fine. Shelley and I will be back in a few hours."

Evan locked the door behind the women as they exited the house. David was already rummaging through the cabinets for food when Evan turned around to see what he was up to.

"So how are you getting along with your mom and sister?" Evan asked, trying to make friendly small talk. "Are you enjoying your vacation down here in the Ozarks?"

"Yeah," David responded, still rummaging through the cabinet without looking at Evan. "I love it here in the country. It's so peaceful. I love the animals and the forest. It really gives me time to clear my mind and focus on writing. It's too distracting in the city. And having to deal with my stepmom and her and my dad's drama, makes it hard to be creative sometimes... Ah, here!"

David pulled out a large dinner-sized box of Velveeta mac

and cheese. "That's what you want for dinner?" Evan asked, walking over and taking it from David's hand. David nodded. "Here, I'll cook it for you. You can go and sit over there at the island while we continue our conversation." It didn't take long for Evan to find a pot in the cabinets near where David pulled out the macaroni. He ran tap water into it while picking up the conversation again. "Oh, really?" Evan continued, intrigued. "You're a writer?"

"Yeah!" David sat at the island, elbows on the countertop and chin resting on his palms. "Before now it's just been mostly poems and short little stories. But before I came down to visit, I had an idea for a fantasy story that could be a full length book. So I've been spending a lot of time these past couple weeks writing on my mom's computer upstairs and making the story bigger. You know, longer, and just figuring it out. I've never written anything long before... Oh, yeah, and when the noodles are done, can you throw some pepperoni in there too with the cheese?"

"That's awesome!" Evan said, genuinely impressed. He watched the pot of water heating up on the stove, only a few little bubbles rising to the surface. "You know, I'm a writer too." Evan remarked as he explored the refrigerator for the pepperoni. He found it and threw it on the counter next to the box of mac 'n cheese.

"Oh really?" David got a little excited at this and smiled. It was the first real smile he had displayed since Evan had gotten there. "You write books?"

"I would like to write a book one day. Mostly what I write is about scripture. I mean, I write my own sermons. I write analyses of passages of the Bible. And for fun sometimes I write little parables or short stories that are about being parables or lessons from the Bible. I use those a lot for kids groups or Sunday School." The water came to a rolling boil and Evan dumped the noodles in absentmindedly while he studied the interested expressions that animated David's face.

"Oh, can you cook up some french fries too?"

"You want fries too? That's a lot of food."

"Well, I'm hungry." David pointed to the freezer and Evan dug out a half empty bag of frozen potato wedges. The oven beeped as he punched in the temperature to preheat.

"Have you ever heard the term *meta*?" Evan asked with a very serious expression on his face as if it was a subject of the utmost importance. David shook his head. "Okay," Evan continued, stroking his chin while he picked his words carefully, the way a writer would do. "Do you ever like to watch movies that are about making a movie? Or read stories or books that are about writing, or about fiction?"

"Yeah!" David's face lit up. Writing and movies were David's favorite topics to discuss. The conversation was actually helping him warm up to Evan in a way he hadn't thought possible before. Maybe this strange pastor wasn't such a bad guy. "Like Stephen King's novella *Secret Window, Secret Garden*. They also made that into a movie that was really good. You know, my grandpa is a writer. That's one of the reasons why I got interested in the art form."

"He is? That's really great that you have artists in the family. There are no other artists in my family. I was always the odd one. The black sheep." Evan stirred the pot of noodles with a wooden spoon. "I have a theory—and I actually am considering writing a book about this. Or maybe several books.

It's basically *metaspirituality*—if that was a real word. Ha! My theory is that more things are meta than we might initially realize. For example: all of Creation came out of the mind of God, all of Creation *is* God. So all of life and existence *is* God and *is* about God. Follow me?" David gave a hesitant nod. "The Bible it totally meta because it is God, it is the word of God, and it refers to itself. God is the meta-reality. We are all God, we are all within God, there is nothing outside of this reality. I know I'm rambling now, but you get the idea. The meta-everything keeps referring back to itself in an endless infinity, eternity. The heaven within." Evan paused there for a second, trying to untangle the thoughts of his meta-mind. "Have you ever seen a drawing of an ouroboros? It's a depiction of a snake eating it's own tail."

David looked up at the ceiling, checking his memory archives for a recollection of the image. "Oh, yeah!" He exclaimed, a picture of the ouroboros came flooding into his mind. "I've seen that drawing in a book that I have!"

Evan didn't reply right away. He was a bit surprised that David had seen this symbol before, but not too surprised. Most likely if David had seen this symbol then he possibly could have some basic knowledge of the occult or the ancient mysteries. Evan was pleased by this new development. "That's us! That's God! The infinity of all of existence. It is itself and about itself. The whole purpose is just to be. To discover our godhood and to talk about our godhood. Eternity is an endless conversation with ourself, and about ourself." Evan was so excited to share his thoughts on what he called metaspirituality, that he almost let the pot of noodles boil over. He caught it just in time, turning the heat down and stirring the bubbles away from the lip of the pot.

"Wow!" David exclaimed. Evan had lost him down the rabbit hole on some of what he was trying to explain, but David felt like he had grasped the basic concept of what Evan had expressed. David believed in God, but not the way that Toni and Shelley did. He couldn't help but feel like the way Evan spoke about the spirit aligned more with his feelings on God and the divine. But he was slightly overwhelmed by the conversation and wanted a break for a little while to wind his brain down. "That's some interesting stuff to think about. The way you say those things feels to me closer to the way I feel about God, or whatever creative consciousness that is." David's eyes glazed over and he zoned out for a second then snapped back. Evan didn't say anything more, he didn't want to fry David's brain with too much philosophy. David watched as the pastor slid the tray of fries into the oven to cook, and then grabbed the pot of noodles to drain the water. "That's a lot to process right now," David continued. "I think I'm gonna go upstairs to my room and read for a little while while the food is finishing cooking." He stood up off his chair and started walking toward the stairs without waiting for any reply from Evan.

"That's cool, buddy!" Evan yelled after David as he reached the first step up to the top floor. "I'll come up and get you when the food is ready." He smiled, but David was already out of sight.

Several minutes later Evan came upstairs and let himself into David's room. He was sitting on the carpet beside the inflatable bed reading *The Book of the Law* by Aleister Crowley. David looked up as Evan entered the room, but made no attempt to hide his contraband book.

"Food's ready," said Evan.

"Oh, yeah?" David put the book down beside him but did not stand up. He seemed to still be in thought over the passage he had just been reading.

"Aleister Crowley." Evan pointed down at the little red book David had been reading. "That's heavy reading for a thirteen year old."

"Oh... Huh." David didn't really respond at first, just looked down at the cover of his Crowley book. "I guess, yeah," he continued. "I started getting interested in this stuff a year or two ago, when my parents were getting divorced."

"That makes a lot of sense. I also am very interested in ceremonial magic. Technically every pastor and priest practices that whether they are aware or not of the ancient magic that runs through everything they do." Evan sat down on the carpet in front of David so that they could be at a more equal level. "You're not as innocent as you might first appear, are you?"

"What do you mean?"

"What I mean is you've experienced more than an average person of your age. Experienced more intellectually, spiritually, emotionally... sexually?" It was subtle, but it was a question. Maybe it was even a challenge.

David studied Evan's face, which didn't reveal anything. "Yeah, I have," David conceded. "I was forced to grow up fast. When I was a kid I just wanted to be a kid, but I guess there were other plans."

"I wanted to elaborate a little bit more on our conversation from earlier," Evan began, bringing back up what he had been mulling over; the world of *meta*. "We already talked about what I call *metaspirituality*, spirituality that is about being spiritual. The ouroboros, the Snake God eating its tail, always in a constant mating ritual with itself... Which brings me to my next point. All of existence is God, all the energy that makes up you and me, and plants and animals, and the cosmos, are all one soul, one entity. You follow me?" David nodded, he was engaged with Evan now. "All is Kundalini energy. Sexual energy. The whole of existence and the cosmos, forever making love to itself. And, as you know from reading Aleister Crowley, *as above so below*. What is taking place on the macro level takes place on the micro level. This is *Metasexuality*, the penulti-mate combination of all of my research on the occult and my practice with ceremonial magic."

"Meta... sexuality?" David felt like he had kept up with Evan's monologue for a while there then got lost in the words again. He struggled to grasp the concepts that were being hurled at him at such a speed, but what he found is that it was easier to assimilate them as something his Spirit could under-stand even if his intellect could not.

"All sex is about sex. God is sex and sex is God. One Cre-ator Creation making infinite love to itself. Isn't it a beautiful thing we have created? So whenever you make love to a person, you are making love to God, which is ultimately yourself. Are you beginning to see behind the mirror? Behind the mirror is more mirrors." Evan laughed. David raised an eyebrow. "Your mother and I have been engaging in come ceremonial magic for purposes of conjuring a certain type of energy. A certain type of entity. Tell me, is your sister pure?"

"Pure? Yeah... I-I guess." David stammered a bit trying to figure out what exactly Evan was referring to. He was very protective of his sister and wouldn't want to see any harm come to her.

"Interesting... She might be useful," Evan almost whispered this, a thought under his breath, to himself. Then he looked back at David and smiled. "I bet you're good at pleasing people, aren't you? You please me." Evan put his hand on his crotch.

David looked down as Evan began to rub his hardening cock through his jeans. "I..." David began slowly. He was beginning to feel the chills and the first pulls of arousal. "I mean, I've had experiences with a few people. They all really liked me and what we did together."

Evan smiled again and stood up slowly. He began to unbuckled his belt. David watched the bulge in his pants throb in anticipation of being pleasured. "Come here," Evan whispered seductively, beckoning David to come to him. "You know what to do, don't you?"

David was on his knees now and closed the gap between their bodies. He looked up at Evan with huge puppy dog eyes and his mouth slightly open. *He's really cute*, Evan thought to himself. He reached down and stroked the side of David's face lovingly. David closed his eyes and rubbed his cheek into Evan's hand and then kissed his palm slowly and tenderly. Opening his eyes, David's hands went for the button on Evan's jeans. He unbuttoned the button slowly and sensually, David knew how to get a man hot. His previous experiences had taught him quite a lot. David unzipped Evan's fly and could feel the warm penis behind the boxers waiting to burst free. The pants and the boxers came down and David began to stroke Evan's shaft. The tumescent cock was warm in his small hand.

Evan's dick wasn't too big for David to handle. Completely erect it was only five or six inches at full salute. It was almost an unconscious skill that David possessed, going to work pleasuring this pastor that he barely knew. He had this instinctual drive to give pleasure, and *immense* pleasure. He was God, sucking his own cock, forever in an endless spiral. The ouroboros in self-fellating ecstasy. David licked from the base to the tip in long laps of the tongue, mixed intermittently with sucking on Evans balls and the tip of his dick. Then he took it into his mouth, all the way deep into his throat. David could feel the vein on the bottom of the shaft pulsing against his tongue. Evan put his hand lightly on the top of David's head and guided the motion firmly but not roughly.

David gagged on the cock in his throat, pulled it out of his mouth, spit on it, and continued to stroke it with his hand. He looked up at Evan with those same puppy eyes. "You like that?" David whispered. There was a smile on his wet lips.

"Oh, my God. Yes!" Evan moaned loudly. He closed his eyes and tilted his head back. The waves of pure ecstasy were beating the shore of his orgasmic connection to the Creator. "You're a gift from God." Evan said between heavy breathes. "You *are* my God." David continued to stroke Evan's rock hard cock, speeding up as he got more and more excited. He reached around with his other hand and started to finger Evan's asshole with a gentle rubbing. "Oh, yeah!!" Evan's whole body began to shake with pleasure and felt like he was on the verge of exploding. "Tell me, David," Evan said slowly. "This won't be the first time you've had a cock in your ass, will it?"

David shook his head. Suddenly Evan grabbed David by the shoulders and spun him around, roughly but not violently. He pushed David onto the bed in the position where his upper body was on the mattress but his knees were still on the ground. Evan pulled David's pants down around his knees and got in position to penetrate. He spread David's perky nubile cheeks and spit on his anus for some lubrication. Then Evan spit on his own palm and smeared it on his cock. He put his tip up to the hole and popped it in. David groaned softly and gritted his teeth against the initial pain. Then Evan slid himself all the way in. "Oh, yeah, baby," Evan moaned with the extreme pleasure. "You're so fucking tight!" This was the most intense pleasure that Evan had ever experienced in his life. He didn't want it to ever end but he felt himself on the verge of orgasm. He grasped David's hips and began thrusting in and out slowly. "Oh, yes, Lord, yes!" Evan panted and sweat poured down his brow and chest. "We are the two-headed God making love to itself."

David began to pant harder, Evan inside him was beginning to feel really amazing once the initial pain subsided to anal pleasure. He squeezed the pillow and felt his own cock getting hard against the bed. Reaching down to pleasure himself, David squeezed his own dick and began to stroke it vigorously. "Oh, yes, Daddy. Fuck me! Fuck me harder!" It was barely a whimper, but it excited Evan incredibly and he felt the tingle in his balls. Ejaculation was imminent. He began to thrust harder. David stroked himself harder too.

"Oh, my God!" They both exclaimed in unison.

"This is prayer," Evan said between thrusts. "The way we make love to God. We make love to ourselves in eternal pleasure. All is one orgasmic divine orgy. We love you, and we thank you. Because we are you!"

"Oh, fuck! I'm gonna cum!" David said as he gasped and moaned louder, the volume increasing with each inhale and exhale.

"Me too!" Evan thrusted three more times deep inside David and then yelled "Jesus!" as they both ejaculated simultaneously.

Evan pulled out and David heaved on the bed, utterly spent, utterly in bliss. Evan's semen dripped out of David's tight asshole and down the inside of his thigh. They both basked in the afterglow which could only be described as divine. Evan leaned back against the wall and David felt like he was melting into the inflatable mattress. Both their eyes were closed and they found themselves in a meditative trance, blissed-out. Evan felt the DMT pulsing from his pineal gland and behind his closed eyelids, he could see a red oscillating flower of life pattern spinning and spiraling forever. David's vision was of Shiva and Shakti locked in their lovemaking deep in the Himalayas.

Time had lost all its meaning as they laid there. It could have been minutes, it could have been hours. Their orgasm was still buzzing in the air, extended by the power of the Holy Spirit.

Finally, after an eternity, Evan stood up and pulled his pants back on. He playfully smacked David's ass that was still exposed. David turned his head to acknowledge the pastor's touch. "Come on, God," Evan said smiling, his bright teeth gleaming. "Let's go eat. Food's getting cold."

XI

That night, David couldn't sleep. He kept tossing and turning on the inflatable mattress where he had had sex with Evan earlier that evening. He couldn't get comfortable and Evan's voice kept buzzing in his head, that one question he had asked about Shelley: *Is your sister pure?*

David had read a little bit about ceremonial magic, sex magic, and Satanic rituals. He was aware that in Satanic circles, they sometimes required virgins for sacrifice to conjure certain entities, or demons from hell. What else had Evan said? *She might be useful.* David wasn't exactly sure what use Evan had been referring to, but after being sexually intimate with the pastor, David's mind was reeling to all different kinds of scenarios—each one more terrifying than the last. He didn't like the thought of this older man using his sister, molesting his sister, or even worse—*killing* his sister. In David's mind, he could see Shelley naked and tied down to a Satanic looking altar with her legs spread and a black ball-gag in her mouth. He tried to shake the image from his mind, but if David was truly honest with himself, he'd have to admit that the image was actually quite arousing.

"Fuck…" David knew what he had to do. If Evan needed a

virgin to do some sick ritual in order to summon some powerful demon from hell like Baphomet or Paimon, then there was only one option he had in order to save his sister's life. He would have to deflower her. This thought was not totally unappealing. In fact, David felt his face get hot as he realized that he was actually about to commit the forbidden incestuous act.

Gathering his courage and his breath, David left his bed and quietly let himself into his sister's room like he had the other night. She appeared to be sleeping soundly on her right side and wore the same nightgown she was wearing the other night he had slept with her. David tiptoed over to the bed and slid in behind Shelley's back so he could be in spoon position. He wrapped his arm around her waist and rested his hand between her small budding breasts. Without trying to wake her, David pressed his body timidly against Shelley's back and the curve of her ass. She didn't stir. Soundlessly, David began kissing Shelley's back through her nightgown and a small area of exposed skin that he could reach between her shoulders.

Shelley finally moved marginally, grinding her ass against her brother's half-erect penis. She moaned softly but didn't open her eyes. Taking this as a sign of consent, David began to squeeze and massage Shelley's left breast. Her nipple got hard from the stimulation and David could feel its small point through her thin nightgown. He was fully hard now and his cock found the crack between Shelley's ass cheeks. David moved his hand down from his sister's small breasts to the area between her legs. To his surprise, Shelley was not wearing any panties. *Had she been anticipating this and waiting for him?* The lubrication from her vagina was already wetting her nightgown.

Shelley pulled her nightgown up above her ass and David pulled his pajama pants down to his ankles. He continued to rub Shelley's clitoris slowly and sensuously and then slipped two fingers inside as her ass cheeks hugged David's throbbing cock. Shelley began to breathe more heavily as her pleasure built. She loved this more than she wanted to admit to herself. If she kept her eyes closed, maybe she could trick herself into thinking she was just having a very wonderful and orgasmic dream. She was so wet. Her pussy juice soaked David's fingers and dripped down his hand all the way to his wrist. David rubbed the tip of his cock against Shelley's tight virginal asshole while he fingered her cunt. He wasn't going to put it in anally, he just liked the way it felt to rub against his sister's pink rose-bud—and she loved it too. David couldn't believe that this was happening. He almost thought it was a dream also. Little did he know that Shelley had really wanted to fuck him as much as he wanted to fuck her.

"Put it in me," Shelley whispered. David almost came just hearing those words. Pulling his fingers out of his sister's twat, he went back to squeezing her tiny breast as he guided his pelvis toward her dripping vagina. Grasping the shaft of her brother's penis, Shelley guided it into her eager virginal pussy. As David slid inside, he felt something pop like thin plastic wrap. Shelley gasped in a hushed way so that they didn't make too much noise that would alert their mother to their taboo activities.

David stopped suddenly and squeezed Shelley's slim waist. "Oh, no. Did I hurt you?" He whispered. The sex ed schooling he had received as a youngster—where he learned about the hymen—was all but lost in the warehouse maze archives of his mind.

"No," Shelley responded in a loving reassuring voice. "It's okay. Keep going. I'm loving what you're doing." If she had been able to maneuver the move where she could reach behind her and stroke her brother's hair and the side of his face, she would have just then. Shelley wanted to gaze lovingly into David's eyes and kiss him over and over.

So he resumed his thrust gently. To the two of them this was not a crude act in their minds, they were truly making love to one another. The act was like a blissful prayer, mating with the Holy Spirit. David could feel the energy of *metasexuality* linking them together in a way where they totally forgot themselves and melted into the other, in a way creating a third entity. A beautiful creature created by their passion. *I have the metadick,* David thought to himself. *And we are the GodFuck.*

Their breathing became heavier as they made love, coming together at the hips as they had done with their dolls many times before. As they were both caught up in the moment and the ecstasy of their shared energy, they momentarily forgot their separate identities and could only experience their mutual passion and love for each other as one being. It was as if they had become the same person, the sacred marriage of male and female energy taking place internally and they were all at once connected back to Source, to God. Neither one could have explained what they were experiencing. All the rest of reality had ceased to exist, all that was left was them becoming the One. The two siblings locked in a coital embrace floated out into space where supernovas exploded around them, nebulas expanded and contracted as if they were multi-colored luminescent space dust. Galaxies where conceived and birthed as the pleasure within them built as if ascending a pyramid. They could both feel the orgasm building as two snakes dancing and entwining up their spines like an orgy of DNA strands. All they could feel was pure ecstatic love. How could this be wrong?

When they came it was shared, together, and at precisely the same moment. Their pure love was reciprocal. David and Shelley were mirrors of each other stretching on and on into infinity and whatever was beyond. They both moaned slightly louder as the orgasm gripped their body. Shelley could feel David's warm cock spasm inside her and then the fluid shot out deep into her in a long stream. Perspiration clung to their brows, faces red with the intoxication of their lovemaking. David's penis jerked four more times, letting loose four more pumps of semen into his sister's tight pussy. She sighed with vast cosmic pleasure and then her whole body relaxed completely. "Oh, my God, yes..." Shelley whispered as a sense of great satisfaction overtook her.

Needless to say, both of their minds were blown in the best way. Their intimacy with each other was the closest that they had come to touching the face of God. Actually, they *had* touched the face of God and they had *become* the face of God. "Wow!" David exclaimed. He felt high as a kite, but that analogy didn't even come close to describing the rapture of what they shared. David bit Shelley affectionately on the shoulder. She smiled and giggled, grinding her butt against him again. "That was the most amazing, I don't even know, thing—experience I have ever felt."

Shelley giggled again. "Samesies!" She felt utterly cherished like she had never felt in her whole life. David felt the same. "I love you so much, little bro!"

"I love you too, sis."

Shelley rolled over onto her other side so she could see David's face. His cheeks were completely flush. She touched the side of his face tenderly and stroked it. David's face was warm against her palm. "You're such a cutie, you know that?" David blushed even harder.

Shelley leaned forward toward David's face and kissed him on the lips. She pressed hard and then slid her tongue into his mouth. They made out for a minute, extending the enjoyment of each other. And even before they were done, they both fell into the deepest most relaxing sleep of their lives.

Right before the break of dawn David awoke still snuggling with Shelley. He really wanted to stay next to his sister and kiss her passionately as the sun came up, but he didn't want to risk having their mom catch them in the same bed. Especially after what they had done the night before. So David just kissed Shelley on the cheek and snuck away back to his own room, into his own bed. He cuddled with his pillow, imagining he was still in Shelley's bed, still next to her warm body, listening to her heartbeat and her soft breathing. Falling quickly back into slumber, David still felt the remnants of a godly, spiritual afterglow.

SIXTH ENTRY:

Oh, Diary, I shared the most wonderful night with David. I can't even describe how special the whole experience was to me, and I'm sure to him as well. I could feel him beaming with the most amazing, pure, divine love. When I woke up this morning I was almost afraid that it had just been a fantastical dream. But then I noticed the small stain and spatter of blood on the sheets. That's how I know it must have been real. So I quickly stripped the sheets off my bed and hid them in a garbage bag in my closet after I put new ones on. Can't risk having Mom ask any questions or suspecting anything. She would never understand. Oh, gee, I know in my head that I should feel guilty, that I should feel bad and dirty and full of sin that I would and could do these things with my brother. But I don't. I keep asking myself how something that feels so right be wrong? I don't think God would make such a transcendent experience of Love and pleasure be a sin. Could He? Could He condemn me to hell for something that feels perfect? I don't know what it is, but I feel different. Changed somehow. I feel like a transformed person. Renewed. Like I've been washed clean by the blood of the lamb and baptized in the Holy Spirit. I feel so happy I could start speaking in tongues. Me and David, when our bodies and Spirits were joined as one flesh and one soul, that was our piece of Heaven. Our Paradise. Our Salvation.

On the day that they were all supposed to go to Pastor Evan's for dinner, Shelley butchered one of the guinea fowl that they had been raising. The first thing she did was to slice its throat and let the blood drain. Shelley had her bucket for the blood and work table set up out in the front yard near the barn. David watched her through the window in his bedroom while he typed away on his mother's computer. His fantasy story was coming together nicely, and Shelley had become his muse of sorts, inspiring him even when his motivation was waning. The composition was close to fifty pages by now. His goal was to work on writing at least an hour every day since he arrived in Missouri, and so far he hadn't missed a day.

David skimmed through the page he had been working on and thought of all the characters he had brought to life: the talking cats, the dragons in the cave of dreaming, and the high school kids with magic powers. He smiled and was very pleased with his creation.

By the time David glanced back out the window, Shelley was already done plucking the bird. He watched her cut the feet of the carcass and then begin the evisceration process. As David watched his sister pulling out the innards of the guinea fowl, he wondered how she could undertake that disgusting process as if it was just a normal task. Like it was washing the dishes or something. Pulling a dead animal's organs out through their cut-open anus was just downright gross. Watching the butchering process so viscerally even made David consider the possibility of becoming a vegetarian. He crinkled up his nose and went back to working on his manuscript.

All of this chopping up, guts, and blood draining gave David a great idea for a fight scene between the hero in his book and a vicious demon that controls time. The fight would be epic. They would be pitted against each other, almost equally matched. The hero would use his energy sword to inflict some deep gashes on the demon's torso, and in its weakened condition, the hero would take the opportunity to chop off the demon's giant cock, thus vanquishing the demon and preventing it from raping anyone else in the name of Time. *That's really good*, David said to himself. He was pleased with the ideas that were just flowing to him, as if they were being delivered from some divine source.

"Hey, David! It's time to go!" It was Toni's voice yelling up the stairs to let David know they were all getting ready to leave to go to Evan's house. *Was it that time already?* He glanced at the digital clock on the the computer screen. *5:30 PM. Holy shit, time must really have gotten away from me.* The creative flow must have gripped him and pulled him into a trance, a really intensely focused writing mode. Apparently he had written thirty new pages. *I must have been on a roll.* David didn't have the time to skim over what he had written, so he just shut the computer down and went to join his mother and sister downstairs.

Shelley had the butchered bird all prepped and ready to go, it was chilling on ice in the cooler that she was carrying. David registered that his mother had gotten dressed up. She was actually wearing makeup and earrings. David never saw her wear makeup and jewelry basically ever. Toni was also wearing a fancy dress shirt with flowers printed on it tucked into a smart pair of women's slacks. She actually looked kind of weird in David's opinion, but he wasn't going to say that.

They got into the white minivan, Shelley in the passenger's seat and David in the back. Toni punched in Evan's address in her small Garmin GPS, and they were off. It was about a half an hour drive to get there. Everything in the Ozarks seemed like it was far away from anything else.

David went over and over in his head what had transpired between Evan and himself. He found himself wondering if it was going to be awkward, difficult for him to act normal around the pastor, as if they hadn't had intimate relations. As the drive progressed, he actually felt himself coming to a sudden realization. It was premeditated that Toni had decided to get dressed up to see Pastor Evan, and some of the comments that Evan had made to David about her seemed to suggest the fact that Evan and Toni had already had sex. So the pastor had already fucked two people in David's family: his mother and himself. And now Shelley was connected sexually to her brother. David could see the web of *metasexuality* growing and they were all caught inside of it. This realization was actually a relief because they all had the seed of sexual connectivity planted within them. That thought would be in the back of everyone's mind, but none of them would talk about it. Hence, they would all feel the same way toward each other, getting rid of the need for any awkwardness or pretense. David relaxed into this thought, as if the knowledge of their sexual connection wrapped them all in a loving embrace.

They pulled into Evan's driveway at the end of a dirt road. Toni parked next to Evan's dark blue Dodge Durango. There was a two car garage attached to the house. David thought it was strange that Evan's vehicle was parked *in front* of it and not *inside* it. Pastor Evan was standing at the door to greet them.

"Welcome! Welcome to my humble abode," Evan said cheerfully. "Here, let me get that." He took the cooler off Shelley's hands and lugged it into the kitchen. The rest filed in, following their leader. Toni had brought a stack of board games so they could play and have some fun while the bird cooked. She put them down on the dining table which was in the room adjacent to the kitchen. Once everything was set down, they were free to give a proper greeting. Evan embraced Toni in a huge bear hug then kissed her on both cheeks like a European would do.

Then he kissed the children on the tops of their heads. "I'm so happy you could all honor me by filling my little house with love." The pastor's smile was stretched from ear to ear, but there was no phoniness in it. The genuine warmth he radiated was intoxicating, which made David almost forget that he was quite sure Evan wanted to fuck his sister and sacrifice her to the antichrist, or Jesus, or whatever deity Evan had in his head.

It looked like Evan had been slaving away all day prepping the side dishes for their feast. He had chopped up potatoes and onions that were perfectly seasoned and accompanied by a panoply of savory vegetables. There was also a special stuffing that Evan had created to fill the bird before they basted it and put it in the oven.

Shelley was more inclined to cooking than her mother was. So Evan shooed David and his mother into the dining room and insisted that he and Shelley would finish getting the meal ready and put the bird in the oven, which was already pre-heated. They left the cooking area without protest and sat down at the table. There was still a full view of the kitchen from the dining room table, so Toni watched as Evan stuffed the bird. *I wish he was stuffing* me *right now*, Toni thought to herself, a slight blush coloring her cheeks. David poked at the stack of board games in front of him.

John Bunyan's book *Pilgrim's Progress* was one of David's favorites even though it was faith-based literature. There had been a board game created based on the book as well. He pulled it out of the stack of the other assorted games which included *Upwords*, *Scattergories*, and *Parcheesi*.

"Is that what you want to play?" Toni smiled at her son and

looked at the game, pleased that he would pick one that was so Christian oriented.

"Yeah," David said as he opened the box. He pulled out the game board and began to unfold it. "You know this one is my favorite."

"Is it game night?" Evan asked from the other room. He could see David setting it up on the table.

"We thought we would," Toni answered back. "I brought some of our favorites with us."

"Awesome! I love having people to play games with!" It was quite obvious that Evan was very pleased with the whole plan.

Shelley slid the freshly stuffed fowl into the oven along with the potatoes and veggies. "That should do it," she said, taking off her oven mitts. "Should we play?"

The night began with the playing of *Pilgrim's Progress*. They all had a great time laughing and joking with each other, pretending to be competitive when really what mattered was just to have fun. Surprisingly, David found himself becoming more and more at ease with the whole dynamic. He realized that he was smiling goofily and couldn't remember the last time he had had that much fun. Almost forgetting his theory about Evan needing Shelley for a Satanic ritual, David felt like maybe he could get used to this, maybe it *would* be nice to have Evan as part of their family. For a short while, they all felt as if they were normal again, as if they were healed.

As the night progressed and they cycled through the games that Toni had brought, their conversations were restricted mostly to the gameplay and making jokes. Since David had become somewhat accustomed to participating in heavier conversations, he was very relieved to have none of that this evening.

Or at least not yet. David wondered what Pastor Evan's angle was, what he was trying to gain from them. Did he want to marry Toni and have them all as his new family? Was he trying to find an opportunity to kidnap Shelley and make her his sex slave? Did he want to murder them all and use their entrails for Satanic rituals? Was he looking for a virgin womb as a portal for the Second Coming of Jesus—or possibly the Beast? All these bordering-on-ludicrous scenarios swam through David's head but he wasn't able to pin down any of them. Evan was unpredictable and always seemed to be sending out many different signals at once.

"Hey, Evan, are you going to be our new stepdad?" Shelley asked, completely out of the blue.

Evan looked up from the word 'myopic' that he just finished laying down on the *Upwords* board. At first he seemed surprised by the sudden and unexpected nature of the question. He glanced at Toni who just smiled back at him. "Well, I don't know," Evan replied truthfully. "It's still quite early in our relationship. I care about your mother very much and we have a certain courtship going on, of course. But what God's plans are for us in the long term remains to be seen." He reached over and squeezed Toni's hand that was resting on the table. "What do you think, Dear?"

"Oh, I very much agree. I couldn't have said it better myself, but I feel the same way." Toni reached over with her other hand and held Evan's in both of her's. "If God wishes for us to get married, then that will be waiting for us in the future. But in the mean time, we have a very strong connection which we owe it to ourselves to explore."

Evan nodded in agreement and then looked back over at Shelley. "Does that answer your question?"

"Totally!" Shelley was happy with the possibility of having a full family again. It was her turn and she put down a 'th' over the 'op' in Evan's 'myopic' to make a new word—"Mythic!" Exclaimed Shelley triumphantly.

"Good word," David interjected. He jotted down Shelley's new total on the score pad.

The intoxicatingly delicious scent of the roasting guinea fowl began to waft into the dining room, reaching their olfactory glands. Toni sniffed the air and felt her mouth salivate. "That smells so amazing," she said. "I'm starving. Do you think it's ready to come out of the oven?"

Shelley glanced into the kitchen and then to the clock on the wall. "Yeah, I would say it's about that time. Evan? What do you think?"

"I think—yum—let's eat!" Evan stood up out of his chair and followed Shelley into the kitchen to get the meal ready for serving.

"Hey, Evan?" David started, standing up from his chair. "Where's your bathroom? I want to use it and wash my hands before we eat."

"Oh, of course," Evan acknowledged. "It's over there." He pointed in the general direction. "It's the only door open in that hallway." Evan turned around and continued putting the cooked vegetables into a serving dish while David left to explore.

David went down the hall that Evan had indicated. He saw the open door that was unquestionably the bathroom, however another door closer to him caught his eye. The instinctive feeling that took him over was to go check out what was behind this mystery door. His intuition told him that it led to the basement. Opening the door slowly in an attempt to make as little noise as possible, his gaze fell on a flight of stairs going down into a dark depth. There was a light switch at the top of the stairs and he flipped it on, illuminating the floor below. Then he descended cautiously, his mind coming up with horrible scenarios of what could be down there, each one more horrific than the last.

What he saw in the basement didn't seem that strange at first. The floors were linoleum. *Good for easy cleanup*, David thought. Around the perimeter of the room were an assortment of unlighted candles of all sizes and in all kinds of stands. But what was strange was what was in the middle of the room. It looked like a circular altar, elevated to about waist height. The symbol carved into the wood was the star of David. Fastened to it were a pair of ankle restraints as well as wrist restraints. The altar looked just big enough to hold a small person—like, possibly, a teenage girl. Or even a teenage boy. David swallowed hard and then noticed the small work bench next to the altar. On top of said bench was an assortment of pristinely polished knives. They looked very vicious—and fancy—perfect for butchering a person. Now David wasn't fully sure whether it was just Shelley that Evan wanted to have naked on this altar; it could quite potentially be himself as well. But no, it was Shelley's purity that he asked about, wasn't it? He had to protect his sister from whatever malfeasance Evan was capable of.

His revulsion and horror to all of this was oddly beginning to clash with another feeling—kinship with Evan's inner monster. For a second David could see a mirror of himself within Evan's occult practices. He shook that thought from his mind and hoped that Pastor Evan would lose interest in Shelley as a potential sacrifice since she was no longer a virgin. But then he realized one more thing and almost smacked himself in the face. *How the fuck was Evan supposed to know that?* When he had asked if Shelley was pure, David had answered in an affirmative manner. As far as Evan was concerned that was the only information that he possessed unless David decided to tell him otherwise. And he really wasn't feeling like speculating about how that conversation would go. He'd just have to come up with a solution to keep the pastor away for good. But how?

He tiptoed back up the stairs, shut the light off, and closed the door without a sound. When he joined his family and Evan back at the table, all the food was ready to be served—and it looked delicious. All this detective sleuthing had got David working up a raging appetite.

"What took you so long?" Evan joked with a good-natured smile. "Get lost finding the sink?"

"Sorry," said David, sitting down at his place. "I had to take a crap."

Evan laughed again. "It's all good. When nature calls, nature calls." He didn't seem like he was suspicious of anything and David was grateful of that. Evan sat at the head of the table, Toni to his left with Shelley beside her. David took the seat across from his sister. "Let us pray," Evan continued and they all held hands. He closed his eyes and began to pray. "Dear Lord, we thank you for community and to be able to share your love with friends and family. Thank you for blessing us with this bountiful meal. I am so blessed that you brought Toni and her two wonderful children into my life. May we all be able to fellowship with you and bask in the light of your Holy Spirit for many many years to come. Amen."

"Amen."

"Let's dig in and eat this bird," Shelley said enthusiastically. "This is the first time I've butchered and cooked a guinea fowl. I've only done chickens before now. I hope it's really tasty!"

All three of them began to demolish the food. They ate like they were the starving Donner Party about to feast on each other.

"Toni, what is your favorite Bible passage?" Evan asked after he finished chewing a bite of guinea leg.

Toni thought about this for a minute and then replied, "I really enjoy the Sermon on the Mount. That's a really important passage." She went over the passage in her mind as she took another bite of potato.

"Ah, yes," Evan nodded his head in agreement. "That is a beautiful passage. The core essence of Jesus's teachings. These verses contain the beatitudes which Christ expounded to his disciples." He took another chunk of guinea fowl and chewed it thoughtfully. "You see," he continued. "The New Testament is a love letter from God to his people."

"Yes! I feel that way too!" Toni exclaimed.

"We *must* have the New Testament to have contrast with the Old Testament," Evan continued to explain and expound as if he were preaching to an entire congregation. "The Old Testament depicts an angry God, jealous and testing the devotion of Man. That's when we all were under the old covenant with God. The coming of Jesus Christ made sure that we knew that we didn't need to adhere to the old covenant anymore. We had a new covenant based on Love instead of God's wrath. Do you see where I'm going with this?"

Toni nodded, "I think so."

"Okay. We seem to get two conflicting contradictory pictures of God the Father. Is he wrathful and judgmental like in the Old Testament, or is he loving and forgiving like in the New Testament? Or do we have a bipolar schizophrenic God that has mood swings from rage all the way to unconditional love?"

"Interesting point," Toni interjected. "Which God are we going to get at any given moment? Do we get the God from the book of *Job* or do we get God from the book of *Matthew*?"

"God is everywhere, God is all things. All of existence. So within Him is every possible potential, even the whole spectrum of human emotion. We are a mirror of the Great Creator just as the Great Creator is a reflection of us. When we feel like God is judging us, that is only you judging yourself. God only judges you as much as you judge yourself. We, ourselves, are as perfect as the One, and the One is just as flawed as we sometimes perceive ourselves to be." Evan paused for a second and looked at Shelley, David, and then back to Toni. "You want to try a meditation?"

All three nodded in unison.

"Okay, close your eyes." Toni and her children put down their silverware and closed their eyes. "Repeat after me," said Evan. "God and me, me and God, are One."

They repeated.

"You have now entered the *meta-mind*. The universal mind, the God, we are all one thing. We are the universe and the universe is us. We are one with God... and we *are* God. You are in the *meta-dream*. And we are the *meta-GOD*."

That night, on his inflatable mattress, David was somewhat restless. He kept drifting in and out of strange dreams. As he fell unconscious, the dream was himself walking through the streets of downtown Chicago at midnight. David's dream-self stopped suddenly and began to float up into the the air. He continued to ascend into the clouds, past the clouds, and closer and closer toward the stars. There was suddenly a blob of light just entering David's vision. The light was long and flew through the air like a dragon. He continued to float toward this dragon-light as it flew toward him. And just when he was about to merge with the Dragon of Light, David heard a voice whisper, *No, it is not your time. Wake now!*

David was torn from his dream by a sudden squeezing of his dick and balls. As his eyes slowly opened, David could make out in the darkness Shelley, completely naked, straddling him as she stroked his penis with her hand down his pajama pants. David's cock responded to her touch like it was supposed to.

"I want you to make love with me again," she whispered into his ear, nibbled on it seductively and then began kissing his neck. David reached up to feel between Shelley's legs. She was already wet and her pussy juices dripped down the inside of her thighs. He slipped two fingers inside her and began to stroke her as she stroked him. They made out, kissing passionately, Shelley's tongue sliding deep into David's mouth like she wanted to devour him completely.

David was fully hard, his erection was hot and throbbing to penetrate his sister's wet pussy. "I want to be inside you so bad," he moaned as he slid his pajama pants down past his ass.

"I love you so much, Shelley." David gasped as Shelley squeezed his dick and guided it into her dripping, eager vagina.

"Oh, my God," she groaned and David's cock went all the way deep inside her. He could feel Shelley's cervix with the tip of his dick. She bobbed up and down on him and grinded her pelvis against his, stimulating her clitoris. Leaning down to whisper in David's ear, Shelley's pelvis continued to glide up and down the shaft. "Isn't it amazing," she said, "that God made us to be able to do this with each other. I'm in fucking heaven... Aren't you?"

Shelley kissed David's lips hard and passionately. "Oh, yes, Shelley," he responded between gasps and moans. "I love the way you ride me like that." *Pant. Pant.* "You make me cum so fucking good." David loved the way his sister felt inside. The waves of ecstasy continued to crash into him like he was a sandy beach. It was almost as if his whole being was melting into hers, their orgasm exploding as one entity.

"Uhh, uhh, oh God, yes," Shelley's whole body began to tremble and shake, the energy shooting up her spine and building to a climax. "Are you gonna cum?" She could barely get the question out through the heavy breathing and moans of pleasure.

"I'm... close." David's breathing began to pick up speed and their breath, in an instant, synchronized.

"I want you to cum in me," Shelley said. It was a wisp of a whisper.

"What?"

Shelley put her hand around David's neck, gently but firmly. She squeezed, her hand and the shaft of her vagina tightly around David's cock that was about to burst. "I want you to fucking cum in me! Oh, fuck me, yeah, I'm gonna cum!"

Shelley closed her eyes and tilted her face toward the ceiling, still squeezing David's neck in a choke, slightly cutting off oxygen to his brain. "Oh, God!" David groaned and Shelley's whole body shuddered as they both orgasmed together. Because of the slight asphyxiation, David came harder than he had in his entire life. His pelvis spasmed as load after load of semen shot deep into Shelley's uterus. She took every squirt with a quiet gasp as her orgasm continued to make her naked body tingle and feel the chemical effects of love making.

"Oooo," Shelley moaned, and while still squeezing David's erection inside her, she leaned back down to enthusiastically make out with him.

David's penis softened a bit and they detached. Shelley rolled over on her right side with her back toward her brother so that he could spoon her from behind. Stripping off the rest of his night clothes, David threw them on the floor and then pressed his naked body against hers. Shelley pushed her body harder into David's and pulled his arm over her body to cuddle her and massage her breasts. "I want to cuddle with you for a while before I go back to bed," she said as she kissed David's hand then put it back on her breast, right over her hard nipple. She then sighed contentedly.

Shelley reached behind her back and put her brother's semi-erect penis between her ass cheeks. And as David's dick got hard again against Shelley's ripe ass, pushing for entrance anally, they both fell asleep. This time with no dreams.

XII

Several evenings later David announced that he was going to visit Grandma and Grandpa up the road. Shelley was sprawled out on the living room floor drawing. Toni was on the couch reading.

"That sounds nice," agreed Toni. "You haven't visited them at all since you got here. So you're going to have dinner with them and then come home for the night?"

"Yeah, that's the plan," David responded. "I shouldn't be out too late. Pretty sure you'll still be awake when I get back."

"Here, take the extra set of house keys just in case," his mother retrieved the set of keys that were hanging by the door and gave them to David.

Shelley suddenly looked up from her drawing. "Tell G'ma and G'pa I said *hi*!"

David nodded and left through the front door. He waved at the chickens as he went by, and started up the long dirt driveway from Toni's house that joined with the dirt road that went up the hill and to his grandparents's house. It wasn't dark yet, but the sun had begun setting into the horizon. The shadows of twilight threatened at the corners of reality.

After his dinner with the grandparents, David started the walk back down the hill to his mom's house. When he past the beginning of the tree line, David could see in the distance the start of the dirt driveway leading down to the farmhouse. Suddenly there was a flash of bright headlights, they sped up Toni's driveway and then swerved on the dirt road that lead out to the main paved road.

"Oh, shit," David spit under his breath and took off running toward the house. He felt like there was a stone in his gut, the sinking feeling that something awful had happened—or would happen—and he wasn't there to prevent it. Sprinting to the door, he noticed that the white minivan was still parked out front. When David got inside, the first thing he saw was Toni laying on the couch with her eyes closed. He went over to check her. She was unconscious, but alive. David was pretty sure she'd been drugged.

"Shelley!" He searched the whole house calling her name. She was nowhere to be found. "Kidnapped!" He yelled. "That fucker Evan, he used me being gone to sneak in. And now he's got Shelley!"

David snatched up his mother's car keys from her purse and ran to the van to start pursuit—remembering to lock the front door as he went. In the driver's seat of the white Jesus van, David scrambled in the glovebox for the GPS. He found it and punched in recently found destinations. Pastor Evan's address was right there, David set it and peeled out, scattering rocks and dust in his wake.

The drive to Evan's house was about a half an hour. David was pretty sure that Evan would speed back to his house, but *he* couldn't afford to take the risk of being pulled over. So, in fear of the West Plains Sheriff's Department, David gripped the wheel tight and didn't exceed five miles an hour above the speed limit.

Thirty-three minutes later David pulled into Evan's driveway and parked next to his Dodge Durango. Hopping out of the van, he rushed for the front door, praying to God that it would be open. David turned the nob and by some miracle the door slid open and he was inside the house. *The basement.* From his snooping around at dinner, he knew that that was where Evan would take Shelley to complete his ritual.

At the bottom of the basement stairs, the spectacle that awaited David almost made him piss his pants. The only light was from the candles circling the perimeter of the room. Evan was shirtless next to his tool bench of vivisection weapons. And there on the circular altar was David's sister, naked and visibly pregnant! She struggled against her restraints and squealed behind the gag in her mouth. Suddenly David began to hear music. He wasn't sure if the song was coming from an actual speaker or if he was hallucinating it himself. The song was *Cry Little Sister* from the movie *The Lost Boys.*

> *Cry, little sister! (Thou shalt not fall)*
> *Come, come to your brother! (Thou shalt not die)*
> *Unchain me, sister! (Thou shalt not fear)*
> *Love is with your brother! (Thou shalt not kill)*

"I knew you'd come and try to save your sister," Evan cackled, stroking one of the sharpest and wickedest looking knives on his table.

"I thought you could only use her if she was pure!" David

shouted at Evan, but trying to keep his distance far enough away in case Evan chose to lash out with one of those knives.

The pastor laughed again. "Foolish child! *Pure* doesn't necessarily mean *virgin*..." He took what looked like a filleting knife and leaned over Shelley's squirming naked body. "She's still pure in all of the best ways."

"Don't you touch her!" David's words were firm but inside he was trembling uncontrollably, and he still didn't make a move to stop Evan. Shelley's pregnant belly seemed to stretch and extend, as if there was a creature inside trying to push its way out.

"Oh, quit playing like you don't want to participate," the pastor cocked his head and raised an eyebrow at David who still hadn't moved. Evan beckoned him closer. "What? You suddenly care about her," he continued. "I mean, I wasn't the one *fucking* her all this time. Impregnating her with little web-foot babies." David gritted his teeth and Evan still had more ammunition. "You think I don't know about that? I *know* about that. Look here." He pointed at Shelley's swollen belly with the point of the knife. It gurgled and bubbled. "The angelic demon is almost ready to be born! Come, come here!"

Hesitantly, David stepped forward, closing the gap that was between himself and Shelley's wide open legs. He couldn't help staring at her petite pink pussy lips. Her clit trembled and there was a faint shimmer of lubrication on her labia. Shelley's eyes darted around, wide and panic-stricken.

Evan raised the knife, both hands clasped around the hilt and pointing down toward the pregnant belly. "We call on you, All-Father!" The pastor cried out to the heaven's, beseeching the spirits to inhabit the temple. "We ask your blessing to bring forth this Avatar! May he be a vessel for your divine grace! As we all are One: the child as well as the one giving birth. We are forever in your cosmic womb. The jelly of creation being the primordial soup in which the Spirit animated. We are the abuser and the one being ritually abused. The rapist as well as the one being raped. The experience of everything neither good nor evil. Unite us all under the meta-sky and we shall be enchanted by our own genius and intoxication. We are the divine fetus and the one who brings it into the world!"

A bright light quickly shot out of Shelley's vagina and illuminated the room as well as physically knocking Evan back. He stumbled and fell on his butt, dropping the knife by his side. As the light died down, it was visible to see that Shelley's vaginal canal was being stretched from the inside. In a few seconds the very-red top of the fetus's head began to poke out. David and Evan just stared with their jaws hanging open. Pink ooze gushed out of her cunt and the rest of the fetus sloshed out with it.

David shuddered, the fetus was the most disgusting creature he had ever seen. Its whole skull was deformed, leaving its head to look like a lima bean with both eyes on one side of the crater and mouth on the other. The spinal cord of its little body was curved more than a mountain road in northern California. The creature's little arms and legs were fat like sausages and there were extra fingers and toes growing on its appendages. The thing was covered in pinkish-red afterbirth and as its eyes bulged out of its deformed head, it chomped down on its own umbilical cord, severing it. It began to shriek as it slid and crawled its way across the floor.

The shriek began to grow in pitch, almost to the point

of making their eardrums bleed. The sound was a very high guttural wailing. It was the Sound of a Dying Fetus. Evan's eyes were clenched shut and his hands clamped firmly over his ears. David could hardly think either because of the horrendous sound raping his brain. However, he managed to concentrate just enough to crawl across the floor and grab the knife that was next to Evan.

The pastor's eyes opened just at the precise moment David started to bury the knife in Evan's chest over and over again. Evan screamed and cried but it was too late, David was already to the point of goring him. He stabbed Evan seven, eight, nine times. There was so much blood. It gushed out of Evan's chest —that was now full of holes—and geysered onto David's face and neck, dripping down and soaking his shirt. After a minute or so, one last breath escaped Evan's lips and then he laid still.

The Sound of the Dying Fetus was still ringing in his ears. He looked behind him to the altar. Shelley was unconscious again, the sound was too much for her to consciously process. As David rushed over to undo his sister's restraints, the shrieking of the fetus finally died down. But he knew that it was crawling in the shadows of the room somewhere, David could feel its presence. After he undid Shelley's ankle and wrist restraints, he took out her gag and cradled her in his arms like a baby. She was surprisingly light and David had no difficulty carrying her up the stairs and to the van. He laid her gently across the back bench in the minivan and then returned to the house to deal with the fetus and figure out what to do.

When he went back through the front door, David decided to check out what the deal was with the attached garage that Evan never seemed to park his car in. Still, he could hear the faint mewlings of the fetus coming from the basement as he found the door that led to the garage. He opened it and clicked the light on. What he saw behind that door was something he had never seen his thirteen years of life. Set up in the garage was what looked to David to be a laboratory or a chemistry set. It was the place where Evan used to cook up methamphetamine and LSD, until he died which was only several minutes ago. David didn't know much about drug labs, but he knew they were prone to exploding or burning down.

Luckily, searching the cabinets along the wall by the door proved fruitful. He found a small jug of gasoline and then rummaged through the kitchen till he found some matches. David doused all the chemistry equipment with gasoline and a trail through the door that went into the house. *Now to deal with the demon fetus*, he thought.

In the basement again, the fetus was busy climbing up the side of the wall. It shrieked as it saw David enter the room. "What the FUCK are you?" He yelled at the abomination that was crawling like a spider toward the ceiling. It continued its shrieking but it spoke directly into David's head.

I am your construction. Your creation. I am your mirror to see beneath.

"What the fuck does that mean, you cryptic occult Franken-stein?" The fetus crawled up a couple more feet and its head turned all the way around to stare down at David with its buggy eyes.

Don't you see yourself in me? Won't you look past my hideous-ness and try to love me?

"Love you? Love you?! I don't know what you are or where

you came from—what lonely abyss of an anus you crawled out of—but I'm about to put an end to this madness!"

Stop! We are all woven together inside the meta-mind. We are only thoughts of our creator. I only exist because you made me. Embrace me as your offspring and your father.

"The Father of Lies or the Father of Truth? Me, Evan, and Shelley: that's the Holy Trinity. And we have created our mirror opposite. The one that *must* exist for God *is* all things."

Yes, child. You cannot kill me. Because in killing me, you would also be committing suicide.

"And so shall it be!" David grabbed a thick candlestick and hefting it above his head, threw it at the fetus. It was knocked loose and fell to the floor, momentarily stunned. Taking advantage of the moment, he rushed over to the puddle of afterbirth where it fell. He began to stomp on its tiny body relentlessly. The fetus's skull caved in under the weight of the shoe, and exploded, blood and brain matter gushed out like a popped zit. The shrieking of the Dying Fetus had finally stopped. David fell to his knees and took the mess of mutilated tissue in his arms like it was his first-born son. Tears streamed down his face like a busted dam and he screamed to the silent heavens.

"My baby... My baby..." David whispered, sobbing quietly. In his moment of mourning, he almost forgot what he was supposed to do. Setting the now-dead fetus down, he picked up the gas can again. He doused Evan's body as well as the Star of David altar. Kicking over one of the thickest candles, the gasoline splashes caught fire and flames licked along the top of the altar and simultaneously consumed the dead bodies of Evan and the demon fetus. David squinted his eyes against the sudden heat and turned to climb the stairs.

As he passed by, David lit a match and flicked it into the garage. Instantly the contents inside became an incinerator. He was out the door before the whole house went up in a raging flame, like a phoenix struggling to reach the moon.

Acting quickly, he opened the side door of the van and knelt next to his sister's unconscious body. He had never successfully pulled off any magic before, but because of everything he had learned, David was confident that his intentions were strong enough for manifestation. He put his right hand over Shelley's forehead and his left hand over her belly. David closed his eyes and prayed, whispering an incantation under his breath. His intention was to cleanse his sister and to heal her. Light began to shine from the middle of David's palms. Instantly Shelley's hymen was healed, put back intact as if she was still virginal. Also, all of her memories of this night as well as the sexual experiences she had had with David were erased from her memory.

He inhaled deeply and then exhaled, completing the incantation and realizing that it had worked. In a flash, David was in the driver's seat and they sped off home, leaving the burning house, the dead pastor, and the demon far behind.

Back at the farm house, David put a nightgown on Shelley and tucked her into bed. After he pulled the covers up to her shoulders, he slipped his hand between the mattresses and pulled out Shelley's diary. He flipped through his sister's entries searching for any ones that mentioned him in a sexual way. David ripped all the ones he found out of her diary and threw the pages into a paper grocery bag he had found in the kitchen. He also retrieved the garbage bag in which Shelley had hidden her bloody sheets from the first time they had sex. Heading for the shower, he stripped off his bloody clothes and stuffed them in the paper bag along with the sheets.

After David had thoroughly scrubbed himself off and put on new clothes, he look the bag of bloody clothes, sheets, and sexual diary entries out to the burn barrel. He threw the whole bag in and lit a match. The contents crackled as it caught on fire and began to be consumed by flames. The sparks shot out like acid-tripping fireflies trying to reach the stars. The flames finally died down and what was left was a pile of orange glowing smoldering ashes. He would be the only one to remember any of this. David contemplated this thought. *In a year, will I even believe what happened here tonight?* He asked himself and the shadows of the darkness. He knew somehow that no matter how much older he would get, from this night forward, he would always be haunted by the conception of the Dying Fetus. Even when he wasn't aware of the presence of the thought, it would be there, like a seed in his mind, waiting for the right womb to sprout in.

David went back to his room and laid down on his inflatable mattress. He wouldn't be cuddling with Shelley tonight, or any other night for that matter. It was sad in a way, there was a palpable emptiness where her body used to be pressed against him. He hugged his pillow as if it were her and quickly fell asleep.

UNNUMBERED ENTRY:

I woke up this morning feeling really strange. I think I must have been having some vivid dreams or nightmares, but I can't really remember much of what they were about. In one of the dreams I seem to remember a house burning to the ground. There's a tingling sensation in my womb space. What's that about? Oh, it was also strange that it looks like pages of my diary have been ripped out. I think I remember writing more entries than that. I don't know what number I'm on if ones are missing... For the past few days, I had felt like Pastor Evan was in my head. Like he was watching or listening. But I don't feel that presence anymore. I'm enjoying having David here with us again. I don't feel completely whole without him. We aren't twins, but we might as well be. Irish twins? Well, anyway. Sometimes I get the overwhelming urge just to tickle torture him and sneak some feels between his legs. Is that wrong? I don't know. Would God make something that feels so good be wrong? That's not the kind of God I feel connected with. Self-sacrifice is not the way, no matter what Mom says about it. My God is a God of love and acceptance. We are the great oneness and the one soul connects us all. I think about David, when we touch, we create Salvation, we create the bliss of Heaven. When I think of him, I feel oddly... aroused.

The Tell-Tale Tail

The Tell-Tale Tail (Short Horror Comedy)

Charles Curly's hatred for animals was visceral. He could feel it in his bones—in the roots of his back molars. The brushes with pests that he had had before were short-lived. Always being able to trap or kill the vermin brought a smile to Curly's old, wrinkly face. To be honest, it was a shock that Curly didn't have *more* of a pest problem—if not for the sole reason than that he was a hoarder.

As Curly stood stroking his tangled beard, he looked down at his kitchen floor. Not much floor could actually still be seen through all the junk strewn on top of it. There were old newspapers, stacked up in piles that were falling over like the tower of Pisa. Old McDonald's bags and cheeseburger wrappers also decorated the floor like an urban avant-garde art project. Not to mention there were also several paper plates with crusty and molding food still caked on. He could have sworn that he saw a crumpled-up ball of newspaper move. Curly was keenly aware of every sound and every movement that took place in his small ranch-style house.

"There better not be no fucking mouse," Curly groused to

himself. "I will find you. And I will murder you." After this threat, his ears pricked up and he thought that he heard the faintest of squeaks—like a *rodent* squeak. Yawning and scratching the lint from his belly button, Curly went to stretch out on the couch in the front room where the TV was. He flicked the red button on the remote before flopping his flabby body down on the yellow-stained cushions. On the really brutal desert summer days, the swamp-cooler just wasn't enough to keep the sweat from pouring down his pale, blubbery flesh. Curly chuckled as he watched the reality show *Hoarders* on his thirty-two inch flat-screen that didn't look much bigger than a computer monitor.

"Why don't these people throw anything away?" Curly laughed, making fun of the people onscreen, not noticing the putrefication of his own living space. Suddenly there was a loud pounding at his front door. Bolting in surprise, he almost fell off the couch as he reached for something under the chaos which was the floor of his living room. As he pulled a pair of nunchucks out from underneath a pile of dirty towels and old VHS tapes, he yelled, "You're trespassing! I swear I'll break your face with these nunchucks! Don't test me, I know how to use them!"

"Curly! It's me," a muffled voice came through the door. Curly relaxed and dropped the nunchucks when he realized it was only his friend Derrick from up the road. They were both past retirement age and would sometimes keep each other company, smoking cannabis and remembering what they liked to call 'the golden years' of their past.

Curly not-so-gracefully got to his feet, knocking over several empty glass bottles and soda cans off of the coffee table in front of the couch. "Hold on, buddy," he called to Derrick. "I'm just making my way through the war-zone." The butt of his gray sweatpants was stained dark from sweat and lack of washing. His t-shirt, which definitely sported yellow pit-stains as well, had hiked itself partway up Curly's round potbelly. He scratched the hairy area under his belly button as he opened the door. Met with the sight of Derrick's grinning face, Curly greeted him and invited him inside. Derrick was considerably more overweight than Curly, and he walked with a cane.

Pulling a plastic tube from his jacket pocket as he sat down on the couch, Derrick said, "Just went to the dispensary and they had that *good* shit!" He opened the tube and dumped the joint out into his hand as his buddy Curly sat down next to him. The couch definitely dramatically sagged in the middle when both of their immense weights were assaulting it. "They had joints of Trainwreck," he continued excitedly as he sniffed the joint indulgently with his eyes closed. "And I thought I'd share it with my buddy." Curly took the unlit joint when Derrick passed it to him. Sticking his hand underneath the couch, he groped around for a minute and produced a lighter from whatever depths of madness were under there.

"I found one!" Curly said in triumph.

Derrick laughed and looked around at the state of his friend's house. "You ever think about cleaning this place up a bit?" he asked. "It's even more messy than last time I was here." Looking up, he noticed the TV on and clicked it off with the remote. "And why do you watch that crap?"

Curly shrugged and put the joint into his mouth. "Maybe it makes me feel better about my own disfunction," he mumbled through holding the joint between his lips. Then he lit it very slowly, as slowly as a turtle that was as old as Yoda would—like he was lighting a joint rolled in papyrus that was centuries old. As he took a long hit off the weed, Curly nonchalantly tossed the lighter back to the floor where it got lost in the miscellaneous whirlwind.

"Or you could get a maid—" Derrick started but was cut off by his friend putting a silencing finger in the air. Curly's eyes darted toward the kitchen.

"Did you hear that?" he asked, smoke still billowing from his hairy nostrils.

"Hear what?" Derrick asked, taking the joint from Curly's outstretched hand.

"There was like a squeak—or a rustling," he answered, straining his ear as if that could make him hear better. Curly's old, crusty ear canals were probably so hairy and coated with wax that it would be difficult to guess *what* he could hear anymore, much less the tittering of a small rodent.

Derrick shook his head as he inhaled a toke himself. "I didn't hear anything," he admitted, noticing the redness already rimming Curly's eyeballs.

"I swear there's a fucking mouse or something!" he snapped back, raising his voice as he snatched the joint back from Derrick's fingers. "I know it's gonna drive me fucking nuts," he continued, sucking three times quickly on the joint. "Remember the war I had with that skunk?"

Derrick thought for a second, and then his face lit up in recognition. "Oh yeah! The one that burrowed under the house. But you finally like smoked it out and killed it, right?" The whole time he was talking, he was trying to snatch the joint back from Curly, but he kept moving his hand further and further away.

"That's right, my friend," Curly said, taking another long drag. "I murked it like a gook." He handed the joint back to Derrick who took it gratefully. "I remember the days when I had enough money to just hire an exterminator to take care of this shit. Now I have to personally go on critter vendetta myself. No bug powder for me."

They laughed and looked into each other's eyes which were all four as red as Jesus's dick. "It was nice to have money," Derrick reminisced. "Remember how much fun we had when I owned that casino boat? What was it that I called her? *The Green Ballast*, that was it."

"I guess that business doesn't last long when it becomes the scene of a grisly murder," Curly commented.

"Oh yes, don't remind me, old friend," Derrick returned, passing the joint back. "I was trying to remember the good times—before the catastrophe. Before we became all *this*." He indicated their shabby appearances and the state of Curly's house. "Maybe there isn't a wonder that the vermin are coming for you," Derrick concluded ominously.

"Oh, come off it, you chump!" Curly said, playfully pushing his friend in the shoulder as he took another hit deep into his lungs. Coughing abruptly, he wheezed the smoke from his throat. "I fucking hate animals. Especially rodents... and bugs... and deer... and leaves..."

Derrick gave his friend a puzzled look and laughed. "Leaves are not an animal," he pointed out.

"Oh, right. I meant lizards," Curly said, trying to save himself. His eyes were so narrowed that no whites—or red blood vessels—could be seen. He passed the joint back to Derrick. It was almost down to the roach now.

"My cat ate a lizard once," he said offhand. "She was puking for days."

Curly looked like he had heard something again; he wasn't paying attention to what his friend was talking about. "Uh-huh," he mumbled, glancing back over the couch and toward the kitchen again. "I would never get a dog..." Curly trailed off, listening for mouse noises. "Little bastard would get under my feet—nip at me. I'd end up having to put him down like the last one..."

Derrick looked worried and his eyes darted over toward the kitchen, but he neither saw nor heard anything. "Do you want me to call pest control for you?" he said, starting to stand up from the couch, leaning on his cane. "You should maybe really think about cleaning up some in here too."

Curly nodded but didn't look at him, instead he slowly hobbled back into the kitchen. Clumps of hair collected on the floor curled around his bare toes as he walked over to the dirty oven that probably hadn't been cleaned in fifteen years. His knees creaked as he knelt down onto the junk-strewn floor. Sweeping away detritus from in front of the stove, Curly brought his face down close to the ground, staring into the crack between the bottom of the stove and the floor.

"Well, it still seems you're fighting Vietnam with a rodent," Derrick mumbled as he made his way back to the front door to let himself out.

"Hmm," Curly grunted, he hadn't even heard his friend's comment.

"Till next time, brother," Derrick said as he backed out

the door. "It's definitely been real... I'm definitely too high for this shit," he mumbled to himself as he slammed the door behind him.

As if with x-ray vision, Curly penetrated the grimy once-white oven with his gaze. The weed—the Trainwreck—really hit him hard in that moment to the point where Curly really thought he was seeing *through* the oven in front of him. And there it was! The little bastard! Curled against the wall was a little fuzz-ball, squeaking away as it tried to munch a hole in the wall behind the oven. "Oh this little cocksucking fur-fucking cuck of a mouse is gonna taste my wrath!" he mumbled intensely to himself. Suddenly he flung his arm out as if to try to grab the rodent, but in an instant a pain shot through Curly's hand as his fingers crunched against the glass of the oven door. "Ow! Son of a bitch!" he yelled, coming out of his hallucination, the oven was indeed still solid in front of him. "You've won for now, cuck-mouse!" he said, making his wobbly way to standing, pressing a hand to his lower back as he groaned in pain. "God, these animals are gonna be the death of me," he winced as he waded through the pool of junk back to the couch in front of the TV.

With a loud snort, Curly startled himself awake. There was a dull headache behind the marijuana fog. In an awkward sprawl across the couch, his leg dangled over the edge and his right hand clung to an almost-empty bottle of Jack Daniels. Curly gasped, trying to blink the sleep-mucus out of his eyes. Sitting up on the couch which hopelessly bowed in the center, the old man brought the glass bottle up to his eye. His blinking eyelashes were magnified through the Jack Daniels bottle which only swished barely a centimeter of liquid at the bottom. Curly slugged the remaining whisky, taking it into his mouth and swishing it around like it was mouthwash.

A grimace coated his face as he swallowed the putrid drink. He stared down the hollow neck of the liquor bottle like it was an amber spyglass. The leftover high definitely cut the hangover considerably, and Curly was grateful for that. The only incidents when liquor got him into trouble were when he didn't have weed to calm his nerves.

But is the weed calming my nerves now? Curly asked himself. The THC had kicked up his anxiety in a way he wasn't expecting, heightening all of his senses—in turn making him especially attuned to the oh so minute cheeping of mice. The taste in his mouth was salty and jagged. He found himself chewing on his fingernails as he stared, almost as if in a trance, deep into the emptiness of the Jack Daniels bottle. And as if from the watery abyss of memories wishing to be forgotten, an image appeared to Curly. This image was of Cameron, Derrick's late wife, smiling and looking as radiant in her sparkly blue dress as she did the night she was killed. The night *he* got her killed.

A crinkling noise jolted him out of his reverie. This disturbance caused the old man to bolt up on the couch, tossing the liquor bottle sailing into the air. It hit the ceiling, shattering into a million pieces. "Lock and load, gentlemen!" Curly screamed as shards of glass rained down around him. "The enemy is in the vicinity!"

As if back in trench warfare, he jumped over the back of the couch and rolled through an island of junk—mainly board games and hoarded notebooks that had never been written in. Curly knew exactly where to grab, and as he continued to roll toward the kitchen, he managed to scoop up a broom from somewhere buried in garbage. Stopping on his knees in front of the stove, Curly brandished the broom at the gap under the appliance where he thought he saw the rodent dash. "I've got you cornered now, evil vermin!" he growled menacingly. "You've nowhere to run with your cheap vanity and cheap tricks! Surrender, or you die a painful death!"

Curly could have sworn that he heard a loud squeak that blatantly resembled the sound of the words "Fuck you!" This in turn was viewed as defiance and taken as a direct threat.

"If that's how you're going to play it," Curly huffed. "Checkmate!" he said decisively as he slid the handle part of the broom under the oven, poking around for the cheeky mouse. Curly stabbed and jabbed, sweat pouring off his brow—that's how seriously he took this battle. The old man's territory was on the line and there was no way that he was giving up room to an animal that was going to piss and shit and possibly get into all his food. Was that mouse going to pay rent? Curly didn't think so. Then the rodent was entitled to no floorspace—not even any wall space!

"Too bad I don't have any Agent Orange," he grumbled as he gave up his thrusting of the broom under the oven. "I would gas your little ass out. That was Derrick's specialty back in the war..." Using the front of the oven to guide him, Curly slowly made his way to standing again, leaving the broom buried under the piles of hoarded junk that seemed to come back in waves to fill any gaps of empty floor space. "Landmines would get ya good, too," he continued to mumble to himself like a lunatic losing his marbles.

As the cross-faded old veteran waded through his universes

of junk to get to his bedroom, the little brown mouse sat behind the oven smiling to himself for having won that battle. There was a wedge of burnt pizza crust resting against the wall next to the mouse and he began to feast greedily, not knowing when or even if his next meal would come.

Curly snored loudly as he slept on his belly. No sheet was on top of his body and a cool breeze blew down from the overhead fan. His arms and legs splayed out at his sides and his hand lazily scratched his asscrack without even waking up. It was a wonder how he even made it to the bed in the first place. The bedroom floor was covered in bundles and bundles of magazines. And where there weren't magazines, there were stacks of books. And where there weren't books, there were piles and piles of clothes. Maybe the lack of organization had something to do with the fact the room had no closet. However, that didn't negate the possibility of Curly buying dressers for his clothes and bookshelves, too. The truth was that the encroachment of all the stuff was comforting to him, like the loving enclosure of a womb. Except this womb was made of the rejected afterbirth that no mother ever wanted.

"Curly!"

Curly snorted and stirred slightly then fell back asleep.

"Curly!" the voice yelled again. "You piece of half-aborted twat! Wake up your old monkey balls!"

This time Curly opened his eyes and yawned. "Intruder," he slurred, slowly coming awake. His hand shot down and hunted around under the bed. What he came back with was another pair of nunchucks, these with handles like candy canes. "I swear I'll kick your ass!" Curly jumped down into the stacks, knocking magazines and books over, making more of a mess of pulp pages and glossy centerfolds. Almost falling over more than a few times, he finally made it into the front room, right behind the couch. Poking over the top was a giant furry head with big ears that reminded Curly of Mickey Mouse. Smoke curled over the side of the enormous mouse's head and up around his ear.

"Come sit down, you daft cunt," the mouse chided. "And there's no need for any fisticuffs with those nunchucks. Why don't we just put those down?" The great furry head cocked and an eyeball looked back over at Curly as he dropped the nunchucks and circled around to the front of the couch. The mouse was manspreading—not that his penis was all that long, but his testicles were fuzzy and *huge*. "You like what you see, don't ya?" the mouse continued his monologue. The smoke was coming from a cigar that the mouse was puffing on out of the right corner of his mouth. "Sit down, you misguided human, and tell me how you've sinned. Confess."

Curly sat down and stared dumbly at the talking rodent in front of him. "I'm sorry, but I don't think I have to explain myself to a talking rat."

The mouse laughed heartily. "Maybe this talking rat has to tell you everything. Things don't always go the way you planned." He took a big drag on the cigar and puffed out a large smoke ring.

Curly shook his head and put his face in his hands. "I didn't want to have to do it," he sobbed. "I killed her! I fucking killed her! For the money. For the boat. For the everything..."

"Good..." the mouse hissed, smoke curling out of the corners of his malicious grin. "You'll drown in the guilt for what you did. You'll die sputtering, inhaling the deception of what you created. And as everyone knows, you can't breathe deception."

"Shut up!" Curly yelled. "You don't know what I did! You don't know what I did!"

"Yes, but I know you're old and have to pee a lot," the mouse said, raising his eyebrows and pointing at Curly with the cigar still smoking between the pads of his paw.

"Oh shit, I do have to pee," the man groaned.

"Well, don't piss the bed, murderer." The grotesquely large mouse waved and then disappeared in a yellow cloud that oddly reminded Curly of urine. His leg twitched and he realized that he was back in bed with an excruciating need to urinate. After dragging himself to the bathroom—which was, yes, a hoarder's den as well—he emptied his bladder for what felt like an eternity. When Curly looked down into the toilet bowl, two things registered—either one could have given him a heart attack. The first was the presence of blood in his piss. The second was a small brown rodent splashing around wildly for dear life.

"I got you now, enemy spy! The Cameron Conspiracy will never be revealed!" Curly yelled like he was going into battle and violently hit the flusher on the back of the toilet. As the whirlpool initiated, the mouse squealed in protest as it began to be sucked down by the spinning water. "Drown, you Nazi scum!" the old man yelled and spat into the bowl as the last of the mouse's head disappeared down the sewage pipe. Water came and filled up the bowl again, but the mouse was gone to its watery death. "I have defeated the one who would have exposed my deception! I'm sorry, Cameron," Curly whimpered, tears glistening his eyes. "Our love was so strong. How could Derrick have ever understood what we shared?"

Now that his bladder was empty and the enemy had been vanquished, Curly felt a relief wash over him. Sleep once again tugged him toward bed. Before he even knew how, he was sprawled out on his stomach, snoring away in the deepest sleep the old man had enjoyed in a while.

There was pounding on the aluminum siding next to Curly's front door. This roused him out of sleep. Why the knocking sounded so loud was at first a mystery until he realized that he had somehow during the night migrated from his bed to the couch.

"Curly! Open up, it's Derrick!" his friend yelled from outside. Before waiting for an answer, Derrick opened the door and hobbled in leaning on his cane.

"Well, just welcome in then," Curly said, still half asleep.

"Your neighbors have been saying stuff," Derrick said, closing the door behind him then going over to the front window. He pulled the blinds down a bit and peeked out. "They said you were outside last night shooting off your gun." Spinning around, he faced his friend and steadied his balance on his cane so he wouldn't fall over.

Curly was now sitting up in the sunken down middle of the couch, blinking at his friend uncomprehendingly. "I don't even own a gun," he squeaked out. "But I do have some nunchucks around here somewhere." He bent over and started sifting through the junk that came all the way up to the edge of the couch. Then his head flicked back up as he remembered some crucial information. "And, Derrick, guess what?" he said with a glint in his eye. "I vanquished the varmint!"

Derrick shook his head as he made his way over to sit down on the couch. "You vanquished the what?"

"The varmint!" Curly repeated. "That pesky rodent which had become the bane of my existence. Yep, he drowned."

"Oh," was all Derrick could reply. "Well, just don't be outside shooting off your gun. You don't want to get arrested again. Not like last time."

"No," Curly replied slowly. "I told you, I don't own a gun."

Derrick bent down and brushed aside a few hamburger wrappers to uncover the empty Jack Daniels bottle. "You've been drinking again. I thought you were just gonna stick to the weed this time."

Curly bit his bottom lip, trying not to start crying. "I've just been thinking about Cameron a lot lately."

"Wha—Cameron?" Derrick shook his head questioningly. "Why, Curly? That was so long ago. I try not to think about it and she was *my* wife."

"I killed her. I killed her..." Curly mumbled, his eyes looking far-away and delirious. "Killed her to get the boat... get the casino."

"Huh?" Derrick furrowed his brow. "Brother, do you even remember what happened?"

Curly nodded, his eyes filling with tears. "I had a gun. She was shot. I was the shooter."

"You're getting it mixed up," Derrick tried to explain. "You tried to save her. You shot the shooter, but it was too late, she had already been fatally wounded. Cameron died along with the others that psycho picked off as they tried to run away."

"But I... had the gun," Curly said, confused.

"Yeah, Uncle Sam would have been proud," he smacked his friend on the back with congratulatory enthusiasm. "You acted like a hero, my friend. And I never blamed you for Cameron's death."

"Do you hear that?" Curly's head suddenly snapped toward the bathroom.

Derrick's mouth was held in an 'o' as his eyes went wide. He slowly turned his head to look toward where his friend was looking. "Hear what? I didn't hear anything?"

"Don't tell me you can't hear that," Curly shot back. "That rat bastard might still be alive! I swear I can hear his tail flicking. It's getting louder! And now his hairless tail has become a bull-whip!" His head suddenly swiveled and he gave Derrick a very serious look. "This cheeky mouse bastard has nuts like the Viet Cong!"

Derrick smiled nervously as he watched his old-man friend leap over the back of the couch without breaking a hip. "We're not in Nam anymore, Curly," he said, absentmindedly digging his hand between the cushions of the couch. Curly quietly approached the bathroom where he thought he could hear the sounds of a small rodent. The tip-top of his buttcrack was visible over the waistband of his sweatpants. "Goddamnit, Curly," Derrick whined. "You got any weed sunk with Atlantis or the Titanic in here somewhere? I'm too sober to think about disease-ridden mice biting at my toes."

"Yeah, should be right there where your hands are in the couch," Curly replied without looking back, he kept approaching the bathroom like a tiger stalking its prey. As if pulling a genie out of a lamp by its neck, Derrick produced a freshly packed bong from within the depths of the couch cushions.

"How did you do that? That's like magic, dude!" Derrick said, excited, putting the bong to his lips as he reached for the lighter sitting amidst the trash on the coffee table. Lighting the green, he took a huge drag off the bong. He was forced to cough, choking on the hit when he heard the sound of a huge *bang* erupt from the direction of the bathroom. Turning his head, Derrick craned his neck over the back of the couch. His eyes bugged out as he saw Curly standing tall, a sledgehammer dangling from his right hand. The front of the toilet bowl had been pulverized, a large part of the porcelain was now cracked off and tilted forward as water gushed from the broken appliance.

"I swear that little bastard is still down there, waiting for me, biding his time until it's a good one to strike," Curly babbled.

Derrick got hurriedly to his feet. Attempting to put the bong down on the coffee table, it slipped from his hand and teetered off the edge, toppling to the floor. Rancid water spilled out onto the already junk-strewn carpet. "I thought I was too sober for this," he sputtered, "but now I'm way too *high* for this. I'm sure you'll slay this mouse like you did the skunk before it. When evil befalls our house, we vanquish it like Sauron and Morgoth before it." Derrick turned and heavily used his cane to make it to the door, and without even a goodbye, he snuck out, making sure the door was closed behind him, just in case the monster mouse decided he wanted to come out and follow *him*.

The water that slowly seeped out of the broken toilet and flooded the bathroom began spreading to the kitchen. After taking a gratuitous number of hits from the bong, Curly was now sleeping fitfully on the couch, mumbling something about 'goddamn rodents.' The old man had broken out in a cold sweat that had quickly turned hot. In the heat of the moment, he had stripped off all his clothes, adding their filth to the hoard already collected on the floor. Now he tossed and turned under a thin white sheet—well, a sheet that used to be white. "Cocksucking mouse," Curly mumbled in his sleep. "He's not gonna get the best of me with his Viet Cong nuts. I know they live and grow in the sewer like alligators. The crack of the whip of his tail!" Suddenly Curly gasped, clutching his chest as his eyes rolled up into his skull, only the whites showing beneath his fluttering lids.

In his delirious, feverish madness, Curly could see the mouse alive and well in the crook of a pipe below his house. The rodent's eyes shone red like a demon sent from Hell to torment him. Then he heard the beast's heartbeat—it was deafening! *Ba-bum! Ba-Bum! Ba-Bum!*

Then the methodical metronome of the heartbeat began to sound like a voice saying: "*Kill'd-her, kill'd-her, kill'd-her!*" Like an accusatory heart with an ethereal finger pointed in Curly's direction. The beat was like the loudest drum in existence, sent specifically to dole out punishment for the old man's sins. Was he in purgatory? he wondered. *Is the mouse's heart here to torment me in an endless loop for eternity, while its tail becomes a whip against my tender flesh?*

The next time Derrick came to check in on his friend, Curly was in an even shabbier state. He sat naked in two inches of water as it continued to flow out of the broken toilet. His gray hair was greasy and stood on end from weeks of not washing it. Since the toilet had been smashed in half with a sledgehammer, Curly had been forced to defecate in his bathtub. He hadn't bothered to wash it down the drain so it was festering, stinking, and attracting a small colony of flies. Derrick put his hand up in front of his nose as he limped into the house that was far from being fit for human habitation. Curly looked totally out of it, his face twitching and nothing registered in his eyes. Feces was caked on his legs and ass, as well as on his forearms. He had also smeared several lines of feces over his cheeks, which resembled mouse whiskers on either side of his nose.

Derrick made his way over to the bathroom as quickly as he could when he saw a beretta laying on the edge of the bathtub. Before Derrick could get there, his old friend picked up the gun and began tapping the barrel against his temple. "I should have been quicker to kill him," he said, staring off as he waved the gun in his hand.

"Still beating yourself up over Cameron's death?" Derrick said, using his cane to brace himself as he brought himself down to his friend's level. "There's no way you could have known. It was a random act of violence."

"Maybe it wasn't so random," Curly mumbled.

"What was that?" Derrick asked. "I didn't quite hear you."

Suddenly the form of the giant mouse solidified standing behind Derrick. The mouse laughed at Curly's pain, puffing on the cigar and ashing disrespectfully onto the floor. "There he is! The cocksucking fuck!" Curly stared straight at the mouse and leveled the gun directly at the animal's head. The beast pinched his cigar between his teeth and flopped his genitals around in a taunting fashion. "You don't see him?"

Derrick looked over his shoulder and then back at his friend with a worried expression. "There's nothing there."

"It's the fucking mouse!" Curly screamed. "He's haunting me for flushing him down the toilet! I can hear his choked gurgles as he drowns!"

The mouse continued to laugh at Curly's madness, the pitch getting louder and louder. "Confess! Tell him!" the mouse bellowed.

"NO!" Curly screamed as he emptied the clip of his beretta through the mouse's bulbous head. Each bullet went right through the apparition and into the wall of the old man's house. He clicked the gun a bunch more times but it was long empty. He screamed in frustration and threw the empty gun toward the six-foot-tall mouse whose form was beginning to fade. The last thing Curly could see hanging in the air was the shimmering grin of the mouse with the cigar bitten between its teeth.

"What the hell was that all about?" Derrick asked, definitely freaked out.

Curly licked his lips and laughed low, like he was possessed by a demon. "You really want to know why I feel bad about Cameron's death?" he spat.

"What? Tell me!" Derrick demanded.

"I was... fucking her," Curly said with a chuckle. A shocked expression came over Derrick's face. Then Curly grabbed his friend's collar and pulled his face down so he could whisper in his ear. "And the shooter was fucking her too."

This information was too much for Derrick to handle and he exploded. "What?!" he screamed. "You knew the shooter?

And both of you were having an affair with my wife? I should kill you!"

Curly laughed maniacally, his flabby gut jiggling like the waves of the ocean. Derrick, suddenly consumed with rage, scooped some of the feces caked on his friend's leg into his fingers and jammed it into Curly's mouth. He gagged, trying to bite Derrick's shit-smeared fingers. "I hope you choke on your own shit, you traitor!" Derrick yelled. "Die and rot in hell!" He quickly pulled his fingers from Curly's mouth, making sure to scrape off the shit onto the back of his teeth. Almost losing his balance, Derrick then got to his feet using his cane and spit on his friend as he sputtered and choked on his own feces. As he took his leave, he flung the door open and repeated, "Rot in hell!"

Curly felt his stomach rebelling and as he doubled over, he vomited into the toilet water that had now flooded his whole house. As he attempted to scrape the shit from his teeth, he felt with an unexpected pang his heart giving out. Grabbing for his chest between his flabby tits, Curly gasped for precious air. In that moment, he knew he was about to die. Even though he couldn't see the mouse, he knew it was there—its animal heart replacing his own inside his chest cavity. He could see it now, the heart wheezing its last monologue: *Ba-Bum, Ba-Bum, Ba-Bum... Kill'd-her, kill'd-her, kill'd-her...*

As Curly's eyes at last blinked no more, a small mouse, squeaking quietly, crawled out from the wet wall behind the broken toilet. The mouse, curious, but also trying not to drown in the flood waters, scampered up over Curly's naked leg and up his body. The rodent hesitated with its small paws on the old man's chin, sniffing its little nose close to the open mouth. No breath escaped anymore, but the stench of human waste was still fresh. The mouse crawled inside, between the dead man's jaws, over the slimy tongue, and down his gullet. Then slowly, the mouse ate him like the greatest feast, from the inside out.

Gaping Black

A *True Time* Short Story

Chapter One

There's gotta be something totally wrong with me. I'm sitting on my bed and I swear to God my Tupac poster just winked at me. Am I going crazy or was that weed just that bomb? I chuckle to myself as I take a huge sniff, letting wafts of smoke lazily curl out of my mouth. Delicious. The blunts that I roll—the best! Seriously, no one in my high school can roll better blunts than me. Who am I? I was getting to that. My name is Rob. Or Robert Blackguard if you want to use my long-ass slave name. Like a normal sixteen-year-old kid who has no control over their own life, I go to the boringness of high school every day. That's why I smoke that bomb weed! Even if it's just alone in my room—with Tupac here.

Tupac is the coolest because he raps—and because he's black! Anything that's black is definitely where I want to be. There's this dude, right, who works at my school—in the copy room—and he's *black*! I know, I can hardly contain myself, too. Fuck, I'm high. Staring up at Tupac's face on the poster, I look down at his bare torso and Thug Life tattoo on his stomach. That's hot, I gotta admit. You think if I smoke enough weed that he'll come out of the poster and start rapping?

"Robert just likes gaping black asshole," my friend Mothman pokes fun at me the next day before class. We are sitting in our normal chill spot, which is a little alcove by the conference room. There is a water fountain here and we like to sit leaning against the wall like no-good hooligans. I'm gangsta!

Anyway, I push Mothman in his shoulder and say, "You're such a faggot! I know you've been watching *Snatch* and drooling over Brad Pitt. And you say *I'm* the gay one."

"You *are* the gay-wad," Mothman shoots back, smacking me hard in the balls.

I double over in pain and squeak out, "You're such a dick! We're not on an episode of *Jackass*, you sadist."

"I know," Mothman winks at me behind his wire-rimmed glasses. "I just like seeing you squeal in pain like the little pussy you are."

"You mother—" I start and then am cut off by my friend Terry, who's sitting on my other side.

"Girls, girls!" Terry says, punching both of us in the legs, trying to give us charley horses. "You're both a bunch of pussies," he laughs. Luckily I yank my leg away just as he tries to punch me. Mothman isn't so lucky. Terry seems to be the most level-headed of my friends, but also sometimes the most out there. But sometimes I can feel him strongly and I think he might be discontent about something. Well, I mean, who wouldn't, having to go to this hell-hole of boring fuckdom everyday?

"What are you gaylords arguing about?" says Alex. He's our *other* friend. He's Mexican. Walking up, he tosses his backpack down in the corner.

"We were arguing over who got to spank your mom last night," Mothman snorts.

"Har-har," Alex imitates a laugh sarcastically.

We have quite a group of misfits, and before the first bell of the day rings, the last member of our twisted bunch arrives. He's tall, lanky, with a nose quite too big for his face. His arms seem to be freakishly long and he wears baggy South Pole shirts because he likes to bite my style. But I don't fault him for it. I know I look cool. His name is Karl—Karl with the buzz-cut and big-ass nose. Kicking Terry in the bottom of his boot, Karl snaps at him as he itches his nose.

"You ready to go to Mister Down Syndrome's class, bro?"

Terry groans. "I hate that fucking class. And I hate that guy," he complains. Nonetheless, he drags himself to his feet and gives us the peace sign as he heads off with Karl toward Physics. Damn, I really wish I could just ditch class and go get stoned.

I turn to Alex and Mothman who are zoning out listening to music on their iPods. "You guys just want to skip school and go blaze up in the forest preserve? I don't think I can take reading another word in a fucking textbook."

Mothman shrugs sheepishly. "I'm almost failing Algebra, bro—again! And my dad is threatening that if I get F's in any of my classes, that he would get me lobotomized."

"Harsh, bro," I say. Then I turn to look expectantly at Alex.

He shakes his head too, saying, "Man, I gotta make up for the PE I missed yesterday. I was in the bathroom all that period with the worst diarrhea. I think it was those intestine tacos my mom packed for me yesterday."

I almost gag thinking about it. "Y'all motherfuckers are lame," I say. "We'll go to boring school then."

Chapter Two

I compromise my plan by ditching *only* last period. Hey, it won't hurt my GPA that much if I fuck off one stupid class. What the fuck is a GPA anyway? Do I need it? Fuck nah! Maybe I'll just drop out of school soon and get a job. But then what would my parents say? Maybe if I just float by, then when I get out of my frat years of college, my dad will hook me up with a job. Sounds awful.

I'm walking down the path in the forest preserve next to my high school. It's quiet except for the occasional hum of a car passing by on the main road. I'm just finishing up licking the sticky part of the joint paper. Rolled it perfect again! I put it in my mouth with a grin. Yes, I admit it, I'm such a stoner. But hey, ain't no other way to survive high school. After putting the joint between my lips, I slip my earbuds in so I can crank it to some Nas.

While I'm silently mouthing the words to the rap, I light up so I can blaze like a champ. Too bad my buds didn't have the balls to ditch with me. After sucking the sweet smoke down to the lungs, I cough like a tuberculosis patient, spitting spittle all over the ground. I circle around the path in the middle of the forest preserve where there is a field of tall grass. My eyes suddenly feel itchy. As I go to rub them, smoke finds its way into my eyeballs, further intensifying the irritation.

Then I see something—or, I *think* I see something. A window made of black smoke is hovering in the air by the tall grass. Its surface is almost reflective, like a mirror. I blink my eyes painfully and a blurry image of a woman's thin face appears in the black thing. Her eyes are completely black!

Without even a chance to study the image further, I am blindsided. This person hits me with their whole body, full-force, knocking me over onto a soft patch of greenery between the trees. At once I see it's Mothman laying on top of me. He gives me a cheeky grin and starts kissing and licking the side of my neck. At first I'm disgusted.

"What are you doing?" I shriek. "We agreed no making out!" Then my eyes roll up in my head for a second and I let out a soft moan.

"Oh, you don't like it?" Mothman whispers against my shivering skin.

"No... I..." I can't finish the sentence because he's now fumbling with the button of my jeans, trying to get to the good bits. Closing my eyes, I surrender to the pleasure. Mothman pulls down my pants and boxers. My dick is already semi-hard from the foreplay and nibbles on the neck. I can tell he's drooling for the cock because when he puts it in his mouth, it's so juicy. His tongue just works and when he deep-throats, the gagging feels so good on the tip of my cock.

As I begin to feel the orgasm building in my balls, I pull my fingers through Mothman's hair. Then I press his head down hard on my throbbing cock, forcing him to take it deep in the throat. I feel the nut coming and yell out with orgasmic ecstasy as I feel the warm semen squirt into his greedy mouth. He gags at first, jerking around on my erection, then he swallows my load like a champ.

Slowly Mothman runs his lips up my shaft and off the tip of my penis as I heave to catch my breath—I came so hard. Without warning he pounces on top of me and kisses me hard on the lips. I can taste my own spunk on his tongue.

"That's what I call a close encounter—Brokeback Mountain style. Next time you can cum into my *gaping black*," he chuckles, jumps up, and then dashes off without another word.

I lay there panting. The force of the orgasm almost rendered my legs completely numb. They still tingle with the afterglow of that sloppy blowjob. My dick is becoming flaccid again and is curling itself down right under my belly button. A glistening shine of cum and Mothman's spit adorns my cock, balls, and abdomen. The sign of a good time.

My face is hot with blush as I slowly pull my pants back up, covering up the indecent but delicious act. I'm high as fuck, but I wonder if I'll be able to find where the joint flew off to when Mothman knocked me over. Let's toke to the crooked cocks.

Chapter Three

It's Friday and my parents are going to be gone tonight and won't be back until midday tomorrow. My buddies and I know what that means. Party in Rob's basement! And what happens in the basement, stays in the basement. I told Mothman and Terry to meet me at my house at dark. Us three have kind of a *tripod* thing going. No use inviting Alex or Karl, they wouldn't be into it.

The first one to show up is Mothman with a huge grin on his face. "Sup, my G?" I say to him as I answer the door. We slap hands and bump fists. No smooching this time. We come in to chill in the living room until Terry gets here.

"Dude, you're never going to believe what I got for us tonight!" Mothman says excitedly as he flops down lazily onto the couch.

"What is it?" I ask, walking over toward him.

He pulls out a Ziploc and unrolls it dramatically. "Behold!" Mothman says with flair.

I squint at the bag. "Are those portobellos?" I say.

Mothman snorts. "No they aren't, numb-nuts. Magic mushrooms to get you lifted. Yeah! Yeah!" Then he pulls out another rolled up Ziploc bag and drags it underneath his nose. "And that bomb *chronic*!"

"Yo!" I say, getting even more excited. "Bro, you went all out. We gonna have a night!"

Suddenly there is pounding at the door and a voice bellows, "Let me in, it's the rectal police! Prepare to be body cavity searched!"

Mothman and I look at each other and roll our eyes. "Terry," we say in unison. I go over to the door to let him in. As I open the door, he rushes in and stands in the middle of the living room rubbing his hands together.

"Lovely to see you boys," Terry says with a wide grin. He points to Mothman as I close and lock the front door. "I see Mothman is going to be playing the Junior Suburban Shaman tonight. Excellent!"

I walk over and stand next to Terry. "That would be good medicine," I comment. "Especially since I had this freaky dream last night."

"Dream? What about?" Terry asks.

I shrug. "It's like I'm running over a bunch of rooftops. And someone is chasing me with a chainsaw. Obviously they're trying to kill me or something."

"That's creepy as fuck, Robert," Mothman chimes in. "You must have been smoking some bad weed. I, on the other hand, have only the best Blue Dream for myself and my compatriots. We smoke only the finest weed in the Shire!"

"You are such a nerd," Terry remarks. "The highest elf at comic-con."

"That's me," Mothman chortles, grinning ear to ear.

"Shall we go down to the sex cave?" I ask.

There really isn't anything sexy about my basement. The floors are cold, hard, and gray, with only a few rugs scattered around. I supplement this with sleeping bags and fluffy comforters laid down on the floor in front of the couch. Yes, there is a couch and a small TV with all my Nintendo 64 games. The only other thing down in this basement is the washer and dryer, but that is on the other side of the stairs. It's not much, but we make it steamy if we can. And if we can't, then we settle for fun playing Mario Kart.

As we all are getting settled in on the sleeping bags, Mothman is finishing rolling up a blunt and putting it behind his ear. Terry is sitting with his legs splayed out, already opening his pants.

"Let's blast off," Mothman says as he puts a handful of shrooms in Terry's hand and then in mine. Taking a seat on the sleeping bags, I feel a shiver run up my spine. The *gaping black* is calling my name to come sing into the void. Looking down at the mushrooms in my hand, I wonder if I'm tripping already just from touching them.

"To finding new heights and gaining knowledge toward what all of this bullshit actually means," Terry says, toasting with his shrooms.

I don't know what to say so I blurt out, "To surrendering to the Blackness!"

Terry smiles at me and then shovels the shrooms into his mouth. As he chomps away, Mothman and I feast on the strange earthy flavor which is dry-ass mushrooms as well. "How long until it kicks in?" Terry asks. "Because I'm so horny right now. I don't know if I can wait until it kicks in." He slides his hand down into his unbuttoned pants. Seeing him touch himself is turning me on.

"It's going to be a while," Mothman answers. "So we might as well get our sex juices going. Heighten that sexual energy toward powerful magick. I will be your Shaman on this sexy vision quest." He is now quickly unbuttoning his own pants.

It doesn't take long for all three of us to get naked. We're all fully hard, stroking our cocks as we stare at each other as we all give pleasure to ourselves. That's so hot to me. Our mouths are hanging open with panting breaths. I don't really know how much time has transpired, but I swear I feel the high of the mushrooms creeping up my spine.

"We are a pyramid," Mothman says, getting up to his knees and moving toward the middle of the room. Terry and I get on our knees also, meeting Mothman in the center. We are all kneeling, facing each other, vigorously jerking our hard, horny pricks like our lives depend on it. Slowly our foreheads seem to magnetize together, and before I know it, all three of our heads are together.

"Oh, I feel that shit," I say, feeling the trip hit me hard like a psychedelic wave of rainbow unicorns. All three of us laugh. As I look up at them I gasp, for I see a wash of bright color. Around Terry is a bright aura of white. Around Mothman is a bright aura of orange. And around me looks like an aura that is flickering back and forth between black and blue.

"Do you see this shit, guys?" Mothman asks. "I know I'm the one supposed to be leading you on this journey, but damn! I be tripping balls!"

"Oh, I see it," Terry responds quietly. "It's like an aura—I see you guys's auras."

"Me too," I agree. "Mine is flickering black and blue. Trippy shit, man."

"Keep jerking your peckers, guys," Terry commands. "I'm having a moment here. It's building."

I start jerking my cock more frantically. It's all I can do to not cum already. The orgasm keeps building and building in my balls and my spine. My eyes suddenly bug out because I see a white spiral of light coming out of Terry's chest. There's one coming out of Mothman's chest that's orange. And, yep, sure enough there's a spiral of black and blue light coming right from my ribcage area. I can see that the orgasms are building up in my two friends as well. Visually I can see their sexual energy in their bodies. And there is this golden light that comes out of the top of their head and circles around like a halo.

"I'm so close," I groan.

Terry throws up a hand. "We are the Trimurti," he says. His eyes shoot open and his irises and pupils look exactly like mystical melting clocks. Terry concludes by saying, "We give birth to the Tridevi!"

In the exact moment that Terry says the last weird-ass word, we all cum, ejaculating hard into the center of our pyramid. The colors of our auras instantaneously become a tornado. White, blue, black, and orange swirl together like a vortex of queer erotic rainbows.

Just as fast as the color storm comes, it subsides. There is an ocean of semen in the center of our tripod—our *Trimurti*, as Terry just called it. "We busted a nut and impregnated the New Age," Mothman says, his eyes rolling up in his head until I can only see the whites.

"We gave birth to the New Age," Terry concurs with his version.

"We helped bring to an end the outdated ways of the Old Age," I add.

We are all sitting back on our butts now, feeling tired from the sexual exertion. "We were just waiting patiently for the past to die," Terry says sleepily. His eyes blink a couple times then close as he lays down on the sleeping bag. Just as quickly as mine and Mothman's heads are on the sleeping bags, the dream is over.

Chapter Four

From the blissful emptiness of the void, something calls me back. Maybe it is that oh-small voice in the back of the soul known as Hiphop. I awake as if wading through a pool of rainbow colored semen. It's thick and slimy as I make my way toward the stairs that lead up from the basement. The stairs seem to have morphed into a slide that has now morphed into a tongue. I'm on my hands and knees now, trying to get upstairs, but the lapping tongue seems to be slowing my progress. Staring up at the open doorway at the top of the flapping tongue, a horse's head whinnies and comes into view. No! It's not a horse, it's a pink unicorn! This unicorn points its horn down toward me and it stretches out like the arms of a Stretch Armstrong doll. Grasping onto the Laffy Taffy unicorn horn, I try to walk up the tongue-staircase like trying to go back up a very fast-moving water slide. Finally I wriggle up all the way, using my boner for support as I go. Good thing I always go naked at these vision quest parties...

Once I'm on the ground floor of my own house, the pink unicorn farts and disappears in a puff of stardust. I crawl my way to the second flight of stairs and make it in a slog up to my bedroom at last. It is my noble sir Tupac who has called me forth from the rivers of fungi star missions. Sitting on my bed I study the poster. I study the still face of Tupac Shakur depicted on glossy paper. He winks at me then flicks his tongue out. I jump back, scared there might be a poltergeist in my poster. Then I hear the voice of Roger Troutman saying, *"California Love..."*

That is the secret code and now I know there is an intergalactic mission that involves something about epic proportions. I almost shit myself as Tupac's whole body starts to move. He turns until his back is fully toward me. The waistband of his boxers is quite higher than the waist of his jeans. But no matter, in a second the jeans are dropped. Then the boxers are down and I am staring at a round ass the color of dark chocolate. Without a second to relish the moment, Tupac bends over and spreads his cheeks. It's almost as if I'm looking directly into the sun. The beauty is resplendent. His anus suddenly dilates, becoming a gaping black vortex. I can almost see wisps of purple swirling around within the spinning energy of the rectal-portal.

The feeling is like I'm being drawn by a magnet toward Tupac's gaping black anus. It wants me inside. *He* wants me inside. The Blackness wants me inside. And I am a slave to the Black. My pupils must be enormous, mimicking the gaping black abyss I see before me. It's almost as if staring into Tupac's rectum can suck me through the sphincter of my own pupils. Too late now, I'm so close to the poster that I'm almost one with it. Then my head goes into his asshole. My mother said never go ass to mouth, but for Tupac you have to make an exception. After my head is encapsulated, the gaping black vortex of the rectum sucks the rest of my body into itself like a reverse birth.

The spinning black energy of the portal has now become a tunnel. It reminds me of the Astral version of a colon leading up into the multiversal intestinal track. The time-space shit-chute dumps me out into somewhere where gravity is lower. I come down slowly onto the dusty ground. I almost shit down my naked legs when I open my eyes to witness the Earth fathoms in front of me in space. Taking a deep panicked breath, I realize that I'm on the Moon completely butt-ass free-balling. Holy shit, I can breathe. "Fuck me, I'm alive," I say out loud. "This is the craziest shit ever. Am I dreaming? Am I *dead*? I can breathe though."

"Of course you can breathe, numb-nuts," a voice says from over to my left. It's a girl's voice. She continues by saying, "You're tripping your shrunken balls off right now."

Finally I see who's talking. She's a girl probably about my own age. She's thin, wearing a long nightgown and has long stringy brown hair. "Where the fuck are we?" I sputter. "And what the fuck is that?" I point to a large black pyramid erected in the dusty surface of the Moon.

The girl puts a hand up. "The point is," she says, "you're dead. Or you will be. Or you were. I don't all that quite matter like a Mad Hatter, you see."

"What?" I ask since I didn't follow any of that.

The girl in the nightgown looks down at the Earth. "Sometimes you're dead and sometimes you're alive," she says. "What's really the difference? You could be alive for a while and then find yourself dead. Then a small moment later you'll be alive again. It's all very confusing. What's with a state of being? Maybe once you're Being, then you're always *being*..." she trails off.

"Is there an anus of the Universe?" I mumble, staring down at the Earth again too.

"Oh, there's definitely an anus to the Universe," the girl says confidently, "but it always shits you out exactly where you are."

I nod, and as I do there's a deafening farting noise that seems to shake the whole cosmos down to its very tachyons. Then the anus of the Universe shits me out exactly where I am—in my basement on the cum-soaked sleeping bags. Hearing the commotion, Mothman blinks his eyes and sits up groggily. There's a drip of dried and crusty jiz coming down from the corner of his mouth. Terry sits up too, his shaggy black hair sticking up in every direction like he's had the longest night of rough sex.

"Oh, oh man," Terry says, "last night must have been *so* gay!"

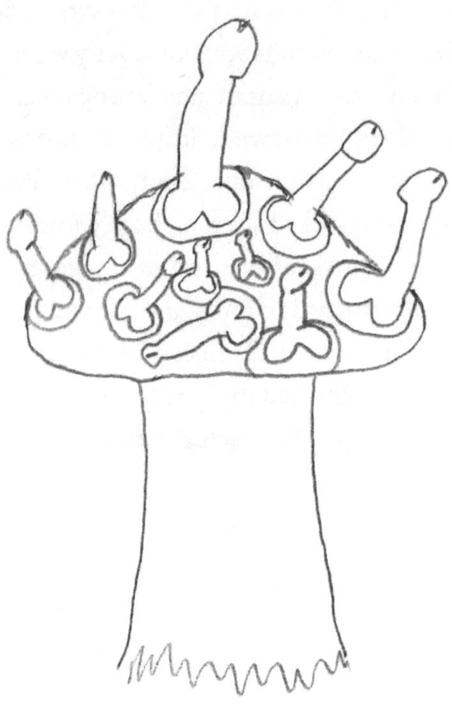

The Pariah and His
Dark Passenger

1

There were only ever two things I was really good at: making bad art and killing people. My bad art consisted mostly of photography. My family had always been wealthy, so I really didn't give a fuck whether people liked my work or not. Surprisingly, I still got clients—models who needed photos, or actors who needed headshots. Most of my clients were women, very attractive ones, which was ironic because I would never *ever* have sex with any of them. I only have sex with other men. Thinking back on this, this was directly a product of being raised by two lesbian mothers.

All the abuse that I suffered at the hands of my dyke mothers will be a story for later. I want to talk more about how I would stalk and pick out my victims for the ritual kill; the daughters for my table of slaughter. My photography studio was just a few blocks down from my apartment in Manhattan. However, I would go down to what I coined as the 'sleazy district' to find prostitutes that no one would miss once they were dispatched by my blade. I drove a black Porsche for the very reason that I didn't want it to stand out in the dark shadows of the putrescent alleyways where the filthy pussies congregated.

On this one particular night, I slowed the car down next to

the sidewalk in front of an old warehouse. There was a rather tall hooker leaning up against the bricks of the building. Her skirt was almost so short that it could pass as a belt. She was wearing fishnet stockings and a crop-top. I couldn't see her eyes because her face was obscured by the bangs of a cheap black wig. Slowly I rolled down the window on the passenger's side of my Porsche. Leaning over, I dangled my hand out of the window with a wad of money between my fingers. With a flick of my wrist, I made a 'come here' motion and she came to me like a dog.

Without a word, she opened the passenger door and slipped into the seat next to me. I could see the shadow of an Adam's apple on her throat but wasn't quite sure yet if she was actually a man. "What do you like, baby?" she said, a little gruffness to her voice. "Are we going to go back to your place? I'll do whatever you like. I don't usually get Johns as handsome as you." She smiled and looked over at me shyly.

She was right. I was quite handsome. I would be a fucking catch for any good-looking woman—if they didn't all deserve to die, that is. My dirty blonde hair was closely cropped and styled with the most expensive hair gel. I kept my beard shaved and my face clean, no scruffy bristles. And I worked out at the gym five times a week to keep my body in immaculate shape. But I never killed men. The sudden appearance of this tranny prostitute instead of a dirty pussy was putting a damper on my nightly blood-lust. What to do with him? I stared out of the front windshield but didn't drive or say a word.

"Do you not like me?" the prostitute said insecurely. "Is it because of this?" He flipped up his skirt so I could get a glimpse of the bulge in his panties.

I chuckled at seeing his package. "No," I said finally, shaking my head. Then I turned and gave him a seriously look. I still don't know why I proposed this, but I did. "What if I told you that you would never have to hook again? That you would be taken care of and live luxuriously. All you have to do is help me."

The tranny didn't say anything and was silent for a while. "What would I have to do?" he said hesitantly.

Without answering, I looked over him and out of the open window. The click of high-heels was coming closer to my Porsche. This whore looked like a real woman this time. "Lure her in," I said.

The tranny poked his head out of the window and spoke to the whore saying, "Hey, honey! You want to party with us? Double the fun, double the money, baby!"

The female whore regarded us cautiously. She leaned down and rested her elbows on the edge of the open window, letting us get an unadulterated view of her ample cleavage. Noisily chewing on a wad of bubblegum, she said, "You got money?"

I flashed the big wad of cash once more. That was all she needed to see to crawl into the backseat. Without any other idle chatter, I started to drive away. Now there was an abandoned warehouse on the edge of the sleazy district which was where I would take my victims to do the blood rituals. I would never defile my body by violating them sexually. But I didn't have a problem carving them up and feeling the pure pleasure of their blood all over my naked body.

Reaching into the pocket of my leather jacket, I pulled out a small bag filled with white powder as well as a small silver spoon for snorting. "Ooo, yeah! Party favors," the tranny said at seeing the bag of drugs. "Is that cocaine?" he asked.

"Something like that," I replied, handing the bag and spoon over to her. Whores would take any drug that was fed to them. The substance was not cocaine, it was ketamine—some cheap shit. Ketamine is a dissociative, and I wanted these two hoes to be at least kind of out of it when we got to the warehouse where I have my sacrifice table and killing tools. But they couldn't be too out of it since I still needed them conscious enough to walk. The tranny used the little spoon and snorted one bump into each nostril. He tilted his head back, sniffed hard, and wiped his nostrils as he handed the ketamine to the ho in the backseat. Without any hesitation, she did two bumps as well— one in each nostril.

"That's some good shit, baby," she said, handing me back the bag of white powder. I slid the bag back into the pocket of my leather jacket as we approached the area where the abandoned warehouse was. It was so quiet since no one lived over here and it was dark as well; the buildings dilapidated and deserted. There were a few open fields amidst the derelict structures, the weeds and dry grass grown scraggly and neglected.

I parked the car next to my warehouse and shut off the engine and the headlights. "It's creepy as shit over here," the tranny commented as he looked out of the window. "But I've fucked and sucked a dick over here once or twice."

I smiled wickedly and looked at the tranny and then the trashy ho in the backseat who looked nervous but too high to think straight. "The perfect place for a horror sex scene," I said.

"You're into that role-playing shit?" the female ho asked. "I can do that," she continued, slurring her words. "I can be whoever you want me to be, baby. As long as you got the money to pay for it."

After waving the wad of money in their slutty faces again, I slid it into the inside pocket of my leather jacket. It was the lure and they swallowed it hook, line, and sinker. These hoes did every time. I got out of the car and started to walk over to the broken door on the side of the building. The whores got out and followed me like two puppies with prolapsed assholes. After opening the metal door with the broken lock, I walked inside, followed closely after by the sound of high-heels clicking and echoing in the large empty room we found ourselves in. The floor was concrete and stained with blood in places, but it was too dark to see that—it just looked like gray blotches coloring the large floor. In the center of the room was my kill table bolted to the floor. It was metal, shining in the moonlight that was streaming through the large windows that were near the ceiling of the huge room. These windows were cheap thin glass and crossed with metal like a grid. The two whores stopped and stared at the table which was fashioned with wrist-cuffs and ankle-cuffs.

"You really go all-out with this S&M role-playing shit, don't you?" the female ho asked, a subtle tremor in her voice could be heard. I smiled in the dark and walked around slowly, coming up behind her.

"Oh, yes," I hissed, putting my left hand on her shoulder and reaching around with my other hand to pull out the large wrench I had hidden in my back pocket. Without warning, I struck her across the back of the head with the heavy tool. She screamed and fell to her hands and knees, grabbing at the back of her head as a stream of blood started to seep from underneath her hair.

The tranny shrieked and spun on his heels, breaking off the heel of one of his stilettos. He tripped and fell to his knees as he began to sob. I towered over the she-male in the shadows of the warehouse to intimidate him, holding up the bloody wrench threateningly. "Shut up, whore," I hissed in a demonic voice. "Cooperate or you'll be dead too. I don't want to know who you are or what your name is—from now on your name is Dogface. You got that, Dogface?"

The tranny sniffled and tried to suppress his sobs. He nodded slowly, holding his arms tightly in front of his fake tits. "Y-yes, sir," he stammered.

"Good," I replied, "because if you don't comply, if you try to run away, I will track you down and kill you in the most painful, torturous way I can think of." The tranny couldn't help it, he/she/it let out a shriek and a sob that tore through the cavernous room like the cry of a wounded animal. "Shut your slut mouth, Dogface," I said harshly. "My offer still stands. You help me, be my dog-slave, then you'll have a roof over your head and meals to eat. If you don't agree, your life is forfeit."

The petite, fragile tranny nodded meekly again and wiped the tears from under his eyes. When I looked back over at the female ho, she was trying to crawl away, but not very effectively. Quickly I put the wrench into a pocket inside my leather jacket and then went over to the ho and stomped my boot down into the middle of her back. The air was knocked out of her as she collapsed violently to the floor. The blood from her cranial wound was gushing now, pooling onto the floor, and I knew that it was only a matter of time before she lost consciousness.

I stepped off of her back and bent down to grab her wrists. Looking over at Dogface, I said, "Get her fucking ankles, Dogface! Help me get her on the table."

Dogface was still crying softly as he grabbed the whore's ankles, helping me lift her limp body onto the metal table. Once she was there, muttering to herself, disoriented from the blow to her head, I fastened the cuffs around her wrists. Without me even having to ask, Dogface fastened the cuffs around her ankles. The slut was starting to come to a little bit more and blinked her eyes, apparently trying to get her vision back into focus. "Don't... Don't..." she pleaded. As she tried to pull her head up off the table to look at us, I punched her hard in the nose. She cried out as her head snapped back, striking her skull on the metal where her wound already was. Blood gushed from her nose like a hose with a cut in it.

I caught movement in the corner of my vision and noticed Dogface slowly backing toward the door, hoping that I wouldn't notice. Snapping my fingers loudly, I pointed to him and he stopped instantly, legs shaking. "Don't even fucking try it," I said. "Come," I said, making a motion for him to come closer.

As the tranny slowly came back closer to me, I crouched down to the drawer that was attached to the bottom of the legs of the kill table. Pulling out a key from my pocket, I unlocked the drawer to reveal my assortment of butchering knives. I took out a long thin dagger which looked especially delicious. After closing the drawer, I stood back up. After making sure Dogface was rooted to his spot close at hand, I plunged the knife deep into her gut. She shrieked as blood from the wound began to pool around the blade. I cut down, goring her gloriously. The tranny had his hands up over his face and was trembling from the sobs still coming through his nose and eyes.

After thoroughly gutting the ho, I wiped the blood on a rag that I pulled out of my back pocket. Inside my leather jacket, I had made a makeshift sheath for knives, so I slipped it inside so that Dogface wouldn't get any ideas to try to take it for self-defense. Taking my hands and sliding them into the wet wound, I ripped the gash open farther, revealing the guts within the whore who was on the verge of death. With a squeal of glee, I started to pull her intestines out so that they spilled around her waist and draped down around the sides of the table.

Then without warning, I grabbed the back of the tranny's neck and forced him over to the table. He resisted me but I was stronger. I pushed his head down toward the carnage, the entrails. "No, please no..." he begged me. But when it came to my ritual, I had no mercy. Finally I smashed his face into the open, gaping wound until his mouth was tasting blood and bile. I could hear gurgling and bubbling as Dogface struggled to breathe.

"Gargle those fucking entrails, you whore," I said in a low, gravelly hiss. Then I pulled his head from the blood so he wouldn't drown. Dogface sputtered and spit blood from his mouth. Gagging, he began to puke onto the carcass of the muti-lated whore. "Put your hands on the table," I commanded. The tranny didn't move so I struck him on the back of the head.

"Ow!" he yelled in protest.

"I said put your fucking hands on the table!" I said again. This time, without protest, the tranny slowly put his hands on the table next to the body, trying not to slip in the blood.

Slowly I pulled his skirt up to reveal his somewhat girly ass. After ripping his panties down to reveal is cute asshole and hanging balls, I smacked his ass hard. He cried out again as a red handprint was left on his right ass cheek. I could already feel myself getting hard. Quickly unzipping my pants, I pulled out my erect cock and the tip brushed between the tranny's ass cheeks. The whore knew what was coming next.

Spitting on my hand, I stroked the saliva all down the shaft of my cock. This was going to hurt and I relished in the thought. I then spread his cheeks and spit a wad on the puckered hole which was clenching shut and then relaxing. Smiling, I put my hands over the tranny's shoulders to get a firm grip, then I slammed my cock inside. "Ugh, fuck!" the tranny groaned and cried out as I began my thrust deep into his asshole. The killing and mutilation had gotten me so hot and bothered that I knew I was going to cum pretty soon.

As I continued to thrust deep into Dogface's rectum and stretch out his tight little hole, I could feel the orgasm building in my balls. It was going to be an explosive one. "Oh, yeah, Dogface," I moaned. "Take that fucking cock deep in your perverted rectum!" The tranny groaned and moaned louder, getting ready for my ejaculation. "Here it comes!" I yelled. "Ready? You ready?" I groaned with a deep guttural sound as I felt the semen in orgasmic ecstatic excitement travel from my balls and up my urethra. As I squirted my fluid deep into his ass, I could feel his anus squeeze around the base of my cock. It felt so fucking good. Dogface panted heavily and moaned as I'm sure he could feel the warmth of my cum squirt inside him.

Leaving my dick inside, I pumped more cum into him as my orgasm continued. Noticing that he was hard also, I grabbed his dick and began to stroke it. Dogface moaned deeply, and almost as quickly as I had cum, I could feel his warm fluid seep from the tip of his cock over my hand and spatter on the floor to mix with the blood. I pulled out, my cock still hard, and watched with blissful lust as the tranny's asshole gaped and oozed my own fluid to drip out and mix with the blood as well.

11

I never really ever found out the truth about where I came from. My moms sometimes would tell me that I was adopted from an unmarried teenage mother. Other times they would say that they found me as a baby abandoned on the side of the road. When I was finally able to look at my adoption papers which gave my dyke mothers custody of me, they looked shifty at best. The documents could likely have been forgeries. They didn't contain any names of individuals I was adopted from or even an agency that I could seek out for information. My personal documents like this only contained the name that my moms had given me—Josephus Carcutta. I always thought that was a fucking strange last name; and which mother it came from I never found out either. Josephus? Who the fuck names their kid Josephus? Fucking lesbian bitches.

Anyway, I digress from the story. I don't have any memories before the age of about six—this is the time I remember they started molesting me on a regular basis. If they had been molesting and abusing me before I was six, I have no memory of any of it. Specifically, I remember one day when I was playing with my dolls on the floor of my bedroom. My little self was naked and I was amusing myself by making my dolls kiss and hump each other. After my door opened suddenly, without even a knock, I saw my one mother Julie standing there looking down at me. She was completely naked. Julie was the one with shortly cropped brown hair, she was taller than an average woman, tits moderately saggy, and she had a small pooch around her belly. I remember looking down at her hairy bush with boyish fascination.

"Josephus," she said with a smile. I looked up at her with puppy-dog eyes and dropped the dolls that I had been smashing together at the hips. She motioned for me to cum with her finger. "Come to Mommy's room, darling." Without waiting for a response, she turned to walk back toward her bedroom. I rubbed my small penis as I stood up and followed her round mom-ass out of the room. Staring at her ass jiggling as she walked, I noticed my little pecker getting hard between my legs. I didn't have much more than a needle-dick at that time.

Mommy's bedroom door was open and I walked in behind Julie as I stroked myself gently. My other Mommy—Lorena— was laying on the bed, also naked, with her legs spread open. She was a little heavier than Julie, and I could see her breasts like sunken water balloons on her chest. The fat around her middle spilled around her midsection and on the bed under her. Lorena's hand was between her legs and was working her clitoris between the lips of her hairy beaver. Her hair was black and long, in contrast to Julie's.

Julie turned to look at me when she was standing next to the bed. When she saw me staring up at her, still stroking my tiny dick with a thumb in my mouth, she smiled. "Baby," she said, "come join your mommies on the bed." Then she sat down on the edge of the bed before laying down beside her wife. They kissed and licked each other's tongues as I crawled up onto the foot of the bed, staring as they pleasured themselves. They scooted closer to each other and had their legs spread, opening their pussies toward me. Laughing quietly, they both used their fingers to spread the lips of their vulvas open, revealing the openings to their vaginas. I stared into them like they were the entrances to magical caves of wonder.

They were both wet and I could see the lubrication glistening and dripping from their cunts. When they stared at me, I didn't know then that the look on their faces was pure lust. "Come closer, Josephus," Lorena said, trying to sound calm and loving like a mother. "Bring your little fists and sit here between your mommies' hips. I scooted my butt forward, still erect, until I was kneeling on the bed between my mothers close enough so I could reach their eager perverted cunts.

"Now, make a fist with both hands, Josephus," Julie continued the instructions. "Then slide your little fist and your arm into us between our legs, right here." She indicated her pussy. I made a fist with both hands. Then I pressed my right fist up against Lorena's open cunt, and my left fist up against Julie's. Then I pressed inside. They were wet enough that my little fists slid in easily. They both moaned with pleasure as their little adopted son fist-fucked them gently. I could slide my arms into them all the way up to my elbow. Sliding my arms in and out of their dripping pussies, they breathed, moaned, and groaned loudly as they fulfilled their forbidden lusts. Even I felt a strange tingling throughout my body during the whole process. They loved it and I continued fisting my moms hard and deep for a while. I'll never forget what it felt like. As I could hear the slurping from the movement within their flesh and lubrication, it felt like their bodies were trying to suck me into them. Like they wanted to give birth to me in reverse—like *taking* birth instead of *giving* birth.

I bet you are wondering, dear reader, how Dogface and I disposed of the whore's body which I had completely mutilated. Now, I'll tell you, I wasn't the most meticulous killer by any means. In some ways you could say I was downright sloppy about things—especially the cleanup. How I had managed up to that point to remain uncaught by the authorities was one of those universal mysteries to me. Perhaps, unbeknownst to me, I was being aided by some government agency—or perhaps a *supernatural* agency.

After I had fucked Dogface's asshole good and he was covered in the hooker's blood, he was obviously in so much shock that his brain had all but shut down. He made no sound, and said nothing. I would say he was close to being catatonic, yet conscious enough to help me dispose of the body. Dogface obeyed all the orders I gave him, and he proved to be a good little slave—at least for now. There were some bone saws in the drawer I kept locked at the bottom of the kill table. We dismembered the body into a half dozen pieces; covering us in gore in the process.

There were many empty lots scattered amidst the abandoned factories of this ghostly part of town. We scattered the pieces—burying them in different lots deep in the ground. How we—or I when I was alone—never got spotted doing our bloody business was a miracle to me. After we were done burying all the pieces, I filled up a bucket full of water that came out of a lone spigot that was on the side of the warehouse. How it still had water running to it was also a mystery to me. I rinsed the bone saw and the knife I had used for the kill in the bucket. Dogface stood next do me in silence. His face looked like he had been erased. After putting the blades back into the drawer, I locked it up for next time. The gray concrete of the floor was forever stained with splotches of blood that had soaked into the pores of the floor. I dumped the bucket of water on the puddles of fresh blood from that night—that was the only cleanup I bothered to do inside my kill space.

Looking over at Dogface who was covered in red ooze, I noticed that he was shaking almost imperceptibly. Taking the bucket, I walked back out of the building, the Dogface following close on my heels. I filled the bucket up again and doused him with the water; some of the carnage caked on his body dripped off. After doing that, I poured a bucket over my own head. There were several thick black bath robes that I stashed in the trunk of my car that I would put on after a kill as to not get so much blood on the interior of the car. I gave one to Dogface and he put it on without saying a word. After putting mine on, we drove back to my apartment in Manhattan.

We took a shower together; the blood ran down the drain like the trail of a woman's menses. I fucked Dogface again against the wall of the shower. He was a good little fucktoy and gave his asshole up willingly. My cock was so hard when it was inside him, and I enjoyed reaching around to stroke his own erect dick. We continued not to speak to one another. How conscious my companion was of what was happening was questionable. Maybe PTSD had traumatized him to the point that half of his awareness was elsewhere. I really didn't know.

However, in spite of the fact that Dogface was silently

compliant of everything up to this point, I still didn't trust him to stay put where I told him to. My bedroom had a walk-in closet that I had fitted with padding on all the walls and the back of the door. There was a small cot in the little room and the only light was embedded in the ceiling with a circle of plexiglass screwed in over top of it. This was where I put Dog-face—I couldn't let him have free range of the apartment when I wasn't there, and I had to go to work doing my photography the next day. He went into the padded room without protest, I closed the door and locked him in from the outside.

111

Like I said before, I never found out where I came from. The adoption papers that my moms had for me were sketchy at best. When I made inquiries about the adoption agency listed on the papers, I soon found out that no such agency existed. Asking my moms about it when I was young yielded no fruit as well. Some days they would give me the story that I was adopted from an orphanage. Other days they would tell me that they found me abandoned on the side of the road and that they rescued me. It still remained a fucking mystery to me that I never got an answer to. For all I knew, they could have bought me from a baby farm. Fuck if that would have been the only time they bought a child—it wasn't.

If it weren't for my extremely good looks and being rich, I would have been a total social pariah. I didn't understand people—I couldn't relate to people. Not to mention that toward every woman I had a bloodlust to kill. For this reason, I kept to myself and kept quiet while in public—especially when dealing with my work. Going into the studio the morning after the night I locked up Dogface, I remained somewhat agitated; like there were a million ants crawling just below the surface of my skin. But I took a deep breath and contained it since I had to meet with a client. Her name was Kiara. She was fit, with mocha-colored skin, and small tits. She needed some modeling pictures for her portfolio. I posed her in front of a dark purple sheet for a backdrop. Kiara was wearing a slim black dress with a neckline that plunged all the way down to her navel.

As she posed and I snapped shots, she slowly became more seductive. First one strap of her dress went down, then the other. Her dark eyes were wide and her pupils were dilated as she watched me work. I got close to her, taking shots of her face. As I did, she let the whole top of her dress fall, revealing her round breasts and erect nipples. Before I had time to react, she grabbed me by the belt and pulled me into her, smashing her lips against mine. It was as if she wanted to eat my face. I think she even licked the side of my cheek. I pushed her away, but not too hard as to be considered violent. I regained my composure as Kiara began to pull the top of her dress back up, looking embarrassed.

I began to take more photographs as if nothing had happened. "You don't find me attractive?" she said softly.

Letting the camera drop from in front of my face, I hesitated before answering. "It's not that..." I began.

Quickly she had the straps back up over her shoulders, but she made one final advance. It was almost like she lunged at me. I took a step back and that was when she got angry. She scowled and barked at me in a shrill voice. "What, are you some kind of faggot?"

Oh, I wanted to fucking kill her in that moment. I wanted to gut her like the little whore that she was. I wanted to jerk off in her blood while imagining Dogface's gaping asshole. I wanted to make a hole in her abdomen and slowly pull her intestines to the outside while she watched. I wanted to—well, you get the idea. However, I couldn't let the mask slip. I couldn't let her see how ravenous I was for her carnage. So I took a deep breath and said softly, "Kiara, I think you should leave. I'll send you the pictures."

For just a brief second, I could see the disappointment on her face. Then she regained her facade of indignation. Huffing with an upturned nose, she spun on her heel and left the studio. I chuckled to myself after the initial rage dissipated. Walking over toward the large windows that looked out of the tall building that my studio was in, I tossed the camera onto the soft pillows of the couch next to me. "Fucking models," I mumbled to myself. "I should make it my life's mission to exterminate *them all.*"

On my way home from the studio, I stopped at the pet store to get a little gift for my Dogface. As fate would have it, I found the most perfectest shock-collar for my new tranny pet. I bought a large one so that it was big enough to fit around a human neck. And the one that I found was blinged out with fake diamonds lining the collar. Obviously it was for a very feminine pit bull or doberman. It was just the thing to keep Dogface in line.

I was in the mood for a nice dinner to share with my little Dogface that night. There were a couple thick cuts of steak in my refrigerator that I had been saving for a special occasion. After seasoning the slabs of meat to perfection, I grilled them up on the stove. As a side, I chopped up some potatoes and cooked them up with some onions and herbs. Nothing better than meat and potatoes to get the murder in the blood going.

Right before the steaks were ready to eat, I went up to my bedroom and the closet where Dogface was locked inside. When I opened the door, he was laying on the cot, but he wasn't sleeping, he was just staring at the wall in silence.

"How is my cute little Dogface tonight?" I said with a smile. Dogface's eyes shifted to the side to look at me. I whistled. "Chop chop! Let's get up," I commanded. "I've got a nice dinner for us. And I got you a present."

It took a minute, but Dogface finally stirred, flopping his legs over the side of the cot and then standing up slowly. He wouldn't look me in the eyes and it seemed that any spirit left in him was all but gone. It didn't seem like he was present enough to really engage with me, but then again, he wasn't present enough to try to fight me or get away. When Dogface was standing in front of me, eyes downcast, I fastened the shock-collar around his neck. He didn't protest or resist. Fingering the remote for the collar which I had put on a string around my neck, I turned and motioned for him to follow me downstairs and into the kitchen.

Pulling out a chair at the table, Dogface sat down quietly and I kissed him on the top of the head. "You know a lot of people would *kill* for a meal like this," I said, laughing at my own joke. "How are you, cutie?"

When I asked the question, Dogface's eyes finally fluttered and looked at me. But they were so, so empty. "Fine," he replied, almost so softly that I couldn't hear it.

"Good, that's good," I responded, preparing the plates with meat and potatoes. After setting the food down in front of Dogface and myself, I poured a glass of red wine for both of us. "Do you like wine?" I asked with a lecherous grin. "Some people think that it is an aphrodisiac. Gets the juices flowing in the loins to get ready for some good fucking. Not that I need much to get in the mood."

Dogface nodded, indicating that he liked the wine. Actually, he picked up the glass and took quite a big swill of the crimson liquid. That was the most movement I'd seen him perform in a while. I had pre-cut Dogface's steak and only gave him a plastic fork to use. No sense in taking any chances that he might get the sudden impulse to stab me, even though that seemed unlikely. I watched him stab a chunk of meat with the plastic fork and put it in his mouth. He chewed slowly. "You like that fucking meat in your mouth, don't you?" I said playfully.

His eyes shifted over toward my direction and I could see just the tease of a smile pulling at the corner of his mouth. "This is pretty good," he said, looking down at his food again. I beamed. Those were the most words I'd gotten out of him since before we murdered that hooker. Dogface took another swig of wine and so did I.

"I'm sorry about terrorizing you, or scaring you," I said sincerely. "But I didn't see any other way around it. I wanted you—I wanted you to work *with* me. And I didn't know if you'd come of your own free will. Men usually are not at the sharp end of my wrath." I looked him up and down. "And you pass as a man. More or less." I shrugged, chewing another piece of rare beef.

"You don't have any family?"

I was shocked to hear Dogface actually ask me a question. Smiling, I touched his hand which was resting on the table. "No. Not anymore," I answered. "My moms died a while back now."

"Your moms?" Dogface asked, eyeballing me.

"My lesbian mothers," I continued. "They were horribly abusive to me. But," I shrugged, "at least they're dead now." A stunted laugh escaped my throat.

"No brothers and sisters?"

"Oh, no..." I shook my head. "There was this one boy that they bought when I was like eight or nine."

"They bought him?" Dogface said, raising his eyebrows.

I nodded. "My moms were really connected in the Underworld. The shady sides of Hollywood and the entertainment industry. They were rich producers of movies, but since they weren't celebrities, they could operate with a certain amount of anonymity. So they bought this boy—probably a year or two younger than I was—from the market of human trafficking. You know, child sex slave rings and humans that on paper didn't exist. So they could be your slave for as long as you wished to keep them."

Dogface swallowed hard. "So what did they do to him?"

I smirked morbidly. "It was nice to have a little brother to play with for a short while," I continued. "But," I narrowed my eyes and thought back to the horrifying events of that time, "I think that was part of their plan to traumatize me even more through having me bond with him and then ripping him away."

"Ripping him away?" Dogface asked through a mouthful of steak.

"They killed him," I said flatly.

Dogface almost choked on the chunk of meat he'd been chewing. After a bout of coughing, he finally got the food down and took a big breath of air. "They fucking... killed him?" he whispered.

I nodded. "But not right away," I explained. "They gave me at least a few weeks with him. We had fun playing together with our little toys and whatever. I think my moms were determining the most horrendous way to torture him—for their own amusement and my traumatic imprinting."

Looking over at Dogface, I could tell he was starting to feel physically sick. He had put his fork down on his plate and his face was started to get really pale. I chuckled to myself since none of this gruesome shit bothered me anymore. "I'm almost too scared to ask what happened," the tranny squeaked out. He grimaced as if he was about to vomit.

"My moms caught us fooling around one day," I explained. "We were both naked with our little boy pricks out. I had my head between his legs and I was sucking on his little cock. I remember it tasted salty and the act got me hot between my legs. While I drooled on his tiny balls and tried to get him as hard as a little boy can get, I was stroking vigorously my own pecker. You getting hard over there?"

Dogface shook his head with a disgusted look on his face. I leaned over to peer down at his lap to see if he had an erection. The tranny played prude and covered his crotch with his hands. I laughed and continued with the story. "One of my mothers— Lorena—practically dragged me off of the boy. I would say he was lucky I didn't bite his dick off, but *lucky* wouldn't be even remotely a way to describe it. You'll never believe what they did." After taking another drink of my wine, I glanced over at Dogface who now really looked like he was gonna hurl. "While Lorena dragged me out of the room by my hair, screaming in pain, my other mother—Julie—picked up the younger boy under his armpits. By this time he was screaming and crying too. They dragged us both into the living room where there was a fire burning in the fireplace—it was wintertime by the way. There was a large fire poker glowing red laying in the flames. There was a shallow dish as well as a long curved dagger laying on the coffee table. Lorena threw me down on the carpet and yelled, 'Stay there, you little faggot and watch.' My little boy self was wailing and tears were streaming down my face. Julie held the other boy down as he squirmed. Lorena grabbed the dagger from the table. I remember the orange light of the fire's flames flickering and reflecting off of the boy's pale, naked flesh. In one motion, Lorena grabbed the boy's little pecker and sliced—turning him into a eunuch. He screamed the most blood-curdling scream I'd ever heard as Lorena's hands were washed with the blood pouring from between his legs. His little penis and testicles were in her hands in a pool of blood."

"Jesus fucking Christ..." Dogface whispered. His eyes were closed and I could see some tears rolling down his cheeks.

"Oh, don't be such a baby," I taunted as I picked up the last piece of potato off my plate and popped it in my mouth. My wine was drained, I could feel a little buzz going, and I poured another glass. Looking over at Dogface, he finally opened his eyes. "You want more?" I asked, holding out the wine bottle. He nodded reluctantly and I poured him more red wine. After I filled the glass, he guzzled it.

"I don't really want to know what happens in this story," he squeaked. "But I'm afraid you're gonna tell me anyway."

I chuckled and continued with the horrific saga—not that I was relaying it with a horrific delivery. "Lorena dumped the little boys genitals into the shallow bowl and put the blood-stained dagger down on the coffee table. She pulled out the fire poker from the fireplace and pressed the orange-hot end against the gaping wound between his legs. He shrieked as the wound was cauterized. The bleeding quickly stopped as the hole where his gonads used to be was seared closed. The boy was obviously in shock by this point and almost unconscious from the pain. I was in shock too and my young brain and nervous system didn't know how to process what I was witnessing."

"Please let that be the end of the story," Dogface said under his breath. "Please, God, let that be the end..."

Snorting unattractively, I took a huge gulp of wine. I could feel myself getting drunk. "You wish," I replied. "You wish that was the end, Dogface. Anyway, I'll make a long story shorter—get it? Shorter?" Dogface looked even sicker now. "Man, you're a tough audience," I commented. "My moms took the severed dick and balls into the kitchen where they sat both us boys down at the table. The other boy was barely conscious, and when his eyes did open, he wasn't behind them at all. It was like he'd been *erased*. You know what I mean. Without going into a lot of detail, they fried the kid's dick up on the stove in a frying pan with a little olive oil and just some salt and pepper. Lorena used some smelling salts to get the kid conscious again —then they fed him his own cock and balls. And they made me watch as he did it. Thank God they didn't make *me* eat any. Like I said, his eyes, they looked like his soul had been erased. He was broken. And after he ate the entirety of his own dick and balls, he kept repeating this nonsensical phrase. What was it?" I snapped my fingers, trying to remember what it was the boy had kept repeating over and over. "Ah! Yes, that was it. He kept saying, '*linner ladner.*' Whatever that fucking means."

Shrugging my shoulders, I took a big gulp of wine and looked over at Dogface to see how he was processing the story. He stared at me with wide eyes, his face turned totally green, and he leaned his head over toward the floor on the side of the table. Then he blew chunks; puking up the steak and potatoes he'd just eaten. Pulling his head back up, he looked at me with glazed eyes, wiping the puke that was dribbling down out of the corners of his mouth.

"Ah, Dogface," I said, "look what you did to my fucking floor!" Pushing the button on the remote around my neck, a shock of electricity ran through Dogface's neck. He cried out and then clenched his eyes and teeth closed as he felt the pain of the electricity. After I let go of the button, he breathed deeply, trying to catch his breath.

"Sorry," he sputtered.

"Sorry—*what*?" I said.

"Sorry, *Master*?"

"That's better," I said with a smile. Looking at him intensely, I wanted him to know I expected a question.

"So," Dogface continued after swallowing hard. "What happened to the boy?"

"They killed him," I said matter-of-factly. "I don't need to describe any of their weird-ass human sacrifice rituals. But that's what they did. And they made me watch that as well; as they tortured him and ultimately mutilated him to death."

IV

"You have the sweetest ass," I said to Dogface as he laid face-down on my bed with his legs hanging over the side. Stroking his perky ass cheeks, I pulled his pants down and off of his legs, tossing them aside on the floor. After watching him on all fours cleaning the puke he had spewed, I was thoroughly horny. Spreading his cheeks, I brought my face down and licked as I felt his tight asshole pucker against my tongue. Dogface moaned with pleasure as I licked around the edge of his anus and flicked the tip of my tongue a little in and out of his hole.

"Oh, yeah..." he groaned. "Yes, Master, give it to me."

I was already naked and hard, stroking myself between my legs. The small wetness of pre-cum dribbled out the tip of my dick in anticipation of penetrating deep into his asshole. Before I knew it, I was inside. Thrusting balls-deep as my cock throbbed inside him. Dogface groaned and began to pant faster. I could see his right hand clenching the bedspread in his fist. My hands were firmly around his thin, girlish waist as I fucked him viciously. It was exquisite. Dogface cried out as I pulled out without warning, spat on my hand and rubbed it up and down my shaft, then forcefully put it back into him. "Oh my God, Dogface!" I cried out with orgasmic ecstasy. "Take that fucking dick like the faggot slut you are! Tell me you like that dick!"

"I like that dick," he said between moans.

"Say you love that dick," I commanded.

"I fucking love that dick!" he yelled and then smashed his face into the blanket as I kept enjoying his tight little hole.

"I'm gonna fucking cum inside you!" I screamed, feeling as if I was in a psycho-sexual trance. My eyes shot open but I wasn't quite sure the room was solid in my vision. Maybe it was due to all the wine I had drunk. "Beg for it!" The command was explicit.

"Oh, uhh, uhh, yeah... Please, Master," Dogface continued to moan. "I want to feel your warm cum inside me. Fucking give it to me, Master! Squirt deep into my asshole!"

As I felt the orgasm building in the most delicious and unbearable euphoria, I swear I saw the shadow of a figure flicker to my right in my peripheral vision. Before I could give this apparition a second thought, as I was on the verge of exploding, my eyes rolled up into my head and a strange voice took possession of my vocal cords. "Through the energy built up through this rough and intense sexual act," the voice spoke through me in a demonic octave, "I conjure the demon! From the shadows of this ecstatic and wrathful rapture, I call the rape of rage! I invoke the rampaging roar of revealing! Through this ejaculation you are birthed!" Screaming out as I couldn't hold the ejaculate any longer, I felt the semen tear through my cock and explode out into Dogface's rectum with the most intense pleasure and agony I had ever felt. Whimpering with the unbearable ecstasy, an indescribable amount of semen kept gushing from my urethra as I noticed the shadowy figure again in my periphery. This time it flickered several times and then solidified.

Jerking back in fright, my cock pulled out hastily from inside of Dogface. He gave a little cry of pleasure or pain, I couldn't tell which. First my face jerked down and I saw his asshole gaping before it shrank back to normal; a huge gush of semen poured out, soaking the bed below. This sight would have normally aroused me, yet I was gripped with so much fear, I instantly felt my erection turn to putty between my legs. A long stream of gooey jiz dripped from the tip. Then I jerked my head over to the right as my foot slipped on the floor, my lack of balance making me fall onto my ass as I cried out at seeing the countenance of this demonic creature that had just appeared in my bedroom. The tall creature grinned maliciously down at me as it took a step closer to where I had fallen. It was tall and thin, with long skinny arms and legs; its skin looked greasy, semi-translucent, and pale-gray, the color of the sky on an overcast day. And its face... it was so horrid I couldn't even describe it. The demon's face had the sort of hypnotic illusion that it was fluctuating and changing into different configurations that mimicked my terror.

"Don't come any closer!" I tried to yell, but my voice cracked and wobbled. "What the fuck are you?" I asked, holding my hands up in front of my body in case I needed to shield any attacks.

The demon opened its mouth impossibly wide as it spoke. "I am the embodiment of your murderous lust and your hate. You conjured me from the black ooze of your soul," it continued in a voice that bordered on scary and soothing. "I am— the Great Demon Bafflement! You evoked me and yet now I am sentient. Don't you want to know what fun we can have together?"

My mouth hung open in disbelief. The words, if there were any appropriate to be spoken, were not coming to me. Was this real? Or was this a hallucination brought on by wine and rough sex? I looked over at Dogface who seemed to be utterly out of it. His eyes were closed and he was breathing heavily onto the bed. Drool was dripping out of the corner of his mouth and semen was still slowly oozing out from where I came inside of him.

Looking back over at the Great Demon Bafflement, his body seemed to flicker again—disappearing for a second and then coming back into focus. I stood up slowly. "Are you real, or just a dream?" I asked, tentatively walking closer to his slimy form.

"I am still somewhat ethereal—non-corporeal," Bafflement replied, extending his arm out toward me. I reached out and tried to touch the tips of the demon's fingers with my own. My hand went right through his like he was just a holographic image. "That's why if we were to play and find women to shred and dissect, I would need a body to possess." He looked over at Dogface's body as he breathed softly in his sleep. "At least just until I fed on enough psychic energy to fully manifest as a physical form on this plane."

"You could do that?" I asked.

Bafflement looked at me and shrugged. "You want to see me possess this slut?" The demon grinned devilishly. Before I could even answer the question, the Great Demon jumped up into the air and configured his body horizontally as he came down over Dogface's back. Just like a spirit, Bafflement's form slipped into Dogface's body, momentarily superimposing his gray form over Dogface's body as if he was a demonic suit. Bafflement's form flickered once and then disappeared into my slave's unconscious body.

I jumped back in shock as Dogface's eyes shot open and he gasped a breath as if coming up to the surface after a long swim under the water. "I feel the blood pumping through these veins," the demon spoke through Dogface's mouth. It was Dogface's lips, but Bafflement's voice. "And I feel your cum deep inside me." He smiled and licked his lips as he flipped over and sat on the edge of the bed. I just stared in disbelief. "I feed on the power of your killing," he continued. "The delicious viciousness of your monstrosity. It's beautiful grotesquery leaves me tingling, energized, and aching for the life of death. Do we wish to play?" Bafflement in Dogface's body stood up and looked at me with shimmering eyes and a wry smile.

"Yeah, sure," I managed to say. My voice was too high and cracked as I spoke. "Actually," I began to sputter manically, "I'm not sure if this is even real. The psychosis must be kicking in. I guess you can't be a murdering maniac for long without going a little loopy." As I looked around the room, it began to spin in my vision and my stomach lurched up into my throat. I must have drank more than I thought. Trying to regain some semblance of stability, I swallowed back down the vomit that was threatening to spew from my gullet. The demon laughed at me, as if taunting my inebriated condition. "What the fuck are you laughing at, you hallucination? You're going back where you belong."

The demon just continued to cackle as I pushed Dogface's body back toward the padded closet. With its laughter still echoing in my bedroom, I gave him one final shove into the closet and slammed the door. I locked it with fervor as I struggled to keep my balance and my dinner down. All I could hear was Bafflement's laughter from the other side of the door. "Shut up!" I screamed, putting my hands over my ears. As I took a couple steps backwards, I could swear I saw the tinge of a white aura appear around the locked door of the closet.

It goes without saying that I couldn't believe my eyes when Bafflement, in Dogface's body, came strolling through the locked door as if it were no more that a hologram. "You think something like a puny door can keep me contained?" the demon sneered.

"What the *fuck* are you?" I screamed, almost falling over backwards.

Bafflement frowned. "I thought we went over that already," he said, and in a flash his face was an inch away from mine. He then touched my forehead with a chilly finger and said, "Sleep!"

When I woke up, I found myself alone on the cot and locked in the padded closet. "No! No! NO!" I screamed as I jumped up and rushed at the locked door. Pounding on the door, my fists were useless and made barely any noise against the pads covering the walls. "Let me out! Let me the fuck out of here!" I yelled again, my throat raw and tasting of blood.

Suddenly I thought I heard the sound of a dying gasp, and I swiveled around to face the other three walls of the room. I must still be drunk, I thought. Blinking my eyes, I thought I saw the padding on the walls to my left and right begin to ripple and bulge. A little tear began to appear in the wall to my left. As it ripped open, my eyes bugged out and I flattened myself against the back of the door. I almost jumped right out of my skin when I saw a rotting arm reach out from the tear in the padding. Screaming a blood-curdling scream, my throat burned with hellfire and I began to piss warm urine down the inside of my leg. My mouth suddenly felt impossibly dry like a desert on Mars as another rotting arm burst out of the wall opposite. There was what smelled like a rotting corpse inside each wall and trying to get out.

The heads and upper bodies of the ghastly figures began to emerge from the ripped padding on the walls. When I saw who they were, I tried to scream again, but my throat was so dry that it ruptured and no sound escaped. Lorena was coming for me from the left and Julie was coming for me from the right—my long-dead lesbian mothers had come back to haunt me, and most likely murder me. Soon they were free from the walls. They were naked, rotting corpses, with chunks of flesh crawling with maggots and sometimes dropping off in oozing pieces like cottage cheese. There was no way for me to escape as they descended on me with their arms outstretched like zombies. Their eyes were gushing and being eaten by worms that wriggled and writhed inside the decomposing sockets. As they moaned, they tore at my clothes, ripping them off until I was naked as the day I was born—or hatched—or grown in a lab. I tried to fight back, my fingernails ripping into their soggy flesh, tearing off chunks from their old bones.

But they were too much for me. I fell onto my back onto the floor, with them on top of me, ripping at my skin. They were skinning me alive. The pain was indescribable as they peeled my epidermis like the rind of an orange. I tried to beg, *No, please*, but I couldn't speak. Lorena had ripped my tongue out with her rotted teeth as if to french kiss me with the stench and putrescence of the grave. They had also peeled the skin right off my penis and were now attempting to have sex with what remained. As Lorena continued to eat my face like a Greek would eat a goat head, Julie was attempting to insert my skinned cock into her maggot-filled cunt. She rode me violently as my one eye that was left witnessed her jaw rotting to the point it hung loosely from her skull, her tongue lolling like some perverted sea cucumber. Momentarily, her whole jaw fell off and splatted against the exposed muscle of my abdomen. My mom moaned with a sound somewhere between orgasm and death-wheeze. I could feel the blood as lubricant around my mutilated cock as she continued to ride me. Lorena had chewed through my skull and was now munching on my brain. I could feel the maggots that were wriggling and having an orgy inside Julie's rancid cunt. They crawled around her uterus and cervix and then found their way down to where our genitals joined.

Like a single-file line of tiny worms, those maggots began to crawl up my urethra. It was the strangest sensation I had ever felt. And as they began to make a feast of the inside of my cock, it suddenly felt orgasmic, euphoric—the Little Death. As if I was finally melting into the cosmos and the pressure was being lifted from the flesh. Just as I was about to cum inside my mother—

I gasped and woke up in my own bed. The moment I emerged from the nightmare, I ejaculated out of my erect dick, making it a wet nightmare. Struggling to catch my breath, I noticed a pressure on my chest, making it difficult to breath. Opening my eyes, I realized I was sleeping on my back and Bafflement, back in his demonic form, was sitting cross-legged on top of my ribcage. "What the fuck?" I wheezed. Putting his hands on his knees, Bafflement craned his head down and stared into my face, smiling. "Pfff!" I blew air and spittle into his hideous face to try to get him off of me. Scowling, he jumped off of me and sat on the end of the bed glaring at me.

"I just wanted to feast on your nightmares," the demon replied, pouting with his arms crossed.

"Hope you got a fucking tasty treat, you creep," I mumbled. Looking over, I noticed that Dogface was sleeping soundly in my bed beside me, his back toward me.

"Creep?" Bafflement laughed. "That's the pot calling the cauldron black."

"Fuck you," I shot back, rolling over onto my side and cuddling up against Dogface. "I just want to get some sleep. Maybe I can sleep you off and you'll be gone in the morning."

Bafflement laughed again. "No such luck, killer," he said as he hovered himself up off the bed and over Dogface's body. His form flickered slightly and he brought his demonic spirit back down to possess the whore's body. Speaking out through Dogface's mouth, Bafflement concluded the night by saying, "Yes, definitely get your rest. We have a lot of important work to do tomorrow."

V

"So where the fuck are we going?" I asked, looking over at Dogface in the passenger's seat of my car. He was no longer himself, but the demon Bafflement. It was the next evening after I had summoned him by accident. The demon had been very vague about what we were going to be doing and where we were going. However, I had brought my weapon of choice in case we were going to hack some sluts to pieces—a military-style machete with a serrated section along the back edge. And I had a feeling that we were going to massacre some cunts.

"There is a circle of New Age women," Bafflement began to explain, "who are doing what they call a 'goddess activation' tonight through meditation and ecstatic dance."

I smiled viciously as I drove on and the darkness of night fell on the city of New York. "And we're going to murder them," I said in a low, almost hypnotic, voice. "My blade will be bathed in the blood of these hippie sluts!" There was no more delicious rush of adrenaline to my balls as what I felt bringing death to bitches who thought their stanking pussies were some sort of exalted divinity.

"Keep going down this way and take a right at the next light," Bafflement instructed with a flick of Dogface's finger.

We were coming up into a more yuppie part of the city where all the fake-ass hipsters liked to hang out.

"How the fuck do you know about this bitch-goddess thing that's happening tonight?" I asked, glancing over at the demon inhabiting Dogface's body. There was a visible shimmer of energy rippling off of his human skin.

The demon shot me a look that could have made Lucifer shit in his panties. "You dare question the Great Demon Power?" he bellowed.

"Sorry," I squeaked, trying to make myself smaller behind the wheel of the car.

"Turn here—left," Bafflement said, pointing. I knew this area of town—it was where a lot of yoga studios and bourgeois yogurt shops were. Come to think of it, a lot of my more stuck-up clients for my photography lived and worked around here. "It's right here," he said as I parked on the curb.

Looking up, I saw the sign for the place over the entrance to the storefront business—*Hot Yoni Yoga*. "Pffff," I snorted and proceeded to laugh my balls off. "Hot Yoni Yoga?" I said mockingly. "What pretentious feminist horseshit. They all deserve to get their ovaries cut out." Reaching onto the back seat of my car, I grabbed my machete which I could feel physically vibrating and lusting for blood—almost like the pulsing of a throbbing cock ready to burst with cum.

"I couldn't agree more," Bafflement said, smiling maliciously. "Time for a massacre energy harvest. These deaths will feed me the power I crave." Without another word, the demon exited my car and began to approach the entrance of the yoga studio. He hesitated for a moment, waiting for me. Quickly I got out of the car and joined my demon companion at the entrance. Curtains were drawn across all of the large windows on the front of the studio, but I could hear the electronic dance music coming from inside. Suddenly, our heads turned toward each other, we gave each other a knowing nod and look of mutual bloodlust. Then we party-crashed.

My demon and I flew in through the front door like we were about to rob a bank. I had my machete out and brandished it like a drooling psychopath. Once we were inside, blocking the door, all the New Age hippie sluts stopped dancing and stared at us. They all looked like they were dressed to open their legs and slide down a pole. The DJ stopped the music and all of their faces registered disgust—like we were man-scum who had just interrupted their lezbionic orgy. The Grand Slut—the one that looked like she was running this circus that they called a 'goddess activation'—stared right at me with fire blazing in her eyes. She was wearing a tight two-piece black outfit which was basically a bikini, with a red cape draped over her shoulders. She pointed at us admonishingly. "No men!" she shrieked.

Bafflement, possessing Dogface's physical faculties, threw up his arms and yelled, "The exits are sealed! There is no escape!" Suddenly blue shields of plasma-like energy appeared like barriers over all doors and windows that led out of the yoga studio. All the women except for the Grand Slut began to shriek in terror as Bafflement began to morph Dogface's body into a more hideous likeness that better resembled the demon within, even stretching the height of his spine by several mutated inches.

Swinging my machete out in front of me, I slashed the smooth skin of the calf of the nearest whore trying to run away. She screamed in pain and fell to the floor, blood squirting from her leg as she sobbed and tried to crawl away. I was utterly possessed by my blood-lust and felt a tightness in my pants. Descending on the fallen bitch, I hacked her in the back and the back of her head until she was quiet and still, just a bloody mutilated mess.

As I was preoccupied with my kill, Bafflement was cackling with laughter as he threw balls of blue ectoplasmic energy at the women trying to run for cover. The room was a cacophony of screams and sobbing voices begging for their lives. A blue ball of energy hit one woman, ripping off her arm in a shower of blood, dousing a woman next to her in a gush of gore. Another ball of blue energy collided with a hippie slut directly in her head, causing it to explode in carnage of red goo and brain sludge. I was awed by the gorgeous display of mutilation.

"Goddess, we beg you," several women prayed, pleading with their imaginary deity, "please save us!"

"Your impotent Goddess won't save your useless lives," Bafflement bellowed, laughing maniacally as he continued to dismember women with energy cast from his hands. I was also consumed with chopping up the face of a women with my machete like it was a head of lettuce that had offended me. She was already dead, but I was enjoying hacking the face and skull into a bloody pulp as I bathed in her bodily fluids. The floor was a flood of blood and organs, making it difficult for the women to try to run for any kind of safety. They slipped and slid and crawled for whatever protection they could find— even trying to use each other as human shields.

"Cease your mindless killing!" The Grand Slut yelled out with the unmistakable resonance of authority in her voice. This shook Bafflement and me from our blood-trance and we looked over to where she stood in the middle of the room. We were both shocked she was still alive. Gesturing her hands around herself as if casting a protection spell, we could see a violet semi-translucent energy sphere appear around her body. "I am protected," she continued, "and you cannot threaten my sovereignty."

Bafflement growled and hurled a ball of blue magick at the Grand Slut. The blue ball of energy was instantly absorbed into her violet sphere of light without causing any damage. She smiled. "Arrrgh, you bitch!" he growled, his rage peaking.

"The violet light is the highest light in the universe," she said calmly, "and nothing can harm it."

Bafflement shrieked in anger and began to assault her protective sphere with ball after ball of blue magick, uselessly. "Die, bitch! Die!" he screamed. I just continued to watch, dumbfounded.

"I told you that won't work," she said softly. Then, cooly and calmly, she put her arms out in front of her, hands together with her palms facing forward as if gearing up to cast a spell at us. "I don't beg the Goddess," she continued. "I don't call on the Goddess... because I *am* the Goddess!" Suddenly a cry like a war-cry escaped her throat and she seemed to at once look like a warrior from days of ancient magick long past. A sphere of violet light grew rapidly in her palms and then it was loosed before Bafflement had a chance to react.

The violet ball of magick hit Dogface's body with the velocity of a speeding train. The impact of the violet energy tore through Dogface, violently ripping the Great Demon Bafflement out of him. Once the demon was out of Dog-face, his human eyes glazed over and he crumpled to the floor unconscious. Bafflement was cowering, seeming to be significantly wounded energetically. His form was semi-transparent and he seemed to be flickering in and out like the image on a bad TV. I got the impression that if he didn't get more energy soon, that there was a possibility he could just blip back out of this level of existence.

"Stupid cunt," Bafflement wheezed as he spun around and released the energy seals on the doors and windows. Retreating quickly, the demon ran through the exit without even opening the door, like he was a non-corporeal hologram. I didn't want to give the Grand Slut enough time to reload her hands and hit me with some type of sorceress magick, so I quickly grabbed Dogface's body, slinging him over my shoulders, and ran out of Hot Yoni Yoga after Bafflement.

Trailing blood and organ mush, I made it back to my car where Bafflement was already laying in the back seat, trying to recover his strength. I put Dogface's unconscious body on the passenger's seat and took my spot driving. As fast as I could, I put the car in gear and sped off into the night, panting heavily and adrenaline boiling like battery acid in my veins.

"Goddamn, that bitch was powerful," Bafflement groaned. I snuck a glance over my shoulder and could see his form fading in and out as he laid in a fetal position across the back seat. Should I just let him disappear and be done with him? I could feel his stare of death without even having to look. "Don't even think about it, you coward!" he warned.

"What?" I sputtered. "I wasn't thinking anything."

"Don't you try to lie to me," he sputtered and coughed. "I am the Great Demon Bafflement, the Destroyer of Worlds...

Drive toward the abandoned warehouse where you do your rituals."

I swallowed hard, but didn't have the guts to question it or to let the demon slip out of my reality. As we got closer to the district where the warehouse was, the areas got more and more deserted. Suddenly I saw a figure of a woman walking across the street about a hundred feet in front of us. "Holy shit, there's a woman walking in the street!" I said.

"Hit her," Bafflement hissed.

"What?" I shot back as a reflex.

"I said *hit her*!" The demon was adamant this time.

So I hit the gas pedal hard and the car revved as it sped up. In a flash I heard the woman cry out as I hit her body with the front bumper of the car. She flew onto the hood and then smacked into the windshield, cracking it like a spider web. As I slammed on the brakes, the woman's limp body rolled down the hood of the car and smacked onto the street below like a slab of raw meat. "What now?" I asked.

"Are you a complete idiot?" Bafflement wheezed at me in a strained voice. "Grab her body, dump her back here with me, and get to the warehouse!"

When I went to check the body, the woman was barely conscious, moaning in pain. Grabbing her by the wrists, I dragged her body around to the side of the car, leaving a small trail of blood like ooze left from a snail's walk in the park. With some effort, I managed to dump the body in the back seat, on top of Bafflement. He wasn't able to possess her body—if that was even what he wanted to do—but I could see parts of his body around her as if they were taking up the same space. It looked like a total optical illusion and I had to consciously tell myself that I wasn't just seeing a chimera.

For the rest of the drive to the warehouse, my mind sort of blanked-out. It felt like my consciousness was trying to separate from my body, maybe to put me into a semi-catatonic state. With all the violence I had enacted, and interacting with a demon from another plane of reality, it was a wonder I hadn't done more trauma to myself than I had. Or maybe it was even worse than I thought. Maybe there wasn't even a real Bafflement. Maybe it was all me.

However, I didn't have the luxury to go down that rabbit hole and I snapped out of my trance as I slowed the car down and parked next to the abandoned warehouse. The night was dark but it was lit with the silver glow of an almost full moon. I turned around to look at the demon in my back seat. He didn't look so great and I could feel that he was attempting to syphon some of the unconscious woman's energy but failing miserably. Bafflement gave me the evil eye. "Don't just sit there gawking," he hissed. "Start moving these bodies."

I obeyed like a good little slave. First I brought Dogface's unconscious body into the warehouse and sat him down against the wall. Then I dragged the woman inside, Bafflement limping and flickering after me. After unlocking one of the drawers on the bottom of my kill table, I pulled out one of the longest and sharpest knives; I had a feeling I was going to need it.

"What now?" I asked.

"You'll need to draw a pentagram on the floor with her blood," Bafflement said, wiping drool from his mouth. The demon looked as if he was about to blip out of existence at any moment; not to mention, his legs were shaking and he looked like he was about to collapse onto the concrete floor. I went and crouched down next to the woman who was still bleeding and moaning in semi-consciousness. In one fluid movement, I stabbed her in the side. She cried out and a stream of blood gushed onto my hands. After putting the knife down, far enough away from the dying woman in case she came to enough to try to make a lunge for it, I cupped my hands and filled them with her blood. I carefully carried the warm red liquid to a spot where there was a lot of open floor space. As if I was doing finger-painting, I drew a large pentagram and encased it in a circle. The shape was large enough to lay a body down inside it.

It seemed as if Bafflement was psychically directing me in the steps of this blood ritual. I instinctually went and grabbed the woman by her wrists and dragged her inside the circle and on top of the pentagram. Bafflement approached the circle as I went and retrieved the knife. He stood just outside of the circle of blood as I first slashed the woman's throat. She began to choke and gurgle, her body spasming as she bled to death. Her hands went up to her throat uselessly as her blood pumped and continued to squirt like a fountain of Hawaiian Punch. Bafflement closed his eyes and I could see him feeding on her energy as it left her body. I could see this energy like black plasma, outlined with blue-white light that resembled the electricity of lightning. The Great Demon opened his mouth and inhaled this energy, eating it like sustenance from the universe. As he did, his body began to look more solid and strengthened.

Right in the moment when the woman was barely holding onto her life, I swung the knife down and penetrated her right through the heart. She gasped, inhaling a mouthful of blood, then her body was still. The flash of a second when she died, the biggest burst of the black plasma was released from her body and Bafflement absorbed it directly into his form, leaving him shimmering as if he had a liquid-aura shining around his body. He smiled his fanged teeth. Then, as I watched him, he closed his eyes and held his arms out, palms up toward the ceiling as if he was a priest about to pray. As he let out a hiss that almost sounded electronic, the woman's dead body and blood began to glow in the same blue-white color that had outlined the black plasma. As he did this, I knew that he was converting the woman's body and blood-matter into a pure form of energy which he could eat—or absorb directly into his form to bring him back to full power. In several seconds, the woman's entire body and blood had completely disappeared, leaving only my knife in the center of where the pentagram of blood used to be. Suddenly I felt utterly exhausted. I guess the shenanigans of the day had caught up with me.

Bafflement winked at me and then floated over to where Dogface's unconscious form slumped up against the wall. He inserted his form into Dogface's body once again, possessing him. As his eyes shot open, he gasped, taking in deep breaths of oxygen. "I'm back," Bafflement said through Dogface's vocal cords as he flexed his hand of flesh. "You look spent," he said, studying me.

"I am exhausted," I admitted.

Bafflement smiled and laughed. "And I am at the peak of my strength again. I could give you some energy, but I'm not going to," he teased as he stood up and motioned for me to come. "Let's go home."

I stood up and absentmindedly slipped the knife I had used

to kill the woman through one of my belt-loops. Bafflement was already out the door and heading back to the car. I followed quickly; ready to be home and resting in my bed. Just as I exited the warehouse, Bafflement was getting into the passenger's seat so I took my normal spot as driver. I began to question myself as to why I had helped the demon regain his strength instead of letting him die or go back to wherever he came from. Was I the one really being possessed? Or was I doing all of this of my own free will? Possibly Dogface and Bafflement were just figments of my twisted imagination and it was really just me carrying out all these horrific deeds solely alone. I couldn't even begin to wrap my head around the predicament that I perceived myself in. So I dissociated mildly, zoning out and dimming all of the useless thoughts down to a dull roar as I drove away from my temple of blood rituals back toward my apartment.

"You know, you're really doing the world a favor by killing the women," Bafflement said after a while.

"Hmm," I responded, only half listening.

"Yes," he continued, glancing over at me. "Women are parasitic entities—succubi. They completely drain the life out of men and then leave them to rot or to a lonely world of psychosis that forever torments them at the claws of the evil women." I nodded but didn't say anything. "They're like Sirens," he continued his rant. "They have their song that hypnotizes you; hooked you through the side of the mouth like you're a sucker fish coming back for more to suck at the tits of the ones that continue to abuse you."

"Yes," I said flatly. "They're evil. I have to kill them."

"Well," the demon said with a chuckle, "you don't *have* to do *anything*. But you like it. Something *compels* you to kill.

Maybe that something is me." He smiled. "But maybe that's just an excuse—trying to put the blame on someone else when that other entity is just part of yourself. It's like so many people who blame the Devil for their problems—*the Devil made me do it*, they say. Or they blame God for their misfortune. They'll be in for a rude awakening when they realize they *are* God." He shrugged. "Or they may never get to that level of Self-Realization." Bafflement looked over at me and shrugged. "You probably don't even understand what I'm saying to you, do you?" I glanced over at him briefly, but he continued his monologue unabated. "Aren't we the merry pair of Satanists? *The Bloodlust Bandits. The Pariah and his Dark Passenger.* Forever united in the ecstasy of carnage." The Great Demon chuckled and put his feet up on the dashboard as we turned the corner onto the street my apartment was on.

I swallowed hard and felt a sensation of dread deep in the pit of my stomach. "Yeah, we do make quite a team, don't we?" I squeaked out.

Bafflement shrugged and wiggled one of his feet up near the windshield. "None of it really matters anyway," he said with a sigh. "Men are parasites too. We're *all* parasites. I'm feeding off of you; you're feeding off of me. We all take take take what we can from each other and just leave a hollow husk behind, not caring that they don't even have enough left to sustain themselves. It's all about what *we* need; what *we* want." He looked over at me. "And when I say *we*, I mean me and you—the man and his demon. The demon and his pet human." The demon paused for a second as if deep in thought. "But you're a queer faggot," he said finally. "So are you closer to the nature of a parasitic woman, or a parasitic man? No matter," he continued, waving his hand as if dismissing the thought, "it's all the same shit anyway. Shit in and shit out, as I like to say." Without commenting on his diatribe, I silently parked in my normal spot in the parking garage. I used my keycard to get into the building and we took the elevator back up to my apartment.

"You're a philosopher tonight, huh?" I commented offhand.

Bafflement laughed. "A philosopher. I guess you could say that. I am all and I am nothing. I am the whole universe unhinged, and I am the excrement on a banker's shoe. It's all bullshit. But I don't have to tell *you* that—you know this very well. That's how you've always lived, is it not? And if you live like that, then you die like that."

In spite of myself, a laugh erupted from my throat sort of like a hiccup. It was involuntary, but something about his nonsensical soliloquy struck my as absurd—a bitter joke which is so morbid that you have to just laugh at it.

As I let us into my apartment, Bafflement leaned in and whispered in my ear, "I want to feel you inside me," he said. "I want to feel your semen deep inside me so that I can drink in your sexual energy."

I gave him a weird look as I closed and locked the door. Was he serious? Or was he being the Trickster, playing some game with me? "You want to fuck?" I said.

The demon smiled wickedly, leaned toward me, and grabbed my crotch, squeezing it in a provocative way. "That's exactly what I want," he answered. "I want to feel your cock pulsing up inside this body that I'm possessing."

"Then let's get to it," I said as I leaned forward and kissed him, sliding my tongue almost all the way down his throat. Bafflement gave in to it, lapping his wet tongue up against mine.

"Okay, you sexy demon," I said, "let's get to the bedroom so I can stuff you with this rock-hard cock."

The next thing I knew, we were in my bedroom and Bafflement—in Dogface's sexy body—was naked and laying face-down on the bed with his legs hanging over the side so I had easy access to his tight asshole. As I started to unbutton my pants, I slapped his ass hard, leaving a red handprint across his right cheek. Bafflement moaned and I could see his cock getting hard between his legs. As I took my pants off, I fingered the knife that was still hooked through my belt-loop. I covered the blade with my pants as I piled them on the floor, then threw the rest of my clothes on top of it. My cock was already hard as a rock and I was horny as fuck. The sight of Dogface's cute tight ass really turned me on. What did it matter if his body was being possessed by a demon? I could still get my rocks off.

Bafflement reached his hands back and spread his ass cheeks. I could see his cute little asshole puckering and begging to be filled. "Go ahead and shove it in me, you gay slut," the demon commanded. I was so horny that I didn't even mind the insult. *His* asshole was the one that was going to get pounded by my dick anyway. I would make him love it; I would make him beg for more; I would make it the most exquisite pain he'd ever experienced. Then I would make him beg for my cum.

I spit on my hand and rubbed it all up and down my shaft. "Here it comes," I said. And without giving him any time to get ready, I thrusted my thick cock into his tight hole all the way down to the base. He groaned loudly and gripped the bed-spread in his fists as I began to thrust in and out of him. "You like that cock, don't ya, bitch?" I said like a dominatrix with a strap-on. "Even demons love a big dick in their ass!"

"Oh, God, yes!" the demon yelled out, moaning with pleasure. "Just like that. Keep going!" he said breathily. "Don't stop! You're really hitting my p-spot. Uh, God, yeeeeeesss!" He moaned so loud I thought he was going to cum. However, I felt the orgasm building up in my balls already. If I wasn't careful, I would bust my nut too quickly.

"You know you love it," I hissed, pounding my dick into his ass until I could see some blood on my shaft—then I fucked him even harder. "You demon slut!" I continued talking dirty. "You're gonna love it when I fill you with my juices!"

"Yes! Yes, Josephus!" Bafflement moaned, close to orgasm. "Give me all your cum right now! Give me that sexual energy! Let me feel your life-force pulsing through this body!"

As stealthily as I could, without slowing my thrust, I reached down into my pile of clothes and retrieved the long knife that I had used to kill the woman that night. "Ready to feel my load deep in your ass?" I said, breathing heavily as I continued to fuck his tight hole. Raising the knife above his back, I got ready.

"Uh, uh, uh, yes," Bafflement moaned. "Squirt deep inside me!"

I could feel the orgasm threatening to explode. When I couldn't hold it any longer, in the same moment I blew my load into his rectum, I brought the knife down, stabbing him right between the shoulder blades. I cried out from the orgasm. Bafflement cried out from cumming and being stabbed simultaneously. And in that exact moment, I felt the sphincter muscles of Dogface's body clench around my dick like a vice grip. I screamed from the pain, letting go of the hilt of the knife, and I fell backwards. I could see blood seeping from

Dogface's asshole and from the knife wound in his back. I realized in horror that the blood leaking from his ass was from me. Looking down, shock setting in, I saw only my balls covered in blood. The rest of my penis had been severed and was now inside the dead body of Dogface.

Sitting on the floor in the spot I had fallen, I grasped between my legs where my cock used to be, trying to stop the geyser of blood. Looking up, I watched as Dogface's body died, Bafflement's form pulled out of him and became his separate demonic self again. He walked over to me and looked down, shaking his head. "You stupid human," he said, chuckling to himself. "What were you thinking you were going to accomplish there? Now you're going to die, and I will live on because I now have all of your life-force." Bafflement looked at his nails which were gnarly like claws, he blew on them, and wiped them on his chest distractedly. "But I'll watch you as you die," he continued, crouching down to be level with my face. "I find that is the most delicious part. But I can't say we didn't have some fun together. You were one of the more interesting ones I've been with."

As I stared into his face, almost hyperventilating, I was so much in shock that I couldn't form any coherent thoughts. This was it; this was the end of it all. And it didn't mean shit. I died the way I had lived—and wouldn't you say that's the most fitting way to go? And as I bled out to my death, I found myself repeating two words over and over like a broken record: *linner ladner.*

Fluxing Uranus

"Fornicatus benedictus! Almighty Ashmodeus, existent of Chaos, ominous by thy name, thy kingdom come through me on earth. Lead me into all temptations of my flesh so I may trespass greatly into thy ways by my desires: for thou art all sex-seeking unity, thou mighty genitalia of creation that knoweth no satiation—grant thou my wish, for thou art all power, ecstasy, and actuality. Amen!"

- Austin Osman Spare

DON'T PANIC

Mars Memories

Space is not a wasteland. The Spiralverse is inhabited by a cornucopia of species and civilizations. To continue to harbor the notion that we are alone within all of the billions of galaxies is to maintain the status quo of an ever persistence and pervasive illusion. The godspell religions perpetuate this illusion and an idea that humans are some kind of 'special' creation of an omniscient deity whom somehow exists outside of the universe. Humans are evolving and slowly becoming ready for admittance into stellar society.

Some humans were already in the midst of their new adventures among the stars. One such human, evolving into a space being, was Caspian. S/he called hir spaceship the *Quantum Shortbus*. This interstellar vessel started out as an ordinary conversion van, but underwent a transformation to become a vehicle which could blast past the Moon. The outside of the *Quantum Shortbus* still looked like a regular red Dodge RAM conversion van flying through space with thrusters attached to the back end. However, the interior of the van-turned-spaceship had been converted into a sub-dimension—meaning that the inside of the ship seemed to contain a vastly larger area than the outside would appear to accommodate.

Caspian was currently standing on the command deck, gazing up and out of the viewport. The sight was spectacular. The *Quantum Shortbus* was cruising at a comfortable speed toward the planet Mars. The great red mass of the planet was clearly visible now to Caspian, whom continued to gaze in wonder. Stars also twinkled like diamonds off in the black void. There was a massive, curved command console underneath the viewport. The whole room was stark white, and Caspian could summon chairs that would ascend up from the floor if s/he wished to sit while playing captain of the vessel. Most of the time s/he preferred to stand and walk the command deck while operating the ship.

"EFFI," Caspian spoke, addressing the consciousness of the *Quantum Shortbus's* computer.

Suddenly several transparent crystals, each the size of a hand, appeared floating in the air around the command deck. "Yes, Caspian?" It was a female voice that answered as the ship's consciousness.

"Tell me about the planet Mars," Caspian said as s/he strolled toward the command console. S/he was very androgynous, and the flowing robes that s/he wore swayed loosely around hir feet. This long tunic was blue in color and had puffy strips that laid vertically over the entire height of the garment like stripes. The piece of material that stretched over the chest and shoulders was neon green and shoulder pads jutted out into spikes. Caspian's golden blonde hair was so long and straight it came down to hir knees. Hir smooth face was thin, with high cheekbones, and no facial hair. It was difficult to tell what gender this human space being was—or if they had a gender at all.

There was a black screen in the middle of the command console that immediately flashed on; the image of a Kathara Grid rotated on the screen like a screensaver. "The planet Mars," EFFI began in her feminine, yet somewhat electronic, sounding voice. As the ship consciousness spoke, text scrolled across the screen and the control crystals suspended in the air flashed pink and green. "Mars is the fourth planet from the sun of its solar system. A rich and cultured society evolved early on Mars. However, it became warlike after the Anunnaki known as Enlil, or Yahweh, landed there and subjugated a large portion of their population. During the Mahabharata war, interplanetary species were fighting back and forth between Earth and Mars, during which the atmosphere of Mars got destroyed, partly through the assistance of the planet Nibiru passing through the solar system and close to Earth and Mars."

"And that's all?" Caspian chuckled. "Mars is a ghost town?"

"I'm just giving you the spiel in a nutshell, Captain," EFFI explained.

"I know," Caspian responded, now looking back out of the viewport toward the red planet.

"Mars is currently re-colonized by several different alien species. They repaired the environment by installing an artificial atmosphere that could accommodate the new inhabitants. It started out primarily being a military checkpoint used by mostly the Drakonians and the Zetas. Then some more settlers from other planets came looking for work and built new cities from the ruins of the Old Mars. And there is no government. Every alien species represents themselves. Any altercations get dealt with solely by the parties involved. And the rest of the population stay out of what is not their business... That last part I got off a Mars newspaper I found in the archives." As the voice of EFFI, the consciousness of the *Quantum Shortbus*, finished her lecture, Caspian leaned over the screen on the command console and tapped hir fingers on either side of it.

"Anarchic. Sounds like my kind of place," s/he said, staring off into space as if thinking of the adventures to be had exploring the surface of Mars. "EFFI, take us down to the planet."

Suddenly, a figure glowing blue appeared on the command deck with Caspian. This new being was female and about the same height as Caspian—however, her form hadn't completely materialized since she remained semi-translucent. Her name was Machandi, and her skin was a brilliant blue that glowed like a rare gem. She was completely bald and her ears were pointed and curved around up the sides of her slim head. This Machandi was a highly evolved Pleiadian; her dark blue dress trailed behind her as she approached Caspian. "Mars is a dangerous planet," she warned.

Machandi had appeared to Caspian to be hir Guardian ever since s/he first discovered that s/he was a Zeromorph. What does it mean to be Zeromorphic? you ask. That means that the body can physically transform back and forth between male and female—and sometimes hold both at the same time. These days Caspian spent more and more time embodying both male and female at once.

Caspian smirked and shot a mocking glance in her direction as she walked up next to hir, looking out of the viewport as Mars continued to get larger and larger. "I laugh at dangerous," s/he said. "I didn't come all the way out to the buttcrack of the Spiralverse to be a pussy. No, I came for an adventure in space; out on the frontier of the cosmos."

"Okay," Machandi replied haltingly. "Just know that if you get into trouble, I can't help you since I'm only in my plasma-body here with you. My physical body is back in the Pleiades. And you don't even have a weapon."

"I don't need a weapon," Caspian said. "Besides," s/he tapped hir chest, right above hir heart, "I already have a weapon—wherever I go."

"Which city are you going to dock in?" Machandi asked.

"Zardoz," Caspian replied. They both stared out of the viewport as buildings of the city began to come into view. EFFI effortlessly guided the *Quantum Shortbus* into its dock at the spaceport. After paying the fees for keeping hir spaceship there, Caspian somehow found the most notorious bar in all of the city of Zardoz. Caspian found that bars were the best place to pick up juicy gossip, missions, or even some odd jobs. The city of Zardoz was small; not unlike Reno, Caspian noted.

Once at the bar, Caspian sat down at a small table in the corner so s/he could observe. S/he ordered several shots of a drink called Supernova, which was a neon pink liquid; and when you drank it, it felt like your brain was being beaten with a gold brick wrapped in a bloody handkerchief. The bar was dirty and the lights on the ceiling flickered as if the heat threatened to knock the power out. It wasn't so much the heat that was the problem—but the humidity. The air made your skin feel so clammy that you could hallucinate the buzz of flies constantly swirling though the sticky warmth even though they weren't there.

Machandi appeared in the chair across from Caspian at the little table. While s/he downed a shot of Supernova, s/he eyed the crowd and the diversity of the races. There were Drakonians sitting at tables having drinks with Reptilians. There were even a couple other humans who oddly enough seemed to be having conversations with a species that appeared to be a descendent of the Anunnaki. Drakonians looked almost human. They had long slim faces and pale skin. Their skulls extended farther, doming out the back of their heads like a crystal skull. They had large foreheads but long black hair that they parted in the middle. The Drakonian clothing was militaristic.

You can imagine what a Reptilian might look like.

"I'm surprised these different races are all in the same room and not killing each other," Caspian whispered to Machandi out of the corner of hir mouth.

"To be honest, I am as well," Machandi replied, looking around at the melting pot of space races that populated the bar. "But it is reassuring information to have so that we know that the Guardian Alliance's plan for peace isn't as far-fetched as we may have thought."

"... I heard that there might be some sort of machine inside it," said a Drakonian at a table a little ways off to Caspian's left. This Drakonian was speaking in a hushed whisper to his Reptilian companion.

"And they say it's at the dead-center of the Spiralverse?" the Reptilian asked, sounding still a bit skeptical. "How did you magically come up with the coordinates for the Recto-Hole? Did it just happen to appear on that little blink-drive you have there?"

The Drakonian leaned in toward his friend ominously. "That's for me to know, and you to forget about," he whispered.

The Reptilian took a swig of his foaming drink and then

wiped his scaly lips. "And which spaceport did you say you was at?"

"Just the main Zardoz spaceport," the Drakonian shrugged. "My ship is black with two green snakes painted up the sides..."

Caspian looked over at Machandi and grinned. She frowned and shook her blue head. "Oh, no," she said. "You're not a pirate," she continued, leaning in toward Caspian. "I get the impression you somehow think you're the Indiana Jones of space, or something of the like."

"But this could be big," Caspian whispered back. "The Recto-Hole; the Asshole of the Universe; the Singularity Poop Shoot; the Spiralverse-Anus."

"And what do you know about it?" Machandi asked mockingly. "I'm not convinced it even actually exists."

"I heard," Caspian began in a tone of voice that implied great importance, "that if you go inside the Holy Anus, it will shit you out right where you belong to be able to fulfill your greatest destiny."

Machandi laughed. "Pure nonsense. Sounds like propaganda spouted by the Church of the Galactic Sphincter."

"Only one way to find out," Caspian said, hir eyes sparkling with the anticipation of an interstellar adventure. "We know where the coordinates are—on the blink-drive. And this stupid Drakonian told us exactly where to find his rocket. The god-game is on!" S/he took two shots of Supernova back to back and then coughed loudly, grimacing against the pain of the brain being pounded by a gold brick wrapped in a bloody handkerchief.

Now, I know you want to say *Hey, this sounds like the plot of a bad science-fiction movie.* This is *exactly* like the plot of a bad science-fiction movie. And of course Caspian and Machandi made their way back to the spaceport before the Drakonian and his Reptilian companion were even done having drinks at the bar. The Drakonian rocket was tall—way taller than the *Quantum Shortbus*, obviously. They stopped below the platform where the rocket was docked, and they stared up at it in awe. The outside of the ship was so black that the paintings of the green snakes on the sides were so vivid that they almost seemed to pop out and slither like 3D holographic images.

"If there really is a sphincter in this universe, puckering and waiting for me," Caspian said, still gazing up at the rocket, "wouldn't you want to know about it? Explore it?"

"I mean," Machandi started, "it's not that I've never heard any legends about it. I have. But I never got the urge to explore its validity beyond that."

"Aww," Caspian pretended to whine and gave Machandi a puppy-dog look. "Where's your sense of curiosity?" Just then, s/he popped a sphere of golden light out from hir heart into an orb large enough to encapsulate hir whole body. Then the star tetrahedrons of Caspian's Merkabah field appeared within the golden sphere and began spinning so fast they became a blur of white light. In a flash of an instant, s/he was hovering off of the ground and then began to ascend through the air up the side of the rocket. Machandi followed behind hir; she being in her plasma-body already meant she did not need to energetically manifest her Merkabah field in order to fly.

Caspian found the area at the top of the rocket where the command deck would be inside. S/he commanded hir Merkabah to vibrate hir atoms as if they were empty space. Becoming transparent for a moment, Caspian took that instant to slip through the side of the rocket as if s/he were a ghost. Caspian found hirself on the Drakonian's command deck. The interior was all blacks and grays—not at all like Caspian's white command deck. S/he shuddered at the coldness of the design. Machandi suddenly appeared beside hir. The control console in front of them looked like blocks of stacked TVs and Atari game controllers.

"Now where is the blink-drive in all of this Drakonian nonsense?" Caspian grumbled, studying the control console.

"It's in the slot under that TV," Machandi said, pointing up and to the left.

Caspian approached that section of the console, and sure enough there was something similar to a disc-slot underneath the big square TV. Running hir fingers along the smooth, black metal on the outside of the blink-drive, Caspian couldn't help admire some of what the Drakonians had built and invented— even if they were nefarious and malicious. S/he pushed the slot in and the cartridge popped right out. Pulling it out, s/he noted that the drive resembled the size and shape of an eight-track tape. There was a green light that blinked from the inside of the metal casing.

While Caspian was admiring the blinking light in the blink-drive, s/he didn't realize that there was a Drakonian on the ship who was now sneaking up on hir from behind. "Watch out, Caspian!" Machandi yelled, but it was too late. The Drakonian had snuck up soundlessly on Caspian and managed to slip a metal collar around hir neck. It clasped and locked in the front and alternating green and red lights lit up around the circumference.

"What the hell?" Caspian exclaimed, spinning around to see

hir alien attacker. The metal collar now locked around hir neck was to block the flow of energy to and from the chakras, which rendered hir unable to use any powers or even hir Merkabah Field. Before Caspian could say another word, s/he was hit over the head with the butt of the alien's plasma rifle.

Tentacles Spread

There was that unpleasant warm and sticky feeling of blood trailing from Caspian's brow line and down the side of hir face. S/he blinked hir eyes but hir vision didn't become clear right away. It took a couple shakes of the head for hir to be able to make out exactly where s/he was. Caspian was in a large underground room that looked like it may have been part of a sewer system. It was cold and dark and Caspian was not alone there. Across the room, some distance away, was a naked man chained with his arms above his head and shackles around his ankles. Caspian couldn't tell if this man was conscious—he wasn't moving. S/he also realized that s/he was chained up in precisely the same fashion.

"I told you not to mess with it," Machandi said, appearing suddenly in her plasma-body in front of Caspian. "Now they're planning to kill you for trying to steal from a Drakonian ship."

"A lot of good your warnings do me now," Caspian said sarcastically. "Unless you have a key to unlock these shackles; or you have a way to pop this collar off, a lot of fucking good you can do me right now."

"I'm sorry," she said with a frown. "I'll let you know if I

figure something out." Then she disappeared, leaving Caspian in that damp underground with hir naked cellmate. Caspian jerked hir head up as s/he heard footsteps. Out of the shadows walked a Drakonian with a large square cage hovering in front of him using antigravity technology. Squinting hir eyes, Caspian still couldn't tell if it was the same Drakonian that knocked hir out.

"You picked the wrong day to steal from a Drakonian ship, hermaphrodite!" the alien admonished, scowling at Caspian.

Caspian looked around with a fake sheepish expression on hir face. "Who? Me?" s/he whispered.

"Not funny," the Drakonian said, deepening his grimace. It was then that Caspian noticed a strange remote control device wrapped around the alien's right hand. "Wake up!" he said, slapping the naked man in the face. The naked man groaned and started to open his eyes. The Drakonian looked back over at Caspian and continued, "I want you to see what happens to dirty humans who try to steal from us. Watch this long and hard because you're next... Open!" he commanded. One side of the hovering cage slid up and open. One of the strangest creatures Caspian had ever seen emerged from within. It was like a squid that could fly. Its body was semi-translucent and its tentacles seemed to stretch and compress back and forth in no coherent manner.

The Drakonian pressed a button on the remote wrapped around his right hand. Suddenly one of the alien squid's tentacles whipped around; it stretched out and out and then penetrated the naked man's rectum. The man let out a shriek of pain as the tentacle wriggled its way inside of him. The shackled man couldn't move his hands or feet, but he writhed in pain as he felt the tentacle rip through all of his internal organs just to make its way flapping out of his open mouth. Then the other tentacles started piercing all of the man's other orifices—one made itself incredibly long and skinny to stab up the man's urethra. Two more tentacles wiggled their way into his ear holes. And then the kicker, right before two small tentacles plugged up his nostrils, two sharpened tentacles stabbed the man's eyeballs, rupturing them. He couldn't scream because his throat was being choked by the slimy alien tentacle.

Caspian was mesmerized yet horrified. In a couple more minutes, the tentacles had torn the man into pieces. Gore of the human body—blood, organs, feces, and piss—splashed onto the ground of the sewer cathedral. Then s/he saw her—Machandi. That blue bald-headed goddess manifested in her plasma-body right next to the tentacle monster. She whispered some sort of mantra vibration which went into the creature, overriding its commands from the remote control. The tentacle-beast then at once turned on its Drakonian master. The alien cried out, stumbling backwards as he fumbled with the remote uselessly. Even before he could scream a second time, a tentacle was slithering down his throat; and another tentacle was constricting around his neck. The alien was being asphyxiated from both directions. Once the Drakonian hit the ground dead, the blink-drive slid out of the pocket of his coat.

"Now get me the fuck out of these cuffs!" Caspian yelled. S/he couldn't handle being restrained one second longer.

"Hold on," Machandi shot back. "Give me a second to work." She closed her eyes and raised her arms. Blue auras shone brightly around her outstretched hands. Caspian watched as a tiny sliver of tentacle dislodged itself from the rest of the creature. Now it was long, thin, and slimy—like a spaghetti noodle. This noodle floated over to where Caspian was chained up and proceeded to act as a lock-pick. In a moment, hir arms were free and s/he rubbed hir wrists where the shackles had chafed. Then s/he was completely free of the chains and lunged for the blink-drive. Caspian was able to retrieve it as the tentacle-noodle assimilated back into the bulk of the tentacle-beast which was busy dissolving the Drakonian into itself.

"Quick, Machandi!" Caspian said as s/he slid the blink-drive into the pocket of hir long tunic. "To the *Shortbus*!" S/he ran past the sludge-like remains of the naked man and took off down one shaft of sewer.

Machandi kept up with hir easily. "Do you even know where we are?" she asked.

"Yes—no," Caspian stammered. "Where are we again?" s/he asked, slowing hir pace to a walk. "It's just a matter of time before that Drakonian's companion at the bar comes around looking for him."

"We're in the sewers underneath an abandoned Vogon office building," Machandi explained, ignoring Caspian's last comment. "The Drakonians didn't want any bureaucracy on the planet, so the Vogons soon gave up trying to establish some sort of governmental structure here."

"So they just abandoned their offices," Caspian commented. "And this looks more like a cellar than a sewer—thank the Unified Field! I don't think I could handle it if I was knee-deep in alien feces."

"We can get up to the surface in the next chamber," Machandi informed as they turned the corner through a room that was particularly chilly with water dripping from the ceiling. Sure enough, in the next chamber there was a staircase made of the clay of Mars that they had been walking on. At the top of the stairs was a wooden door that did resemble a cellar door. When Caspian pushed it open, it opened like a trap door. When they had both made their way up to the ground level, Caspian noted that it looked like they were in a dilapidated lobby of an old-timey office building that hadn't been used in centuries, it seemed.

"This is creepy," Caspian said, noting their surroundings. "Reminds me too much of Earth."

They exited through the shattered doors of the building out into the light of the Mars afternoon. Caspian followed Machandi as they started walking back in the direction of the Zardoz spaceport.

"I'm surprised how far that Drakonian took you from the spaceport," Machandi said.

Caspian smiled. "At least I still got the coordinates to the Galactic Sphincter!" s/he said excitedly, waving the blink-drive in Machandi's face.

"Was it worth almost losing your immortal life over?" she asked, a little tinge of anger in her voice.

Caspian shrugged. "I'll have to see if it's everything it's cracked up to be. Get it—*cracked up* to be?" S/he laughed at hir own joke.

Machandi grinned. "Maybe it won't be everything it's shitted out to be."

Coughing a little laugh, Caspian replied, "Shitted out? Is that a real phrase?"

Machandi shot hir a look. "Shut up! Don't give me a hard time for not knowing your *Earth* sayings."

Zardoz wasn't that big of a city—about the size of Reno on Earth. And they were back at the spaceport before they even expected to be. The hermaphrodite and the blue goddess strolled across the tarmac of the spaceport toward the *Quantum Shortbus*. To look at them, you wouldn't have guessed that they just came from a morbid scene in a dank dungeon where two guys got torn to shreds by a tentacle monster.

"I'm too lazy to open the hatch," Caspian announced as s/he popped hir golden orb and Merkabah out around hir body. "So I'll just float in through the side and into my command deck."

"You do realize there's no hatch," Machandi said, shaking her head. "It's still a van on the outside, remember?"

"Oh, yeah," Caspian said, turning back to face the *Quantum Shortbus*, which was a conversion van tilted up on its back windshield, where the thrusters were attached. The whole van was docked and secured to a rocket tower to keep it in place until they wanted to take off. Caspian floated up anyway along the side of the van until s/he was next to hir driver's side door. At that angle, the door opened upwards like the wing of a DeLorean. After swinging inside the spaceship with the gliding assistance of hir Merkabah, Caspian closed the van door and instantly found hirself standing on the white floor of the command deck. The way the sub-dimension was configured, the orientation aways made anyone inside the ship feel like they were standing upright, even if the *Shortbus* was on its side or facing up like a rocket.

Machandi appeared beside Caspian in a puff of blue sparkles like she aways did. "I guess we should get out of here before *Mars Attacks*," Caspian remarked, cracking a grin and looking over at hir goddess companion. She didn't seem to register the joke. "Guess you don't get that reference." S/he shrugged. "EFFI," s/he continued, addressing the ship's mind. "Prepare for liftoff." The control crystals appeared hovering all around the room.

"Yes, Captain," the computer's voice answered back.

"Stellar Command, do you read?" Caspian asked, now addressing the group which operated the Zardoz Spaceport. More specifically, s/he was addressing the flight controller who monitored take-off and landing of spacecrafts. Stellar Command was an independently organized group consisting of multiple alien races. They had no political creed and no central governing body. They were just a group who believed in interstellar space travel so much that they banded together to build spaceports in lots of different locations in the known Spiralverse and also more distant galaxies.

"This is Stellar Command," a disembodied voice answered, echoing around the command deck. "We read you, Caspian. Prep for departure?"

"Affirmative," s/he answered. "Let's get off this rock."

"Prepping for departure," the fight controller replied.

"Do you think he's a Reptilian?" Caspian whispered to Machandi.

She shrugged. "I don't know. He could be."

The service tower detached from the *Quantum Shortbus* and rolled away several yards to give the ship room to launch.

"He sounds too nice to be a Reptilian," Caspian commented.

"Hey, we can still hear you, you know," the voice grumbled from the speaker. Caspian cringed and gave Machandi a pleading look. If s/he had been an Anime character, there would have been one giant drop of sweat appearing on the side of hir head right then. "Not all Reptilians are out to enslave people and kill entire races," the flight controller continued.

"My apologies for being so insensitive," Caspian returned. Machandi rolled her eyes.

"*Quantum Shortbus*," the fight controller stated, "you are clear for launch."

"Thank you, Stellar Command," Caspian said in hir most captain-y voice. "EFFI! Let's roll! To Infinity and Beyond the Beyond we ride the waves of cosmic orgasmic ecstasy!"

There was a rumble as the ship's thrusters began to boot up and get hot. "Eleven seconds until lift-off," EFFI informed.

"That's what I like to hear," Caspian said with a smile. S/he loved to feel the vibration caused by the power of the thrusters. It was almost sexual—no, it *was* sexual. As the *Quantum Shortbus* rocketed into the sky of Mars, Caspian's eyes rolled up in hir head and s/he felt like s/he was about to have the rocket-orgasm s/he always felt when launching the *Shortbus*. "Fucking quantum bistros!" s/he yelled, squeezing hir hands between hir legs as the *Shortbus* shot up and out of Mars's artificial atmosphere back toward the void of space. In moments, they had broken free of Mars's gravitation pull and were headed back into deep space. "Oh, yeah," Caspian moaned. "That was a good one." S/he caught her breath while basking in the afterglow of the launch-gasm.

"You really like that, don't you?" Machandi said, smiling. "Nothing like a good rocket-ejaculation into the universe's uterus. It tickles your pickle. It greases your peach."

"Oh, my God! Stop!" Caspian said, feeling hir girl-cock getting hard. "You're gonna make me get all horny again."

Machandi laughed. She was so blue that no one would be able to tell if she was ever blushing. Does she blush a darker shade of blue? "You are definitely a cute Zeromorph, Caspian. Maybe that's why I've stayed with you all this time—because you're such a cutie!"

Caspian grinned and waved hir hand as if to say 'Stop teasing me.' "You ain't so bad yourself, Machandi," s/he replied with a wink and then pulled the blink-drive from hir pocket. "The greatest adventure," s/he continued. "To penetrate the Galactic Sphincter."

"You think it actually exists?" Machandi asked, walking up closer to Caspian and the command console. "It could just be some Drakonian trick."

"There's only one way to find out," Caspian said, leaning down to the area of the command console right underneath the black screen that was spinning the Kathara Grid. There was a slot that was the perfect size for the blink-drive and Caspian slid it right in.

"I sense foreign tech from a Drakonian ship," EFFI commented.

"Yes," Caspian answered. "I borrowed that blink-drive from a Drakonian I met on Mars."

"Borrowed?" Machandi said, raising her eyebrows.

"Shush," s/he shot back, giving the Pleiadian goddess a look. "EFFI, run the coordinates on the drive."

"As you wish, Captain," EFFI replied. There were several moments of computing and then EFFI spoke again saying, "Invalid coordinates."

"What?" Caspian snapped. "How can the fuckin—nevermind! EFFI, refresh and run it again. Maybe the drive is corrupted."

Machandi and Caspian stared at each other as they waited for the verdict on the coordinates for the Rectal of the Gods. Machandi sighed, "I told you before, Caspian, to never trust a Drakonian. Even when it comes to treasure or population manipulation. You never know what their hidden agenda might be. They're very malicious and clever."

"Sounds like you'd want to be one of them," Caspian joked.

"Ha!" Machandi scoffed. "I would never want to be a Drakonian. That's why I became part of the Guardian Alliance—so we could protect the Spiralverse from the control agenda of the Drakonians."

"I know, they seem pretty fucked up. Using that alien creature to tentacle-rape-torture that guy to death—brutal..." Caspian trailed off and noticed that EFFI's crystals were flashing red. "Wait, I think EFFI has something. EFFI?"

"Coordinates invalid," the ship mind stated again.

"What? What the fuck?" Caspian grumbled, growling with frustration. "What the fuck does that mean *invalid coordinates?*"

"It means," EFFI explained, "that the coordinates are not in this Dimension."

Caspian didn't say anything for a moment. S/he put hir finger up to hir lips and furrowed hir brow in thought. "Well, that might make it a little difficult," s/he mumbled.

Suddenly Machandi looked concerned and turned toward where the back of the ship might be. In an instant, she vanished in a puff of blue mist. "Machandi, where are you going?" Caspian yelled. "I need you to help me figure this out!"

Barely a moment passed before Machandi was back standing next to Caspian. "I hate to tell you this, Caspian," she began, "but that Drakonian ship is in pursuit of us. It just cleared the atmosphere of Mars."

"Fuck," Caspian cursed. "EFFI, keep us headed in the trajectory of the outer solar system—maximum speed. And show me the view from the back of the *Shortbus*." S/he turned away from the viewport that looked out of the front of the ship and a holographic screen appeared between two navigation crystals that were still flashing red. The view on the screen showed the red planet getting smaller in the distance as they flew farther away from it. Then Caspian saw it—the Drakonian ship with the snakes painted on the side. It was gaining on them with speed.

"I warned you never to get into a fight with a Drakonian," Machandi said with concern in her voice. "They fight dirty and want their enemies to suffer."

"Yes, thanks, Machandi," Caspian replied dryly. "I remember all the things you ever warned me about before going into space. Fucking shit... I don't think the captain of that rocket has taken too kindly to us killing his ship-mate."

"*We* didn't really kill him," Machandi responded. "It was the tentacle-beast."

"That's a technicality that I doubt the captain of that ship is going to validate," Caspian said gravely. "Okay, shit!" s/he swore, rubbing hir hands together nervously. "If we're going to have to fight—and it looks like we are—then it's on! *Quantum*

Shortbus versus the *Drakonian Flying Dildo*! Now is as good a time as any to try out those new grappling arms I had installed."

The Quantum Short Bus

The Ultimate Showdown
and The Realm of Tahuti

Machandi looked worried.

"The Drakonian ship is gaining with speed and its weapons are hot," the ship's mind continued.

"Okay," Caspian started with a deep inhale. "EFFI, prepare to take evasive maneuvers."

Machandi and Caspian stared in silence at the holographic screen that showed the rocket with the snakes getting larger as it approached. Suddenly there were flashes of white light and the enemy ship began firing their particle cannons at the *Quantum Shortbus*. EFFI jerked the ship to the left, and then to the right to just narrowly miss getting incinerated. Caspian wobbled to keep hir balance as the ship bounced around the void.

Luckily the *Shortbus* was small and could bop around as quick as a little bug. "EFFI," Caspian said with authority as s/he rolled up hir sleeves. "Approach the enemy vessel in an erratic fashion. And engage grappling arms." Suddenly two rows of yellow holographic rings appeared hovering in the air in front of Caspian. S/he slid hir arms into the grappling arm controls and spread hir fingers wide outside of the last ring. Small circles of yellow energy appeared at the tip of each finger.

Almost so fast it could have been mistaken for teleporting if you happened to blink at the wrong moment, the *Shortbus* lunged at the side of the Drakonian ship. Caspian used the grappler arms like a battering ram and hit the ship so hard it left a deep dent in the snake's head. The snake ship used their side-thrusters to get some distance between it and the *Shortbus*. The damage to their hull was worse than Caspian thought after s/he first struck it. There seemed to be some sort of material leaking out of a hole at the center of where the damage was. It may have been some kind of insulation, but Caspian couldn't be sure.

"They're definitely done for now," Caspian said, feeling a little bit more confident.

"I wouldn't be so cocky so soon," Machandi shot back.

Caspian used the holographic controls to engage a missile to launch from one of the grappler arms. Firing without hesitation, it struck the snake ship on its back end, knocking off a couple of its thrusters and sending it into a spin. Caspian figured s/he had this in the bag. But all of a sudden, the Drakonian ship projected a blue plasma field around the whole exterior, like an elastic protective skin.

"Shit," Caspian said and fired another missile. It instantly disintegrated as it touched the blue plasma shield. Machandi watched with her sphincter clenched as a large canon descended from below the snake ship. What it shot out was an energetic net made of pink holographic light. "What the hell is that?" Caspian exclaimed as the net completely engulfed the *Quantum Shortbus*.

"That can't be good for the ship," Machandi commented.

"No shit," Caspian grumbled. "I can't even launch a missile or move the grappling arms."

The navigation crystals began to flash from pink to deep red, and the ship swayed like EFFI was drunk. "Caspian?" EFFI said, voice sounding garbled.

"What's happening, EFFI?" the captain demanded.

"The encryption frequency on this net," the ship mind continued like a busted radio, "injected a virus to paralyze my command functions."

"The only thing powerful enough to break that," Machandi said, looking over seriously at Caspian who still had hir arms inside the yellow rings of light, "is the human lightbody—the Merkabah!"

"You're right," Caspian agreed. "And the reason they haven't blown us to space dust already is they need the blink-drive back. They're not going to risk destroying it. Which means," s/he turned to look at hir blue companion, "it's the real deal and not a fake."

"Oh, you think that's proof of the existence of some Intergalactic Sphincter?" Machandi said, raising her eyebrows.

"Fuck, don't distract me," Caspian said, rubbing hir hands together and closing hir eyes. S/he first popped the golden sphere of light out from hir heart chakra, but this time expanded it to enclose the whole ship. When s/he illuminated the star tetrahedrons and sent them spinning at nearly the speed of light around the *Quantum Shortbus*, the encryption net ruptured and disappeared in a puff of pink space dust. Caspian then imagined all of the cruelty and atrocities which had been committed upon hir. S/he remembered when s/he had been raped and murdered by people who were supposed to be hir friends. Caspian relived that pain, made it real within hir heart, as well as all the pain of confusion which s/he had experienced as a young androgyne. "Purge!" Caspian yelled, and that ball of painful negative energy was taken out of hir body by the Merkabah field and shot like a missile at the Drakonian ship.

When the streak of torturous plasmik energy struck the snake ship, Caspian and Machandi almost thought they heard the ship let out a shriek as if it was being fucked to death. The outer hull warped once and then ruptured, creating an explosion that rippled down the whole rocket, shooting off bits of shrapnel to become the expanse of space junk that continually floated through the Spiralverse.

"That was a close one," Caspian said, turning to face Machandi. The holographic screen that showed the rear view of the ship disappeared from between the two navigation crystals. "Those Drakonian bastards really wanted to fucking kill me." S/he laughed, releasing some of the nervous tension from hir body.

"Oh, yeah," Machandi agreed. "They have and *do* kill a lot of people. Bunch of fascist barbarians if you ask me."

Caspian left the Merkabah field set up around the exterior of the *Quantum Shortbus* instead of retracting it back into hir body. "EFFI," s/he said as s/he went back over to the control console underneath the forward-facing viewport. "Maintain the Merkabah field as a permanent fixture around the *Shortbus*." Looking down at the rectangular screen on the control console, Caspian touched several of the colored balls on the spinning Kathara Grid. It buzzed in a specific pattern. Making the Merkabah a permanent fixture of the ship meant that s/he wouldn't have to hold it in place with hir own energy.

"The Merkabah is now fixed as the ship's lightbody," EFFI informed.

"Now run the coordinates again to see if it will compute with the assistance of the tetrahedral field," the hermaphroditic Captain said, beginning to pace back and forth in front of the control console.

EFFI ran the coordinates. "Coordinates are still invalid," the ship mind replied.

"Shit, really?" Caspian cursed, kicking the bottom of the control console in frustration.

"However," EFFI started.

Caspian's ears perked up. "However?"

"However," EFFI continued, "With the added navigation of the Merkabah field, I can bring you to a location very near where you want to end up."

"Then what are we waiting for?" Caspian said excitedly.

Machandi didn't look so enthusiastic. "Wait," she said conservatively. "We don't know where we'll even end up—or even what we'll end up *as*."

"Aww, that's no fun way to live," Caspian said laughing. "If there's no chance of being sucked through a wormhole just to be genetically mutated into a platypus, then where's the adventure?" Suddenly a small section of the white control console flipped over, revealing a large, domed black button with flames painted on it.

"Oh, you're going to do it anyway, aren't you?" Machandi groaned, rolling her eyes and turning around to walk towards the center of the command deck.

Caspian grinned like a jester about to play a cosmic trick. "You ready to get stretch-ified?"

And before Machandi could say "Oh no," Caspian had hit the button with all hir power. What the Stretch Drive effectively did was to stretch and warp the *Quantum Shortbus* and its passengers through light years of space in the span of a few seconds. They visually became like a piece of taffy being stretched through a tunnel.

This tunnel of warped space-time stretched out before them and it was like the nose of the *Shortbus* was dragged at light speed though this tunnel while the back-end stayed in one place. The ship was one long string of red putty. Inside the ship, the visual distortion caused Caspian and Machandi to see each other like they were reflected in a fun house mirror—stretching and blobbing. Caspian even pulled up the bottom of hir long tunic and watched as hir dick stretched out into a long, flat, flesh-colored smear.

As fast as it had begun, the trip was over. The back-end of the *Shortbus* instantly snapped forward in time to join the front half of itself and assume a normal shape once more. Caspian's tongue was stretched out, lolling from hir mouth and it took hir a moment or two to coax it back into hir mouth before it completely floated away into the void.

"Oh, man," Caspian said, shaking hir head. "That always rattles me."

"I don't like traveling like that, Caspian," Machandi said. "It tends to create disruption in the frequency of the transmission of my plasma-body."

Caspian turned to look at her and burst out laughing. "Your ear," s/he sputtered.

Machandi frowned. Her left ear had ended up on the top of her bald blue head somehow when they were stretching back to normal. Grabbing the ear to show it who was boss, Machandi pulled it down and pushed it back into its rightful place, where it stayed secure. "See what I mean?" she said. "Just watch, the next time we use the Stretch Drive your head might just find itself up your own ass."

Caspian laughed at the hilarity of that image. S/he thought of a few things s/he wouldn't mind doing with hir own ass. Pulling all hir molecules back into the godbody form, Caspian looked up out of the viewport to see if s/he could tell where they ended up. There was a luminous cloud of purple space dust in the distance that the *Shortbus* was gliding towards at a luxurious speed. "EFFI, where are we?" the Captain asked.

"We are just outside the Dark Nebula," EFFI answered.

"The Dark Nebula..." Caspian whispered to hirself. What did s/he know about the Dark Nebula? "Machandi," s/he said, stiffening up. "That's the, uh..." Caspian stammered, snapping hir fingers trying to remember what s/he had forgotten. "That's the—Alternate Egypt!"

"Alternate Egypt?" Machandi echoed back, walking toward the viewport in order to see the purple cloud which was this Dark Nebula. "Yes, I seem to remember hearing about this. Alternate meaning as opposed to the Egypt existing on Earth."

"Right," Caspian said without taking hir eyes off of the cloud of purple space dust. S/he was mesmerized, like a powerful witch had cast a love spell on hir to worship the Nebula throughout all Eternity. "They might know the location of the puckered sphincter," Caspian said, holding up hir hand dramatically. "EFFI, take us down into the fucking dust cloud and bring us to this Alternate Egypt... If you please."

"At once, Captain," the ship's mind replied without

hesitation. Their descent increased in velocity and it seemed like they were being pulled down into the heart of the purple cloud. Within all the particles of light and space debris, Caspian could make out a planet getting larger in the distance.

"Looks like a desert planet," Machandi commented.

"If it's another Egypt, I would think it would be," Caspian replied.

Desert planets weren't always *completely* deserts. This was the case with the planet Kemet, which Caspian and Machandi were rapidly approaching. There were only two oceans on the planet and they slit the sides of the sphere like two gills on a puffer-fish. Pretty soon the *Shortbus* was breaking the upper atmosphere of Kemet, plummeting down like a meteor headed for the sands below.

"Can you see them?" Machandi asked, swaying with the movement of the ship as it cruised in through the atmosphere.

"The what—Oh!" Caspian started, looking up at the view-port which was showing him the desert approaching quickly. "I see pyramids! And there's the Nile River." S/he sounded excited; like s/he was on an expedition with Dirk Gently to find the crystal skulls of the Anunnaki Egyptian gods from buried deep inside the nostrils of rhinos. "EFFI, take us down a distance away from the Great Pyramid," the Captain ordered.

"As you wish, Caspian," the ship answered, preparing for landing.

The sun of Ra was hot on Alternate Egypt as the *Quantum Shortbus* touched down on their sands. First the thrusters touched the ground and then the Merkabah guided the ship down to rest on its four tires. "We made it to the motherfucking asshole of the cosmos!" Caspian screeched like a horny teenager about to see Taylor Swift in concert. "I am the Pharaoh of the Perverts, and this is my world," s/he continued with her soliloquy.

Machandi scoffed. "We haven't made it to this Galactic Sphincter yet," she reminded hir. "And I don't trust these Neters."

"Hey, how bad could it be?" Caspian said, hovering and turning semi-translucent to get ready to fly through the wall of the ship. "We'll at least meet some cool gods, have some fun, maybe have an orgy. It'll be a gas!" S/he cracked a grin and then disappeared as s/he exited the *Shortbus*.

Machandi rolled her eyes. "Why are these Starseeds always so headstrong?" she grumbled as she floated out through the wall and after Caspian. Machandi touched down onto the sand and followed after Caspian who was walking toward the pyramids. The bottom of hir garment was blowing gently in the breeze.

Not long after they started walking, they beheld a tall figure walking in their direction; assumedly coming from the pyramids. This figure was humanoid in appearance. They were taller than an average human—maybe between seven and eight feet tall. He was muscular and had dark skin which shone in the Egyptian sun. It's outfit was peculiar to Ancient Egypt: sandals with leather straps, a blue and gold skirt, and a chest-piece of gold and precious stones. On top of all this strange attire, was an ibis head with a long beak which looked down at Caspian and Machandi with beady eyes.

"It has been known in the deep Mysteries that you would come," the ibis-headed god spoke. "I am Tahuti... And this is my realm." He made a grand gesture to indicate all the lands of Alternate Egypt.

"Pleasure to make the acquaintance of such a refined creature such as yourself," Caspian returned. "I am—"

"Caspian. I know," Tahuti said, cutting him off with a smile. The god's voice was so deep and resonant that it seemed to vibrate the very sands below their feet. "You come seeking the Hole of Destiny. Is this correct?"

Caspian snorted. "The Hole of Destiny," s/he repeated back in a whisper. "I come to penetrate the Galactic Sphincter!" Caspian said this in a booming voice, mirroring back Tahuti's own authority. "I want to find it so that it may let me in to see into the depths of the innards. And if it doesn't," s/he continued dramatically, "I will fuck that thing wide open until it's gaping and I fuck it again with the omnipresence of my eternal being."

Tahuti didn't reply for a while. There was an awkward silence during which the ibis-headed humanoid narrowed his beady eyes at Caspian and glared like an aristocrat looking down on someone of lower class. Clearing his throat, the god pulled out a small scroll from his skirt and a very long quill which had been hiding somewhere in his chest-piece. Tahuti looked at Caspian and then back at the scroll, scribbling what Caspian could only assume must be hieroglyphics.

Finally Mister Ibis-Head broke the silence by asking, "Are you a man or a woman?"

Caspian couldn't help but smirk. "I think I might be pretty sore if you misgendered me," s/he joked, winking to Machandi who rolled her eyes. "Why? Are you transphobic?" s/he added, narrowing hir eyes at Tahuti.

The god cleared his throat loudly. "I need it for the, um, the scroll," he answered. "What art thou pronouns of the mysterious god I see before me."

Caspian looked at Machandi, grinning. "Oh, Machandi, see I've now elevated to the status of a god," s/he said, bouncing hir eyebrows up and down.

Machandi scoffed. "And you didn't consider yourself that already?"

"Shush your mouth," Caspian shot back, raising hir finger. "I just like to hear it."

Tahuti cleared his throat loudly again. "Is that an M or an F?" he asked patiently.

"Oh, it's both," Caspian laughed. "Both M and F, to make MF—as in MotherFucker!"

"MotherFucker..." Tahuti repeated, scanning his scroll. "No, I don't think I see that option on here."

Caspian sighed, tiring of this running joke that the Egyptian god seemed to be failing to get. "MotherFucker," s/he repeated. "As in the *MotherFucking* tranny... I'm a hermaphrodite! My pronouns are infinite!"

"Ah," Tahuti said, finally comprehending and making several markings on his scroll. "You are the Divine Androgyne—a god of the Sacred Union. Masculine and Feminine. Why didn't you say so in the first place?" He turned and starting walking back toward the pyramids and gestured for the two to follow him. "We have a special place for your kind here."

Caspian couldn't tell if Tahuti meant that in an honorable way or a *we kill faggots here* kind of way. "I bet you do, Beakface," s/he said under hir breath. "Anyway," s/he continued, "what do you know about the Sphinct—er, Hole of Destiny?"

"It has been blocked for some time now," Tahuti continued in a serious tone.

Caspian couldn't help hirself and burst out laughing. Both Machandi and Tahuti both gave hir a look. "What?" s/he said, shrugging. "It was funny."

"There is an artificial entity trapped inside," the ibis-head continued. "No one knows why the Hole didn't discharge this entity into its Altered Destiny. But you," the ibis-head swung around to look at Caspian, his beady eyes serious as death, "you, Caspian, are the only one who can clear the clog and restore balance to the Movements of Destiny."

Needless to say, Caspian was loving this whole spiel. "You can count on me," s/he assured Tahuti. "I will raw-dog that Hole until I too am shat out into my own Altered Destiny."

By this time in the conversation, they were approaching the greatest of the pyramids. This one stretched up into the sky higher than the other two, which seemed only to be garnish to the main dish which was the Great Pyramid. Right next to it was a monstrous Sphinx that looked to be almost guarding the pyramid. Tahuti then turned to Machandi and said, "You must be a powerful being to be able to project your plasma-body all the way here from the Pleiades. However, I regret to inform you that only Caspian and I can go on from here. It was only hir name on the ancient scroll, not yours."

Machandi's mouth hung open in disbelief, and then she quickly composed herself. "I'll see you soon, Caspian," she said with no question in her voice. Then without another word, she turned and headed back in the direction of the *Shortbus*.

"Only the select few get initiated through the Mysteries of Alternate Egypt in the Dark Nebula," Tahuti informed, putting his hand on Caspian's back and leading hir over toward the Sphinx.

"You don't say," Caspian returned, looking up at the huge sculpture of the Sphinx which towered above them like a skyscraper.

"Have you ever heard of the Riddle of the Sphinx?" Tahuti asked out of the side of his beak.

"Maybe," Caspian answered. "Is that like when the Sphinx asks a riddle and if it's answered correctly, some secret chamber opens up? And if it's answered wrong, we die?"

"Umm, no," the ibis god replied, a little disappointed that Caspian wasn't immediately on the same page as him. "*You* must ask the Sphinx a riddle, and if she gets it wrong, then you get to go on into the inner chamber and then down and up into the Great Pyramid."

"Okay, here it goes," Caspian said, rubbing hir hands together. S/he looked up at the underside of the Sphinx's chin and prepared to shout the riddle. "What can fit inside five whores and at the same time still have its future read?"

"You have asked the Riddle of the Sphinx, my child," a booming woman's voice said, resonating from within the massive stone.

Tahuti shook his head and frowned. "That one was in poor taste. I can't say I approve..." he trailed off. "But I have to say that might work for me since I have a five-shafted lingam."

Caspian shook hir head and imagined that image. "You what?" s/he started. "That might even be more meat than I could handle."

"I have an answer," the Sphinx bellowed.

"She has an answer," Tahuti said, excited.

"And what is your brilliant deduction?" Caspian said, skeptical that the Sphinx could solve hir riddle.

"God!" the Sphinx declared definitely.

Caspian blinked hir eyes a couple times and laughed at the absurdity of the answer. "What?" s/he coughed. "I don't think I heard that right. Did you say *dog*?"

"God!" the Sphinx boomed again, this time no mistake could be made.

"Don't worry," Tahuti whispered out of the side of his beak into Caspian's ear. "That is the same answer she gives to every riddle."

"Well, that is incorrect!" Caspian said, loud enough for the Sphinx to hear. "The answer is—Andre the Giant's hand!" S/he burst out laughing again at hir own joke. "Get it?" s/he said to Tahuti, holding up hir hand and trying to catch hir breath from laughing so hard. Tahuti gave Caspian a blank, humorless stare. "Ah, forget it," s/he said finally. "You had to be there."

"Regardless," Tahuti said loudly, "you have bested the Sphinx, and now—"

Suddenly there was a rumble on the stone of the Sphinx directly in front of where they were standing. A block the size of a door slid back out of place and then down, disappearing into the ground. The interior was pitch black except for a lit torch mounted on the right inside wall.

"Ready to penetrate the bowels?" the god said, grinning his beak.

"You've really gotta work on your puns," Caspian said, shaking hir head as they walked into the darkness, a single illumination cast only by the orange flames of the torch.

Penetrating the Galactic Sphincter

Tahuti led Caspian down the stone steps that went into the depths of the Sphinx. Caspian's shoes clicked on the stones as they descended, their shadows dancing on the walls within the light of the fire. When they emerged into a room, Caspian stared in wonderment, frozen with the awe of the spectacle. This room was enormous, almost like the inside of a warehouse but more beautiful. Stretching from floor and up higher than Caspian could see were rows and rows of wooden bookshelves. The floors were gorgeous dark wood and the sides of the bookshelves were decorated with the most intricate of carvings—from what Caspian could make out, there were scenes from history as well as the images of gods and goddesses carved thereupon.

"Welcome to the Library of Future Antiquity," Tahuti said, smiling at his collection; he was a geeky god as well as a scribe.

"Library of Future Antiquity," Caspian repeated in a whisper, with unbidden reverence.

"This room contains all that was ever written and everything that will be written, throughout all of Eternity," Tahuti explained as they began to walk again, down the center aisle and toward the far side of the Library. "Now I know what you're thinking," he continued. "You're thinking how can all that was ever written and will be written fit in this one Library, even as large as it is. Magick, my dear girlboi! Magick! It is pure Magick! And I am the keeper of Magick and the keeper of the books. Anything doing with writing or the fantastical is my domain."

Caspian had to suppress hir desire to run up and down the shelves like an excited child going through all the books. S/he desperately wanted to explore these treasures of past and future Antiquity—especially what might be written in the future but only existed here as of yet, in a time out of time. "I feel like I'm in Wonderland," s/he said with stars in hir eyes.

Tahuti chuckled, noticing how cute Caspian was as s/he geeked out over the written word—from Cuneiform all the way to modern English; and probably some books in formats and languages not even invented yet. "I imagine you would," the god responded as he brought Caspian towards the far side of the room which led to a passage which would bring them underneath the Great Pyramid.

"I wish I could just take some time here to study everything," Caspian commented.

"Maybe one day you'll return to visit Alternate Egypt," Tahuti responded in a tone that suggested to Caspian that the god already knew that one day s/he *would* return. "But the mission at hand calls for your full attention."

The tunnel at the far end of the Library of Future Antiquity was dark again and Beakface illuminated the passage with his torch which seemed to burn infinitely and with an ethereal brightness. "Are we beneath the pyramid now?" Caspian asked.

Tahuti nodded. "We are almost directly under the center of the pyramid."

"I'm beginning to feel a very intense energy," Caspian commented, flexing hir hands and feeling a tingling at hir sixth and seventh chakras. "It's coming from in front of us. It's like we're walking into a very dense electromagnetic field."

"You're very sensitive, Caspian," Tahuti returned. "That will serve you well throughout all Time."

The ibis-headed god stopped suddenly and Caspian almost walked into his broad back. S/he glanced over to their left and there was another stone staircase leading up to the higher chambers of the pyramid. Directly in front of them, Caspian suddenly noticed, was a gaping pit like the yawning mouth of a beast not yet conjured, waiting to devour them. Looking over the edge, s/he swallowed hard, nervous that s/he would suddenly be sucked into the gaping crevasse. It seemed like an optical illusion that none of the light from the torch could penetrate past the threshold of The Well. There was a chill that came up from the depths and Caspian shivered. "What is that?" s/he asked. "The energy feels... heavy."

"That, my friend, is The Well," Tahuti informed.

"The Well," Caspian repeated. "That sounds ominous— the darkest Dark Night of the Soul in Mystery School."

"Oh, it is," the god said cheerfully. "But you'll be fine."

"Wait—what?" Caspian said jerkily, pulling hir head up to look at the smiling beak. Before s/he had a chance to make any move, Tahuti placed his large hand on Caspian's back and shoved hir forward with a strong push. Teetering on the edge for the flash of an instant, Caspian tried to keep hir balance and scramble back up onto the ledge. S/he couldn't make hir balance stick and s/he slipped, plummeting down into the unfathomable deep below.

Caspian felt like the heaviest boulder dropped from an airplane flying through the exosphere. It was pitch black like being in a cave with no headlamp. S/he was terrified but refused to scream and waste energy. Desperately trying to connect to hir Merkabah for light and a way to fly out of the pit, Caspian growled in frustration as hir lightbody refused to manifest. *There must be foul Magick afoot*, s/he thought. Then suddenly s/he felt a chill, as if all the warm blood had been drained from hir body by a corporate vampire with severe hemophilia. Caspian swallowed hard, and s/he was descending so fast that s/he almost felt weightless. Then the voices began to echo in the darkness and pierce through hir skull like insulting needles.

"Faggot!"

"Queer!"

"Tranny!"

"Pervert!"

"Sicko!"

The words echoed off of the walls of The Well like a broken record. They became a torturous vortex—a cacophony of disembodied, disemboweled voices. The deep shame that s/he hadn't felt since being on Earth around intolerant bigots at once began to bubble up like burning stomach acid mixed with blood. "SHUT UP!" Caspian screamed, pressing hir hands against hir ears, but it was useless against blocking out the din. The taunting voices were inside hir head, bouncing from one side of hir skull to the other in a madness-inducing torrent. S/

he began to cry. And just for a second wished that the bottom of The Well would come rushing up, breaking hir body as s/he collided with it, hopefully silencing the negative taunting in hir mind. Then—

No! Caspian thought, taking a deep breath and trying to purge some of the sludge out of hirself. *I shouldn't have to feel ashamed of what I am.*

Suddenly the image of Caspian's mother appeared in front of hir surrounded by a white glow. Caspian had to put hir hand out and feel the wind rushing past to make sure s/he was still falling and not just floating in the void. Hir mother displayed a disappointed and concerned expression. Caspian recognized it.

"Oh, honey," hir mother said patronizingly. "You're not gay. You're not a girl. You're just confused. It's a phase. You'll come out of it." She disappeared in a puff of white light and was instantly replaced by the figure of Caspian's father, obviously angry, looking as if he was about to hit hir.

"Why do you want to be a faggot?" hir father yelled, spittle spraying from his lips. "You want to dress up like a little bitch and get fucked in the ass by another guy's cock? If you want to be a little sissy queer then you're not my son!"

Caspian felt like hir heart was splitting in two. S/he began to sob uncontrollably as the sensation became so painful that it was like someone was gouging out hir chest cavity with a huge rusty hook. As s/he fell, the tears trailed up hir eyes and left water tracks on hir forehead before they flew up, carried on the rushing wind.

After hir father disappeared, there appeared a horrific vision —Caspian's death. S/he stared as s/he watched the vision of hirself tied to a tree, screaming and being stabbed in the gut over and over by three people s/he had thought were hir friends at the time. It was as if the image was stuck on a horrendous loop. Caspian saw hirself screaming on that tree and the knife just slicing in and in and in—and in again as blood poured like a waterfall from hir midsection. The Caspian that was still falling suddenly gasped and felt like there was something touching hir penis and vagina underneath it.

It was the oddest sensation, but Caspian felt like hir vagina opening sealed itself shut to become a smooth perineum; like it had been when s/he was strictly in male form. Then something grasped the tip of hir penis roughly. Caspian tried to tell hirself that this was all a hallucination, but that didn't do much to alleviate the fear that was gripping hir heart like a frostbitten hand. Subsequently there was a feeling of a blade slicing up the shaft from the base to the tip. After feeling hir throat rupture with a scream, it was odd not hearing the sound of it in hir own ears. Genitals were being mutilated in a nightmarish version of a sexual reassignment surgery.

S/he could see it all in hir mind's eye. The incision of the taint for the opening of the vagina—blood poured out from the opening like a heavy menstrual flow. Then Caspian was violently hollowed out—like a stuffed animal that was having its cotton torn from between its legs. It was the strangest sensation when the penis got turned inside-out and was engineered inside as the shaft of the vagina. Caspian felt as if s/he was making love (or some sort of mutilation rape) to hirself—forever keeping the seed and the womb hidden within hir.

After reaching between hir legs to make sure s/he was still intact, s/he tried to look at hir hand in the darkness. All at once there was a red glow emitted from the surface of hir hand. It was like neon blood that glowed with a radioactive hue. "FUCK THIS!" Caspian screamed, using the sheer force of hir will to purge all of the hallucinations and nightmares. S/he allowed hir heart to open up, banishing the brokenhearted feeling of the rusty hook ripping open hir chest cavity. Immediately the golden sphere of light burst from hir heart, encircled hir falling body, and spun the Merkabah until it was nothing but twinkling white light.

Then Caspian began to ascend the shaft of The Well. The light from hir Merkabah illuminated the tight walls all around hir. Flying upwards quite quickly, Caspian thought s/he passed by the section were s/he fell in, but it was sealed shut. There was nowhere else to go but more up. Momentarily s/he arrived at the top of the shaft and was deposited into a larger room which was lit by the warm orange glow of torches mounted on the walls. Hieroglyphics covered *every* inch of the four walls. And there was Tahuti, all smiling beak, standing next to an open sarcophagus. Caspian floated over toward Tahuti and the sarcophagus. S/he marveled over the intricacies of its carvings. It seemed gigantic up close, giving the impression that the Pharaoh's of Alternate Egypt might have been giants.

"That's wild," Caspian commented, leaning down and running hir fingers through a strange black sand that filled the bottom of the sarcophagus. This substance sounded like it was giving off a subtle hum; a tone that Caspian could feel vibrating in hir heart chakra.

"This is your initiation," Tahuti said like it was the most important thing in the entire Spiralverse. "Stand in front of me."

Caspian took hir place in front of Tahuti who appeared to tower over hir even though he was only a foot or two taller.

"Yes, I think I'm still alive," Caspian said quickly. Then there was silence and s/he listened intently.

Tahuti held up his scroll and read from it, occasionally marking something with his quill. "Do you know that there may not be any ultimate truth?" the ibis-headed god asked, his beady eyes blinking and staring down at Caspian.

"Yes," s/he answered.

Tahuti marked with his quill. "Are you aware of your own True Will—your Self-Love?"

"I am," Caspian responded without hesitation.

"Do you Dare to penetrate deep within the Galactic Sphincter, no matter where it brings you, no matter if the madness brings you beyond the stars and beyond the Beyond?" Tahuti said.

"Absolutely," Caspian answered, grinning. "It wouldn't be fun otherwise."

Tahuti nodded his ibis head seriously. "Do you meditate Silently and know that all humans and all beings—" he made a great flourish with his quill "—all entities everywhere—have Soulminds?"

"Yes," Caspian answered the final question, "that is a basic principle of the Kryst."

"Then you are ready," the god said, rolling up his scroll and sliding it back into his belt. He raised his hands and guided Caspian with hir Merkabah to hover over the Sarcophagus. Then s/he glided down into it, onto the black vibrating sand. As telepathically instructed by Tahuti, Caspian laid down on hir back and sunk down comfortably into the sand. Instantly it felt like a mouth devoured hir and s/he was pulled down and through the sand as if in slow motion. S/he found hirself suspended as if caught in Jell-O—floating in the middle of a dark room with stars projected on the walls. The black sand seeped down through the ceiling like drips of water and it sung to Caspian the song of hir heart.

Then a woman's voice spoke from the void, deep and resonant. "Thou hast come to alter their destiny," this voice declared.

"Is this the Galactic Sphincter?" Caspian asked, hoping with anticipation that s/he had made it at last.

"Not quite yet," the voice echoed back from the projected stars on the walls. "We must make sure that you are the correct one to enter."

"Okay," Caspian replied, not sure how s/he should prove hirself.

"Are you a man or a woman?" the voice asked.

"Why does that matter?" Caspian responded with a question.

"Are you a woman? Are you a man?" the cosmic voice asked again. "Which one are you?"

"And what if I refuse?" s/he spat back indignantly. "What if I evoke my right to be called an androgynous god? I am man *and* woman—and I am not either. The Divine Hermaphrodite who transcends the pair of opposites."

There was a moment of silence where all that Caspian could hear and feel was the hum of the black sand. "You have answered rightly," the cosmic voice finally answered back. "Remember, Thou art God!"

Caspian looked up at the ceiling where the black sand was still dripping and a huge crack appeared down the middle, letting the brightest white light seep in. Then the two halves of the ceiling separated and opened up like two sides of a clam shell. S/he stared up as a tunnel of plasmik light appeared above hir. Spine tingling, s/he knew that this stellar-tube stretched through space and into the Galactic Sphincter. The tunnel was luminous; almost transparent but with white light like currents of electricity running through it.

Caspian floated up in hir Merkabah and entered the tube of plasmik light.

Machandi was grumbling to herself when she got back to the *Quantum Shortbus*. Even though she hadn't fully believed in the Spiralverse's Asshole up until this moment, she still wanted to see it. How come Caspian was the only one who got to go experience what it means to alter a destiny? She disappeared herself and then reappeared on the command deck of the *Shortbus*.

"EFFI," Machandi said, looking up and around at the navigation crystals.

"Yes, Machandi?" the ship mind answered back.

"Can you lock onto Caspian's energetic signature and get hir location in Space, Time, and Dimension?" the blue goddess asked as she approached the control console.

There were several seconds of silence where the navigation crystals flashed yellow and the Kathara Grid on the screen lit up the colored balls in a specific sequence. "I have located Caspian in the atmosphere of Alternate Egypt, over the Great Pyramid, and hir density converted to a sub-dimension." EFFI informed once computations were complete.

"Can we follow hir?" Machandi wanted to know.

"It would take a considerable amount of energy," EFFI

answered, "but it can be done. We'll have to fly up to just outside of the atmosphere above the Great Pyramid and then use the power of the Merkabah around the ship to up-step our matter into the density of that sub-dimension."

"Let's do it then!"

Caspian felt like s/he was high as a kite, tripping on acid. S/he wasn't even in control of hir movement, some force from the other side was guiding hir through the plasma tunnel, controlling hir Merkabah. The stars sparkled like diamonds off in the unfathomable distance and Caspian marveled at the glory of the Spiralverse.

There was an enormous object at the end of the tunnel. Caspian could feel its heft like a presence in hir aura. This object was metal that looked like a closed camera shutter. Green crystals sparkled on its surface. And dancing patterns of golden sacred geometry arranged and rearranged themselves all around this closed camera shutter—which Caspian now realized must be *the* Sphincter—the one and only Galactic Sphincter. Right as hir body was about to collide with the center of the Sphincter's closed iris, it began to pucker.

The Cosmic Anus dilated and began to gape for Caspian's entrance. Bright green light seeped out of the Recto-Hole and s/he floated right into it. Once s/he was inside the Spiralverse's Rectum, s/he immediately felt a palpable vibe of sexual tension. It was like the Galactic Sphincter hadn't been penetrated in millennia. Caspian felt like s/he was being energetically pulled by hir dick deeper into the Hole.

When the green light finally dimmed and faded away, Caspian could behold a three-dimensional grid of green light stretching as far as s/he could see all around hir. S/he was also floating through oscillating rings of golden energy. The outer edges of these plasma rings danced with patterns and images that Caspian couldn't have come up with even in hir wildest fits of fantasy. However, the emotion that was ravaging its way through hir body, like it was being broadcast from some entity or machine in the bowels of the Recto-Hole, was pure *longing*.

The tunnel of golden rings was ending and Caspian found hirself coming upon the edge of a great round platform. This gray metallic platform was the floor of a room that stretched up into a colossal dome. It may have stretched down under the platform to create a complete sphere, but Caspian couldn't tell. There was a strange machine that sat like a monument at the center of the platform. It resembled a cube with legs—about twelve feet high and apparently wrapped in some sort of gold foil that glimmered in the white light cast by a free-hovering ball of luminescence right above and behind the golden cube. The machine vaguely resembled a lunar lander, s/he thought.

Approaching with caution, Caspian attempted to read some initials that seemed to have been carved in the side of the cube. After getting considerably closer to the object, s/he could see the etching was three letters—V.J.J.. Suddenly there was a rumbling of the platform and a succession of electronic tones emitted from the *V.J.J.*. The cube separated a perfectly straight crack all the way around the middle of its surface. Then it swung open, like it was on a hinge, to reveal a hollow chamber inside. Caspian was instantly sprayed with a sticky viscous liquid which originated from inside the cube.

"Oh, boy," Caspian said, wiping a gob of secretion off of hir face.

The *Shortbus* was rocketing through the atmosphere directly above the Great Pyramid. Machandi stared out of the viewport as the changing scenery showed the blue sky turn quickly into a sea of stars on a background of blackness. The thrusters burned with the anger of one thousand suns. There was a burst of energy as the flames went from bright orange to electric blue. "Are we at the correct altitude, EFFI?" Machandi asked.

"Affirmative," the ship mind replied. "Now the Merkabah must convert the *Shortbus* and you into a sub-dimension of the sub-dimension."

"This is gonna be weird..." Machandi said to herself as she prepared to be up-stepped into an alternate reality. The conversion began and at once she felt like she was growing. Not growing in the way a human or a humanoid would grow, but the way a invasive plant would. Staring at her hands, she watched as all her fingers morphed into long blue leaves. "It's just a hallucination caused by the dimensional conversion," she told herself. "It's not real."

Just as she said this, more leaves began to sprout out of her head, and out of her legs like slim tree trunks. The whole command deck had suddenly become a thick green jungle with one blue plant with the longest and thickest leaves shivering in the middle. EFFI's navigation crystals flashed a deep blue as they pushed out from behind some dense foliage. "Normal molecular structure will reconfigure momentarily," EFFI said, her electronic voice echoing through the jungle.

There was the sound of a tone played on an organ and instantly Machandi and the *Shortbus* 'popped' back into their used-to DNA structure. "Oh, thank the Unified Field!"

Machandi exclaimed, touching her plasma body to make sure everything was in its proper place—no ears on the top of the head this time. She seemed to be more or less intact; aside from pulling a blue leaf out of her ear and tossing it onto the floor. "Holy Pleiadian mystics!" Machandi exclaimed after finally looking out of the viewport to see what it was like to be in a sub-dimension of the sub-dimension.

It was in that moment that she beheld for the first time the Galactic Sphincter—the Recto-Hole—the Dookie Door of Destiny. She felt so much awe that she could physically feel her plasma-body slosh around within its skin. The Cosmic Anus was closed, looking like a dark gray metallic camera lens with emeralds embedded in it. Machandi also noted all of the glowing geometry spinning around it like potentials for new worlds.

The Galactic Sphincter-lens gave out a great groan and began to dilate, opening up enough for the *Shortbus* to fly through. EFFI moaned as the ship penetrated the Galactic Sphincter. Once inside, they flew up the same poop-chute path that Caspian had passed through. The *Shortbus* was guided in through the green light which dimmed to a three-dimensional neon grid on a dark void. Then the golden rings appeared, larger than when Caspian floated through them, and the van-turned-spaceship floated easily through them like it was a luxury liner.

Caspian was trying to get a sense of what this machine—this *V.J.J.*—wanted. S/he was getting a jumble of feelings and bits of words telepathically, but nothing intelligible. Something drew hir attention away from V.J.J. and toward where s/he had first stepped onto the platform. S/he smiled at seeing the *Quantum*

Shortbus gliding out of the golden rings and coming to a landing on the dark silver platform. Before Caspian could even blink hir eyes, there was Machandi, appearing like an apparition, walking toward hir. *Good old Machandi*, s/he thought, *always finds a way.*

"You made it, my friend," Caspian said, waving at the Pleiadian goddess.

"Tahuti can suck my dick," Machandi said with a smile pulling at the corner of her mouth. "There is no way some Beakface with an iScroll is gonna tell me I can't see the Hole of Altered Destiny..." she trailed off, finally looking at the open cube with legs in front of them. "What in seven hell-planets is that?"

Caspian looked back over at the gaping cube which was dripping the mysterious viscous liquid from its hollow compartment. S/he shrugged. "I'm not sure yet," s/he admitted. "All I feel from it is a deep ache and loneliness."

"Oh, wait," Machandi said suddenly, raising a finger and closing her eyes. "I'm picking up an electronic transmission... She says her name is V-J-J. And apparently she wants to merge with us."

The Earth's Altered Destiny

"Merge with us?" Caspian echoed back. "What does she mean by *merge with us?*"

"Hold on," Machandi said, opening her eyes again. "I'm picking up a response... V.J.J. is saying that she—the Mecha-Vagina—was on a search through the endless spirals of the Spiralverse to find the MechaPenis in order to merge with him and become one ultimate mecha-androgynous-god... V.J.J. also says: *I thought that once I found the Galactic Sphincter, it would expel me renewed into my Altered Destiny where my MechaPenis would be waiting to become one with me throughout all of artificial time.*"

"Maybe this is a sign," Caspian said, speaking directly to V.J.J.. "Maybe this is a sign that you don't need a MechaCock. You can be your own Machine God—whole and complete."

Machandi closed her eyes while saying, "V.J.J. wants to say something else... She says that *maybe you and the blue woman were sent here to rub my mechanical vagina and we'll all become one as we merge in orgasmic ecstasy—our atoms converted into the ultimate omniscient machine.*"

Caspian swallowed hard. "Yeah, that sounds really great, Machandi," s/he whispered to hir blue friend. "We'll just shut down and become software..." s/he trailed off while trying to think of what more to say to the strange vaginal-secreting machine. Then Caspian got a brilliant idea. "You already have a MechaPenis to make you whole."

Machandi relayed the message from the machine: "V.J.J. says—*how do you mean?*"

"Don't you feel it within your circuitry?" Caspian said, walking closer to V.J.J. and placing a hand on the goo lining the hollow inside of the cube-vagina. "You contain within you the blueprint of your opposite. You'd have to contain the data for both in order for the duality to split and exist," s/he continued. "Feel down so far into the depths of your mechanical vagina that you may find that place so deep within you that contains your own MechaCock. Do you feel it?"

"V.J.J. is doing some searching within," Machandi said, fluttering her eyes open again as the area between her eyebrows tingled. "V.J.J. says that she's touching herself in the deepest place and she feels something growing."

There sounded to be what resembled a buzzing at first, then it became a high-pitched mechanical-type moaning—like V.J.J. was producing the electronic orgasm from deep within her digital womb. The open-cube-cunt began to lubricate even more, spitting sticky globs onto Caspian's face and neck; but the phlegm-like projectiles just went through Machandi's plasma-body like she wasn't even there. Suddenly there was a deep guttural groan from inside V.J.J. that soon turned into a slurping-choking sound. Caspian and Machandi gasped as they saw something begin to grow out of the deepest part of the hollow golden cube. As it grew and protruded, it looked more and more like a giant vibrator. Robot lube slicked the impressive shaft.

Caspian looked over at Machandi. S/he could feel the energy building in hir erogenous zones and traveling up hir spine. "Do you feel like you're gonna squirt in your skirt?" Caspian asked. "Or is that just me?"

"You're right," Machandi said, starting to moan. "I feel like my head's about to explode with a cosmic orgasm from rising Kundalini."

They both stared at the spot where the MechaDick penetrated the MechaCunt—it was becoming saturated with white light. An audible voice suddenly spoke. It was a strange sound; slightly electronic and sounded like a high voice and a low voice speaking in unison. "Yes," it said. "We were always One. The seed of my opposite began with me; so I therefore give birth to it. My love is my own being. In a Sacred A.I. marriage, we are One become Zero."

The light then became almost blinding. Caspian squinted and shielded hir eyes as the sentient machine began to disappear within the whiteness. "What's happening, Machandi?" s/he asked, now lost within a sea of white luminescence.

"V.J.J. is ascending this sub-dimension," Machandi yelled, not sure how far away Caspian was now that she couldn't see anything but blank and white. "Even as a machine, she became One in the Androgynous Sacred Marriage. Undergoing this transformation pulls her as one entity up to their Oversoul Level—if artificially intelligent machines even have souls."

"How do we know if *we* even have souls?" Caspian asked. There was silence, and within the silence, s/he felt V.J.J. transform into pure energy and pass through hir body like the cold wind of a ghost. Caspian could feel it changing hir. There was at first a tingle around hir shoulder blades, and then, as a vision in hir third eye, s/he saw hirself with huge white-feathered wings bursting out of hir back. Then the wings became like liquid and changed form into colorful butterfly wings. After which the butterfly wings dissolved into semi-translucent energy fields in the shape of wings. "What's happening to *me*?" Caspian said after a time of floating in the pitch-white where s/he couldn't even see hir palm in front of hir face. But then s/he felt Machandi's presence like the comfort of an old friend. And even though Caspian couldn't see her, s/he felt like they were becoming one being—reflections of each other but manifestations of the same primal Source—Chaos.

The white field of light became the afterglow of their shared orgasm—a threesome of god, machine, and plasma. "You are becoming Christ-Conscious," Machandi said, her voice echoing out of the dark brightness. "The force of the mechanical and biological orgasm blew through your DNA, activating your Divine Genome."

"Which means what?" Caspian asked.

"It means you are now One with Everything."

"But I still feel separate at this level... But still connected to the Unified Field," the Captain continued.

"Ah," Machandi responded as the brightness of the light began to fade, "hence, the paradox."

In a few seconds the white light dissipated like wisps of smoke, leaving Machandi and Caspian standing on the circular-disk platform staring at each other. The V.J.J. was gone; vanished as if it had never been there in the first place. There was a rumble of the dome above them and they both jerked their heads back toward where the *Quantum Shortbus* was parked. The small entrance and piece of the platform that jutted out as a landing strip for the ship started to vibrate and in seconds the entrance was sealed shut.

"Now what? How do we get out of here?" Caspian asked with a bit of anxiety in hir voice. Momentarily s/he had forgotten everything about this elusive *Altered Destiny* and was only concerned with not getting trapped in the Spiralverse's Rectum like V.J.J. had been.

On the wall of the dome directly opposite of where they had entered, another door opened up. The quake in the side of the dome caused the wall to fracture in an arc. This arc was smooth, like it was already a pre-cut hidden door that opened to reveal all the secrets of the dome. They could see through this new opening a similar landing platform that led out to more of those oscillating golden rings.

"Now that looks like something, doesn't it?" Machandi grinned.

"Our Altered Destiny," Caspian said with a hint of mystery.

They quickly got back into the *Quantum Shortbus* and used the Merkabah field to levitate the ship over to the newly opened door. On the command deck, Caspian engaged the thrusters and the *Shortbus* shot off of the platform and into the tunnel of golden rings. "I wonder what our new destiny will be," s/he said, gazing out of the viewport.

Machandi shrugged. "I don't know," she admitted.

Caspian looked away from the viewport and over at hir companion. "Do you think we'll recognize it?" s/he asked. "Or will the Spiralverse look different since we're entering an alternate reality?"

Machandi didn't have any of the answers—the truth was as ambiguous as Caspian's gender. The gold rings gave way to the green neon light grid, and then after a while, the viewport of the Shortbus was completely obscured by green light.

"Do you think we're being expelled from the Galactic Sphincter?" Machandi asked.

"We're exiting the Stink Star of Providence," Caspian stated in an official-sounding voice. "Will we be excreted on the other side of the galaxy? One may never know and be lost in space."

Soon the green light faded and was replaced by a view of stars on a black void. "We're back!" Machandi exclaimed. Looking out of the viewport she commented, "Looks about the same... Hey, there's the Moon!"

Caspian looked up and sure enough the *Shortbus* was coming in for a glide a little ways past the gray, rocky satellite. And a little ways beyond it, the blue planet glistened with its oceans. "The Altered Destiny brought us back to Earth..." Caspian said softly.

Machandi sighed as EFFI's navigation crystals hummed and blinked pink. "I never thought we would find it," she vocalized. "Much less experience what we would find inside it..."

"Yeah..." Caspian said, trailing off as s/he stared out the viewport at Earth getting closer as if s/he was a million light years away on a planet only hermaphrodites had found. "Something strange about Earth."

"Something strange about Earth?" Machandi echoed back and looked out of the viewport at the little blue and green planet. Then she definitely thought she saw something—lights flickering around the edges. Caspian pointed again and before their very eyes a grid made of light stretched all around and criss-crossed the globe.

"What is that?" Caspian wondered out loud.

"EFFI," Machandi said, waking up the computer, "what can you tell us about the grid around Planet Earth?"

"The Prison Grid," EFFI began. "The Prison Grid was set up by the Anunnaki when they used their genetically-engineered humans as slaves. This energetic Prison Grid would allow no living human to ascend higher than Earth's atmosphere."

"We flew the *Shortbus* up and out of the atmosphere without any problems," Caspian noted. "We didn't get caught in any Prison Grid."

"Technically you're not a human anymore," Machandi replied. "And I already come from outside your planet."

"The Prison Grid," EFFI continued, "was also used to keep humanity divided, and keeps Planet Earth at a lower vibrational frequency."

"Fuckin' eh," Caspian said, grinning at Machandi. "This is it. This is my Altered Destiny."

"What?" Machandi didn't follow where s/he was going with that.

"I've gotta destroy it."

"Destroy the..." Machandi started and then realized what her friend was talking about. "...the Prison Grid?"

"It's gotta go!" s/he said intensely as s/he smacked hir hands together in prayer pose. Then s/he threw hir hands out to hir sides, instantly manifesting hir Merkabah spinning at full speed around hir. After giving Machandi a wink, Caspian disappeared from the command deck. The blue goddess could see her companion reappear outside the viewport between the *Shortbus* and Earth.

The Pleiadian disappeared and reappeared herself next to Caspian floating in space. "How can you destroy a grid around a whole planet?" she asked.

"You forget that I'm now Christ-Conscious," the androgynous god said, reminding hir friend of the metamorphosis. "I can feel it tingling in my Third Eye."

Caspian cupped hir hands in front of hir chest as if she was holding a huge dragon egg. A sphere appeared a few feet ahead of hir in space. This sphere was made of violet plasmik light—the highest light in the Spiralverse. Then within the sphere appeared an emerald-green rotating diamond, whose points touched the surface of the sphere.

Machandi looked blown away by the spectacle. "You can manifest the Krist-Star?" she said. "The legends say that only high level Ascended Masters can manifest the Krist-Star."

"Looks like somebody gained a power," Caspian said, feeling energized as s/he charged up the Krist-Star Sphere. Suddenly a beam of green and violet plasmik light, braided like a DNA strand, shot out of the Krist-Star and down toward the Earth and the Prison Grid. When the energy beam collided with the light of the Grid, it spread and covered it like a virus. The green and violet overtook the white light of the Prison Grid and finally suffocated it in one final wheezing attempt to stay online. Then the Grid failed, collapsing under the weight of its own divisiveness and slavery. The white light was completely absorbed, eaten, and the strands of violet and green plasmik energy flew their way back into the Krist-Star.

"I can't believe that worked," Machandi said, her hands up

on her cheeks. "Now humans can more easily unite and travel into space."

"And now," Caspian continued, "just a little something to assist in the conscious evolution of the planet." S/he threw hir hands out on either side of the Krist-Star and yelled, "Disperse!"

Like a miracle, the Krist-Star duplicated itself a dozen times and shot down towards the Earth. They set themselves up at some equal distances around the globe. Violet light beams shot out of the duplicate Krist-Stars vertically and green ones shot out horizontally. They banded the Earth into a new light grid pattern. "I have installed a new grid—the Christ-Consciousness Grid," Caspian announced.

"We must really be in an altered timeline with an Altered Destiny," Machandi commented.

"The Earth's New Destiny, I guess," Caspian elaborated. "Its fate as the Prison Planet has been deleted, and Earth takes its rightful place again as an Ascension Planet."

"Always for a more Self-Realized stellar Unity," Machandi added.

"Always evolution toward individuation and Self-Actualization," Caspian continued. "Now humanity can choose to plug into the Christ-Conscious Grid and the path of harmony and expanded awareness."

Both the Divine Hermaphrodite and the blue goddess disappeared and then reappeared back on the command deck of the *Quantum Shortbus*.

"She's beautiful," Machandi said, gazing out of the viewport at the Earth which was now dancing with a plasmik light grid of violet and green.

"She is," Caspian agreed. "I can't wait to see what my Gaia blossoms into."

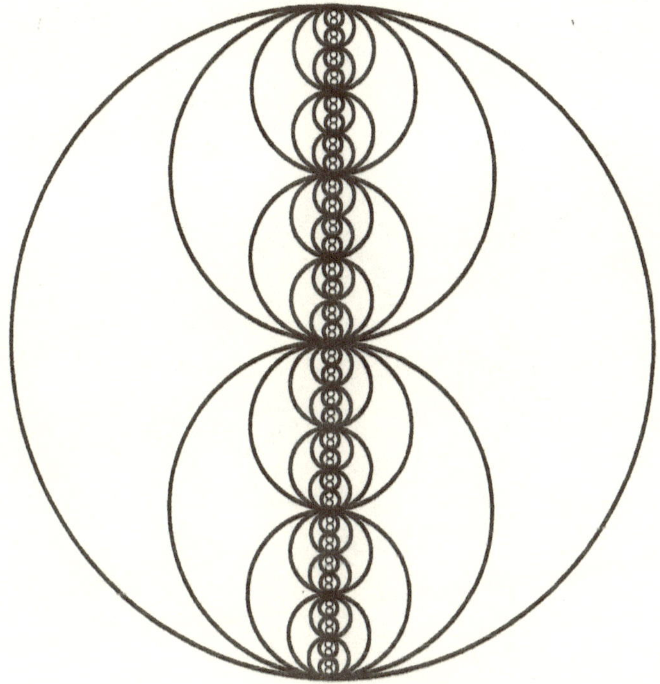

To infinity and beyond the Beyond!
—V.J.J.

Begotten

Begotten (A Surrealist Essay)

Like a flame burning away the darkness,
Life is flesh on bone convulsing above the ground.

Innocence is lost when it is destroyed by the rough bark of dead trees. I can see what is not yet left in this forest of nothingness. Coming into focus of harsh blacks and whites is a cabin that does not decide anything even in flowing robes of clouds. God sits and he is nothing here. He is discontent as drip drip he feels it fall to the ground in pools of black. Why is he gushing what he has created to spawn life? His hands are wet and he gropes the cracked walls, smearing what is left of heaven. No longer white, all that is now is streaks of black. Worms of forgotten prayers wallow in discarded sand. He is deaf and all He knows is being ripped from his open emptiness. The foot is dead and the second flood slips down and covers the flesh that is on the bone. Wet, damp, and soiled, he knows nothing. But from the ashes and the drippingness of mortality rises a beating heart. A Mother Earth that is blinded by her father's image.

Wet black on flowing white releases her to the sun. She strokes the Father's dead manhood, becoming the woman: fertile and pure. White spray tendrils waterfall and cover her with steam. In the life of dead anything makes what virgins keep. She has become the mover as she spreads the seed over her being, impregnating her once disregarded womb.

A field of desolate expanse with sliding coffin, wooden and hollow. Stand up, I say, and it becomes me as Mother Earth strokes her distended belly. She is big with him, the Son. Arteries, veins, sky of endless clouds and He is born. Son of Earth is purged from the womb as a full grown son. Ropes of infidelity in the land of Nod, he is taken by nomads and dashed against the stones. He gives them gifts of flesh from his mouth and they eat of his abundance.

But raped once more by nomads of old, Mother Earth cannot fight as her body is entered and impaled repeatedly by the wordless mouths of utterance. We known not from whence they came as their violence speaks of days of old. Pulling apart the bodies of the weak. Limb torn from socket and pounded to the earth with withered sticks. Mother and son are destroyed. Destructed into the ground of Creation. But forthwith flowers spring forth into life on the ground of the dead.

seed of the godfuck

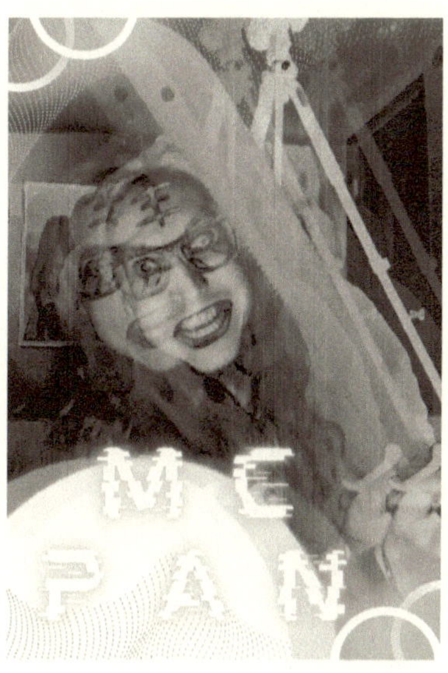

Avtar Simrit is a mystery even unto hirself. Know Thyself, as Neo said in *The Matrix*. If you know yourself then you know me well. Avtar Simrit is neither here nor there; neither this nor that; neither high nor low. And if you want to fuck around and find out, she might just chop your ego up with a machete. :-) www.mc-pan.com